Whispers of
BLUE RIDGE

NINA PURTEE

PORTO BANUS PUBLISHING 2026
St. Petersburg, FL

ISBN 979-8-9911007-7-9 (Digital)
ISBN 979-8-9911007-8-6 (Paperback)

Acknowledgments

In the fall of 2025, I spent a two-month residency in Blue Ridge, Georgia, taking in the beauty of its surroundings, its breathtaking scenery, and driving its curvy roads with their hairpin turns and motorcyclists at daredevil speeds. The rhythm of small-town living and the people of Blue Ridge left a lasting impression on me... along with the rich aromas of Southern cooking, with a special nod to Mountain Mama Coffee and Southern Comfort Restaurant.

Whispers of Blue Ridge was born from that time... shaped by the landscape, the pace, and the stories that seemed to linger in the mountains themselves. I'd like to offer a special thank you to my new friends at Copper Fox Bookstore & Coffee Bar for their support and encouragement throughout my stay and the writing process.

And, last but certainly not least, to Jane Austen, and particularly her book *Persuasion* (written in 1817), for words that remain memorable two centuries later.

ALSO AVAILABLE BY NINA PURTEE

Annie's Journey Series:

Beyond the Sea
Annie's Journey into the Extraordinary

Crossing Paths
The Road to Destiny

Finding Sarah
A Phoenix to Behold

Moroccan Sunset
Dawn of a New Beginning

Grand Illusion
Lesson of a Balinese Lotus

ONE NIGHT. ONE CABIN.
THERE'S NO GOING BACK.

CHAPTER 1

G RAYSTONE Winery was her legacy and her future. Savannah Gray worked steadily, pruning where needed, pausing only to brush a stray curl from her cheek. Northwest of Blue Ridge, nestled in the foothills of North Georgia, the morning air held a faint chill that hinted at the coming harvest. The rows of vines stretched in even lines across the slope, their leaves rustling with every passing breeze. As she carried out the familiar routine, she wondered whether she would have chosen this path if her parents were still alive. Possibly not.

She shook off the unwelcome thought and returned to the steady rhythm of removing the excess leaves to allow more sunlight to reach the grapes. Just as she reached for a sprig that looked damaged, the quiet broke without warning, and she glanced up. In the distance, a low rumble echoed through the vines... a pickup truck climbing the dirt road toward her. Savannah straightened, squinting through the light, frowning at the rising plume of red clay dust that drifted over the vines.

"Unbelievable," she muttered, setting her shears aside as she wiped a bead of sweat from her brow. The truck came into view... big, flashy red, and far too polished for country roads. It rolled to a stop beside the barn, idling like it owned the place.

The driver paused a moment at the crossroads where the driveway to the house forked up a winding road. From the determined set of his jaw, this wasn't a man just passing through.

Savannah felt her irritation climb with the dust. "Can I help you?" she called, shading her eyes from the sun, and pushing the loose strands from her ponytail behind her ear.

The driver swung down, boots hitting the gravel with practiced ease. Tall, broad-shouldered, hat tipped low, he looked every inch the rodeo poster boy she tried not to admire in the banners posted around town. "Afternoon, ma'am," he said, tipping his hat with a confidence that wasn't the least bit apologetic. "Sorry about the dust. I'm lookin' for Duke Gray... got a meetin' about the rodeo sponsorship."

She sighed. *Of course.* Duke and his endless obsession with the annual rodeo. "He's in town," she said, her voice soft but edged with exasperation. "And he didn't say a word about meeting anyone. I guess you'll just have to wait for him."

Jake Rollins smiled, slow and sure, the kind of smile that came naturally to a man used to charm working in his favor. "Then maybe you're the one I'm supposed to talk to. The foreman said something about Duke's granddaughter."

She crossed her arms, mumbling loud enough for him to hear. "Maybe. But next time, try not to coat the block of merlot in Georgia clay. Just creates more work cleaning them up."

He chuckled, deep and unbothered. "I'll keep that in mind."

For a moment, neither spoke. Savannah studied him. Tall, sun-worn, his eyes the cobalt-blue color of the mountain sky, and wavy hair a dark shade of chestnut brown. She tried to decide if he was trouble or just another arrogant cowboy passing through the hills.

Jake's grin didn't fade under her stare. "Well, since I've already disturbed the vineyard, maybe you'll point me to the house before I do any more damage."

Savannah glanced up the hill. "Duke holds his meetings in the main residence at the top of the road. You can wait there if you'd like. He should be back soon."

His eyes slowly roamed over her. Even in worn boots and work-stained clothes, she felt the weight of his assessment. Unpolished. Effortless. *Real.* He nodded toward the passenger door. "Hop in, ma'am. Perhaps you could show me."

She started to protest, then realized Duke would have a fit if she left a guest unattended at the house. Savannah looked at the long, dusty slope with the haze still hanging over the vines. "Fine," she said at last, tossing her gloves and pruning shears into the truck bed before climbing in.

The earthy smell of leather and sunbaked cedar surrounded her. The driver's seat was well-worn, yet the passenger seat looked brand new. It appeared Jake Rollins had driven countless miles across the country from rodeo to rodeo—alone.

Jake settled behind the wheel, glancing her way as he turned the key. With a slow drawl, he smiled and added, "Appreciate the company, ma'am."

Annoyed by the lurch in her stomach that followed the intoxicating sound of his voice, Savannah stiffened. "Don't get used to it."

A lazy grin spread across Jake's face. "Reckon I'll tread lightly then, ma'am. No sense stirrin' up more dust than I already have."

In the cab of his truck, with Savannah seated next to him, a subtle scent of lavender drifted through the air. His mother had always worn lavender, and he felt a tug somewhere deep inside.

As they started up the drive, the air between them felt charged. In his role with the rodeo, Jake was used to the attention he got from women. But there was something about this wisp of a young woman that intrigued him. He glanced over at her, hands steady on her lap, jaw set like someone who'd rather be anywhere else.

CHAPTER 2

*E*ARLIER *that morning—*

Jake Rollins wasn't sure why he'd come back to Blue Ridge. The rodeo circuit was as good an excuse as any, but the truth rode closer than that. It had been years, and still the memory of these hills had a way of tightening in his chest like the pull of a rope.

The highway snaked through the foothills in sharp, familiar curves... the kind that made most folks ease off the gas. Jake didn't. He knew every turn by heart, every scar in the pavement, every place a man could lose control.

When the town came into view below, he let the truck idle at the overlook and stared. Roofs glinting in the morning light. Smoke curling from chimneys. The air smelled like rain and pine and something old he couldn't name. He thought of the road just beyond those hills, the one he never talked about, the one that had changed everything.

He put the truck back in gear and rolled on. The fairgrounds sat quiet on the edge of town, ringed by towering pines and mist. A few trailers were parked near the arena, but most of the crew had already headed out for breakfast. Jake backed into a space and killed the engine. For a while, he didn't move. The stillness of the morning was a stark contrast to the chaos that stirred within him. He leaned back in the seat, letting the calm wash over him.

The wind shifted, carrying the faint echo of a train whistling from the valley below. It was enough to pull him back. Blue Ridge hadn't changed much... one of the few small towns that hadn't. The hills still rose sharp against the sky, the air still held that clean bite of fall, and the past was still waiting, just where he'd left it.

***

"All right, folks. Settle down now. We aren't finished yet." Harold Jennings, the committee chair, tapped his pen against a stack of rodeo flyers to regain the group's attention. "We're expectin' an even bigger crowd than last year with Jake Rollins on the docket, so we'll need extra help to direct traffic down at the fairgrounds," he announced. "We all know what the fall means for this town. Between the leaf lookers, the train riders, and the winery tours, Blue Ridge is gonna be packed to the rafters."

The group attending the meeting at city hall murmured in agreement, several recalling last year's traffic chaos. A few joked about the need for more stoplights in a town that cherished its handshake-driven charm.

The influx of pedestrians, mostly tourists wandering into the streets, continued to be an issue, and this year, with the rodeo tied to the fair, they anticipated traffic from the surrounding counties as well.

For Duke Gray, a veteran of these meetings and a fixture in the community, the discussions were a needed ritual. He leaned back in his chair, observing as the talk wound through parade floats, hay bales, and who'd sponsor the barrel races this year. He'd heard it every autumn for the past twenty years, yet there was comfort in the familiar rhythm of a town that took pride in the events that showcased its beauty. His commitment to Blue Ridge was as unwavering as his devotion to the family winery.

Across the table, Natalie Maxwell, a staple at all these meetings, set down her pen and smiled faintly. "Can't say I mind all the fuss," she said. "Makes the town look downright storybook this time of year."

"Storybook or not," Duke muttered, "we'll be knee-deep in mud if it rains again."

Laughter rippled through the room, and Natalie's glance toward Duke lingered just a second too long.

"Duke," Harold said, flipping through his notes, "we're still good on the winery sponsorship, right? The town's countin' on y'all for the hospitality tent."

Duke gave a small nod, chewing on the tip of an unlit cigar. "Savannah has it under control. She runs the tastings better than I ever could. We'll have the booth throughout the fair, then the sponsor tent during the rodeo."

"That girl's a wonder," Natalie said. "Every tourist in town leaves talkin' about her. The way she's stepped in at the winery and what she does with Lois's old recipes is nothing short of magical."

Duke grunted, not missing the way Natalie's eyes softened when she mentioned Lois's name. He checked his watch again. Nearly half past ten. He was late. He hated to keep anyone waiting, especially someone like Rollins.

As the meeting adjourned, Duke made for the door, only to be caught by Natalie hurrying up behind him, her heels clicking lightly against the old pine floor.

"Duke," she called, a little breathless. "You always leave before I get a chance to say two words."

He stopped and turned, hat in hand, polite but guarded. "You said plenty in there, Natalie. You run half that committee without even tryin'."

She smiled, tilting her head. "Maybe. But I wanted to tell you somethin' important. Lizzie just got her acceptance letter to that art school in Florence. Isn't that wonderful?"

"That so?" Duke's expression softened just enough to pass for pleased. "Good for her. We'll miss her help at the winery."

Natalie hesitated, then added, "She told me she and Savannah used to talk about Italy all the time. Said Savannah's been studyin' wine the way Lizzie studies paint. Wouldn't it be somethin' if they went together?"

Duke's face tightened around the edges of his smile. "Savannah's got her hands full right here. Our vineyard doesn't run itself."

"Oh, I know," Natalie said quickly. "I just thought…"

"I appreciate the suggestion," Duke said, sliding his hat back on. "But her place is with family. Especially now."

Natalie's voice faltered into a soft sigh. "You're a good man, Duke. I know you miss them. I do too. Just don't let that vineyard keep her from livin' a little."

He paused at the door, flinching at Natalie's words. "She's got a good life right here, Natalie, and she won't be needin' your interference. I'm late for an appointment. Goodbye."

The door closed behind him. Natalie stood alone in the hallway for a moment, the echo of his words settling around her. *It's been three years*, she thought, reaching for her purse and heading toward the stairs.

CHAPTER 3

BY the time they reached the house, Savannah wished she'd had five minutes' warning. The truck had left a thin film of dust on her overalls and probably on her hair, and now she was leading a rodeo cowboy into her grandfather's study like it was the most natural thing in the world.

"Have a seat," she said, motioning toward the leather chair near the window. The words came out steadier than she felt. Duke's morning newspaper lay folded neatly on the desk beside his reading glasses, the room carrying the faint scent of his aftershave and lingering smoke from his pipe.

"I'll grab you something to drink," she added quickly, needing an excuse to escape for a moment.

In the kitchen, she pulled open the refrigerator, the cool air washing over her flushed face. A pitcher of sweet tea waited on the top shelf. She poured two glasses, watching the ice crack and float, and tried not to think about the smudge of dirt on her sleeve or the loose strand of hair that kept falling across her cheek.

Of all the days to look like she'd rolled straight out of a hay bale.

Savannah nudged the study door open with her shoulder, balancing the tray.

Jake stood as she entered, hat in hand, the kind of courtesy that belonged to another decade in some parts of the country, but not in the South.

"Sweet tea," she said with a wry smile, setting the tray on the desk. "Figured you could use something cold after all that dust."

He grinned... just a hint this time, slightly cha-grined. "Much obliged, ma'am. Didn't mean to stir up trouble before the day even started."

"Trouble?" she echoed, arching a brow. "Only if you count the grapes."

That earned a low chuckle from him, warm and genuine. "Then I owe you and your vineyard an apology."

She passed him a glass, careful not to meet those soulful eyes again. "Apology accepted," she said, her tone lighter now, "as long as you promise to keep the speed down next time you drive past the barn."

Jake's grin widened, and his wink did not go un-noticed. "Can't make promises I might not keep."

The easy banter surprised her. Was he actually flirting with her? She couldn't remember the last time a man had left her this flustered, and over something as simple as a smile. She lifted her own glass, the con-densation slick against her palm, and took a sip just as a flash of sunlight through the window caught her eye. Her grandfather's truck was easing through the gate.

Her smile faded a little. "That'll be Duke."

Jake nodded, setting his hat back on his knee. "Good. I was hopin' to make a proper impression. I know he's a powerful influence around here."

Savannah straightened, suddenly aware again of the dust on her overalls and the curl escaping near her temple. "He won't be long," she said, crossing to the window. The truck had stopped at the gate. "I know he wouldn't appreciate me entertaining a guest looking like this. I'll introduce you and go change."

Jake followed her glance, the faintest trace of a grin still tugging at his mouth. "You look okay to me," he murmured.

Savannah turned toward him, caught for a moment between amusement and exasperation. "Right."

He lifted his hat and tipped it slightly. "Well, I hope you'll rejoin us soon."

Outside, Duke's truck door slammed, and the moment between them folded into silence.

Savannah met her grandfather at the doorway.

"Duke, this is Jake Rollins," she said, nodding toward the study. "He's here about the rodeo sponsorship."

Duke walked the short distance and extended his hand. "Jake—I hope you don't mind me calling you by your first name. I've heard a fair bit about you on the circuit."

"Sir," Jake replied, rising to shake it. "Appreciate you takin' the time."

Savannah excused herself before Duke could comment on her vineyard attire. "I'll leave you two to talk. I'll be back in a few minutes."

As she slipped out, the murmur of their voices followed her down the hall... Duke's steady baritone, Jake's calm drawl, both low and deliberate.

Duke settled behind the desk and motioned for Jake to sit. "We like to keep the community involved in both the fair and the rodeo," he began. "Graystone's planning to sponsor the opening-night social. Just a bit of a dinner and dance before the week's events."

Jake nodded. "Sounds like a fine idea, sir. Folks like a reason to come out early."

"Please, son, call me Duke. Everyone around here does, including my granddaughter. For the event, we'll be showcasing local wines, a few visiting riders, and I'm told you've won enough buckles to draw a crowd."

Jake smiled. "I've had my share of good rides, but I reckon the crowd's more interested in the show than the man."

"That humility plays well," Duke said, tapping the desk with a satisfied nod. "If you're willing, we'd like to feature you at the event. Bit of a Blue Ridge welcome angle for the rodeo elite."

Jake hesitated, caught between pride and discomfort. "If it helps the cause, Duke, I'll be there."

"Good. My granddaughter handles most of the logistics. She'll see that you get the details."

The hallway door opened, and both men turned.

Savannah stepped back into the study, now in dark jeans and a crisp white blouse, her hair pulled neatly away from her face. The change was simple but striking—vineyard dust traded for quiet confidence.

Jake found himself standing before he even knew why, his jaw slightly ajar. He caught himself a beat later.

Duke glanced between them, unaware of the current that shifted between his granddaughter and the cowboy. "Perfect timing, Savannah. Jake has agreed to be our guest of honor at the opening social."

The smile she gave him seemed edged with a challenge. "Then I'll make sure it's an evening worth remembering."

Jake cleared his throat, forcing his gaze back to Duke. "Reckon you already have."

CHAPTER 4

THE sun had climbed high enough to burn the early-morning mist off the vineyard, leaving the air bright and edged with a slight chill. Savannah wiped her hands on a cloth and leaned against the porch railing, watching the rows of vines shimmer in the light. Harvest season always carried a certain vibe, with tractors in the distance, the faint laughter of workers, and the steady pulse of work that filled every spare moment. It should have been enough to satisfy her wandering mind.

The rodeo was only a week away, and the town of Blue Ridge, as well as the surrounding area, buzzed with excitement. As Graystone Winery's representative, Savannah had volunteered to organize the vineyard's booth for the community fair that would run prior to the rodeo, mostly to keep herself busy. Everyone in Blue Ridge had their part to play, and she preferred keeping her hands occupied to letting her mind drift to her parents' absence, or to the empty spot where row after row of her mom's freshly made jams and relishes once sat, neatly lined and waiting.

The community fair was an annual highlight, bringing together local businesses and residents in a celebration of shared heritage and camaraderie. The event was more than just a showcase of regional talents and produce; it was a testament to the strength and unity of Blue Ridge. She hoped that with time, she'd find her way back to it.

Despite the bustling activities and her involvement in the preparations, Savannah couldn't shake the feeling that something was off. She understood her obligations, but there was also a restlessness in her that whispered of change and possibility. Perhaps it was the anticipation of the rodeo, with its promise of adventure and daring, that spoke to her soul. Or maybe it was the vineyard's timeless beauty that reminded her of life's fleeting moments, urging her to seek her own path.

As she stood on the porch, Savannah felt a mix of anticipation and uncertainty. The week ahead promised to be filled with hard work and laughter, but beyond that lay a horizon she couldn't yet see. For now, she would focus on the tasks at hand, trusting that clarity would come in its own time.

She was halfway through checking the supply crates when a familiar voice called from the path, "Don't tell me you started without coffee again."

Savannah turned to see Lizzie approaching, auburn ponytail swinging, one to-go cup of her favorite Mountain Mama's latte in each hand.

"I was hoping you'd show up," Savannah teased, taking one of the cups. "Mmm, this is delicious. You're late."

Lizzie grinned. "Traffic jam. Duke was holding court at the feed store again... something about a new shipment of hay. You'd think it was front-page news."

Savannah laughed. "That sounds about right. How's Natalie?"

"Neck-deep in that charity luncheon for the rodeo sponsors. I think she's hoping Duke will notice her if she wears one of those sundresses she picked up at Trish's dress shop."

Savannah smirked. "You know Duke. He's no doubt noticed. He just likes pretending he doesn't."

They stood for a moment in comfortable silence, sipping coffee, as the morning chill dissipated and the air warmed.

Then Lizzie's tone shifted, casual but curious. "So... rumor has it Jake Rollins is the star rider at the rodeo this year."

Savannah's hand stilled on the crate she'd been checking. "I heard that. He came by to see Duke yesterday."

Lizzie looked at Savannah in disbelief. "He was here? Is he as handsome as they say? Do tell!"

"I suppose he was nice looking enough," Savannah said too quickly.

Lizzie giggled. "You always say that when you're trying not to sound interested."

"I'm not interested," Savannah replied, though her heartbeat disagreed. "He's just... a cowboy, a drifter. You know how people love to swarm around the cowboys when the rodeo comes through."

"Uh-huh." Lizzie set her cup down and crossed her arms. "And I guess you have your feet planted firmly here in Blue Ridge. You've become a vineyard manager, event planner, and community favorite. Don't tell me this was your plan and that you wouldn't jump at the chance for an adventure."

Savannah rolled her eyes but smiled at her friend who knew her so well. "You're impossible."

"And you're transparent," Lizzie said, grinning. "Anyway, I promised Duke I'd drop off the flyers for the booth setup. Oh, and he said Jake mentioned he might stop by to help."

Savannah frowned. "What? He's not..."

Before she could finish, the familiar rumble of an engine pulled her gaze to the drive—Jake's pickup kicking up a fresh swirl of dust behind it.

Savannah shook her head and mumbled, "You've got to be kidding. Not again."

Lizzie's grin widened. "Speak of the devil. This must be the infamous Jake Rollins!"

Jake pulled into one of the guest spaces and sauntered over, tipping his hat in greeting, his smile easy but his eyes focused on Savannah.

"Mornin'," he said. "Heard you might need a hand haulin' supplies."

Savannah blinked, caught off guard by how casually he said it. Though it wasn't their first encounter, it still felt unexpected. "We're managing fine, but it was nice of you to stop by."

"Didn't ask if you needed me," Jake said, a hint of mischief softening his tone. "Just said I heard."

Lizzie coughed into her cup to hide a laugh.

Savannah, suddenly remembering her manners, said, "Jake, this is my friend, Lizzie Glover. Lizzie, Mr. Rodeo himself—Jake Rollins."

Lizzie extended her hand with a grin. "So, you're the one causing all the commotion in town. Folks can't stop talking about you."

Jake shook her hand lightly. "Hope it's the good kind of talk."

"Oh, depends on who you ask," Lizzie said, her tone teasing. "You've certainly given the ladies something to discuss at Mountain Mama's."

Savannah rolled her eyes. "Lizzie."

Jake's smile deepened, his gaze flicking to Savannah. "Well, I'll have to stop in and thank them, then."

"Oh, I'm sure they'd love that," Savannah said dryly, trying to sound unaffected.

He laughed. The warm, genuine sound settled somewhere in her chest before she could stop it. Jake commented, "You don't seem like the type who's easily impressed."

"I'm not," Savannah replied, picking up a nearby box. "Now, about those crates... are you willing to help me or not?"

Jake nodded toward the truck. "Figured I could haul a few down to the west lot for you. Looks like a sizable load for just you two."

"It is," Lizzie chimed in before Savannah could answer. "And I've got to run, so she could really use the help."

Savannah shot her a look, but Lizzie only smiled sweetly. "Don't worry, I'll make it up to you later." She turned to Jake. "Nice meeting you, Mr. Rollins. Try not to give my friend too hard a time."

"No promises," Jake said with a wink.

Lizzie laughed and headed for her car, leaving her friend to deal with a certain cowboy.

For a moment, the only sounds were the rustle of vines and the distant clatter of a tractor starting up. Jake leaned one shoulder against the fence rail. "Your friend's quick."

"She's helpful, although sometimes too helpful." Savannah set the box down by the crates. "You really don't have to..."

"I know." He reached for one of the heavier crates, muscles flexing under his rolled-up sleeves. "But I'm here anyway."

She hesitated, then bent to grab the other end. "You're persistent."

"I've been called worse."

They lifted the load of boxes together, falling into an easy rhythm while filling up the bed of his truck. The steady motion seemed to fill the quiet between them. Jake set a crate down and glanced over.

"You've got a good setup here," he said. "Didn't expect a vineyard this size in a place like Blue Ridge."

"It's my family's," Savannah said, then hesitated before she added, "Or what's left of them."

Jake studied her for a moment, then nodded. "Sorry. Guess that makes you the heart of it now."

Savannah looked away, busying herself with the next crate. "Something like that."

He didn't push. Instead, just lifted another box—deliberate, unhurried. The silence that followed wasn't awkward, just charged in a way that made her aware of every flex of his muscles.

When the last crate was stacked, Jake brushed his hands on his jeans. "There. Least I could do for the local fair's star volunteer."

"I'm hardly that," Savannah said, though her smile betrayed her. "But thanks."

Jake tipped his hat. "Anytime. I'll have them ready for you once you get to the fairgrounds."

As his truck rumbled down the drive, Savannah stood watching until the sound faded into the distance. The midday sun had grown warmer, and the air shimmered above the vines. She told herself it was just the heat, the long morning... but something about the man and the moment stayed with her.

CHAPTER 5

THE road from Graystone curved along the ridge, sunlight filtering intermittently through the shrouded trees. Jake eased the truck into a lower gear, his hand steady on the wheel. He told himself he'd stopped by the vineyard for no reason other than good manners. Just help with a few crates, lend a hand, and move on. That was what people expected of him: show up, smile, disappear before anyone asked for more.

Still, thoughts of her lingered, not inviting him in so much as daring him closer. *Oh, I'm sure they'd love that*, he recalled with a smile. He caught himself replaying the dry humor in it, the way she didn't flinch beneath his teasing. Not many people met his eyes that long.

The road dipped, and a slight movement caught the corner of his vision. On the outside curve stood a narrow pull-off with a wooden cross, sun-bleached and half-hidden by weeds. Someone had tied flowers to the post. A scrap of ribbon fluttered in the wind.

He recognized the spot before he understood why he had chosen this route. The steering wheel tightened beneath his grip. Three years hadn't dulled the picture... the shriek of tires, the flash of flame, the smell of burning fuel. A car overturned, the motorcycle skidding past him before the world erupted in light.

He slowed, his truck crawling past the guardrail. The patch of scorched pavement was still visible if you knew where to look. Jake forced a breath and pressed harder on the gas. Not now. Not again.

He'd been riding along Wolfpen Gap Road that night. One of many thrill-seekers riding his motorcycle, chasin' curves and quiet roads. He hadn't expected to find himself crawling toward an inferno, pulling at a car door that wouldn't open. Breaking the window where someone he couldn't quite make out screamed for help.

The authorities said there hadn't been anything he could do, but the words never stuck. He'd promised himself he wouldn't come looking, not unless he was ready to face what waited behind that memory. He had to focus on the rodeo, contracts, and the people counting on him.

And yet, as the road straightened, his reflection in the windshield looked back at him... older, quieter, and still carrying the same question he'd left here with.

Blue Ridge wasn't supposed to mean anything. It had been a stop on the map, not a night that changed everything. So why did it feel like coming home to something he'd never fixed?

***

By the time Jake parked at the fairgrounds, securely covered the crates, and headed toward the arena, crews were already busy hauling panels and guiding cattle toward the pens. He headed straight for the arena boss.

"Look what the wind blew in." Graham Branson leaned against the fence, arms crossed, hat tipped back. "Thought you'd given up on us."

"Would've, if I had any sense," Jake said, forcing a grin.

Graham laughed, slapping Jake on the back. "You and sense parted ways long ago. Heard Graystone Winery is one of your sponsors. Not bad. Do you have to do anything other than wear a T-shirt with their logo?"

"Yeah, I have some crates I have to deliver when they get their tent set up and they want me to hang out at their wine-tasting tent when I'm not working," Jake said, though the thought had slipped further from his mind since the vineyard and his meeting with Duke.

They walked the perimeter together, checking rails and banners. Graham talked numbers since they both knew Jake's salary would be determined by the take at the different shows. Jake nodded, answering on autopilot. Every smell, every sound dragged him back toward that roadside marker... the gasoline, the smoke, and the sight of a burning couple he couldn't pull free.

"You all right, buddy?" Graham asked finally.

Jake blinked. "Yeah, sorry. Long drive."

Graham gave him a look that said he didn't quite buy it but let it go. "Keep your head clear, Rollins. Duke Gray is pretty important around here. Those sponsorships are what sets you apart from the other cowboys. Try not to end up in the gossip pages before the end of the week."

"Wouldn't dream of it."

Graham smirked. "Uh-huh. I understand the granddaughter you helped out is a looker. She's on the volunteer board *and* Duke's granddaughter. I'd be careful if I were you. I've heard she's a no-nonsense kind of girl and can see straight through the bullshit."

Jake lazily looked over at Graham, poker face intact. "Didn't notice."

"Right," Graham said with a laugh, walking off. "Keep tellin' yourself that."

***

Normally, Jake loved to get immersed in the rodeo preparations, but today the afternoon had dragged on. Duke had already unloaded his truck, so Jake told Graham he was going to check out the town. He should've turned his truck toward his rental, but instead he slowed in front of a small brick building: Mason & Reed, Attorneys at Law. The painted letters were a dull gold, but the name still caught his attention. It matched the envelope folded inside his glove compartment.

He killed the engine and paused to watch the tourists and locals drift between storefronts. There was a weariness in his eyes, a heaviness that seemed to weigh him down even as he sat still. He'd had no intention of stopping at the law office, but the marker on the hill had been a stark reminder of the past he had tried so hard to escape.

Inside, a bell chimed as the door opened, alerting the young clerk behind the counter. "Can I help you?"

Jake removed his hat. "Maybe. I'm looking for someone who handled a case here a few years back, a car accident up on Wolfpen Gap Road."

She frowned, scanning a ledger. "That might've been Attorney Reed, but he semi-retired last spring. He does still come in occasionally. You would have to speak with him about those older files. I can let him know you came by."

"Any way to find out if... there were survivors?" His voice caught on the word.

The clerk hesitated. "I'm sorry, sir. I really can't release details. You'd have to speak with the attorney."

Jake handed her the letter, but not before noticing that it was signed by Attorney Tyler Reed. "I understand. Can you let Mr. Reed know I'd like to speak with him?"

He left a card, though he wondered whether the attorney would call. Outside, he leaned against the truck, watching the world pass him by.

He'd told himself he only wanted facts, not forgiveness. But the welcoming nature of this small town had a way of pulling at old scars. It was time. He could no longer outrun the truth about that night.

He shoved the envelope deeper into the glove box. The answers could wait, but the questions wouldn't.

CHAPTER 6

J AKE had barely dropped his duffel on his bed when his phone buzzed from the nightstand. He considered ignoring it. He was bone-tired, and the day had already been too long. But habit won out.

"Tell me you didn't forget the photoshoot tonight." The voice was sharp, female, and full of caffeine.

Jake rubbed his hand over his jaw. "What shoot?"

"The Graystone Winery promo," she said. "Restaurant, cameras, wineglasses, local charm. Remember? You, my friend, are their rugged face of refinement. Contractual obligation, page three, clause nine."

He sat down. "You've got to be kidding."

"I never joke about sponsorships." The tone softened into something almost sweet. "Read the small print, sweetheart."

"Catherine," he muttered, remembering the name on his contract, "I ride bulls for a living. I'm not exactly sommelier material."

"Then try acting. The restaurant's expecting you at seven. Wear something clean. Try not to smell like livestock."

The line went dead before he could argue.

Jake was used to the grit and grime of the rodeo circuit, not the clinking of wineglasses and whispered conversations. Yet here he was, about to be thrust into a world he'd never imagined being part of.

He glanced around the cozy cabin, its fireplace beckoning. He had to admit his agent had done well finding this place, especially in peak season. He sighed, knowing he had no choice but to fulfill the contract she'd had him sign. The sponsorship gig was a means to an end, a way to keep competing and living the life he chose, never having to settle in one place for too long.

Jake rummaged through his duffel bag, searching for something presentable. Most of his clothes were practical and well-worn, perfect for the rodeo but not quite suitable for a classy restaurant setting. Eventually, he found a clean shirt miraculously free from dust and wrinkles.

He checked his watch. It was just past five. That gave him enough time to shower and mentally prepare for the unexpected role he was about to play. He chuckled to himself, imagining how out of place he would look among the polished staff and sophisticated patrons.

"Well," he mused, "at least they'll get authenticity."

Jake stared at the phone, then tossed it onto the bed. "City folks and their fine print." He couldn't help think of Graham getting a good laugh out of this whole charade.

***

The drive to the Vine Table, located near Graystone Winery, was a scenic one, with rolling hills and lush vineyards stretching as far as the eye could see. It was a stark contrast to the rodeo arenas he was accustomed to. As he approached, Jake took a deep breath, trying to shake off the nerves that had been building since Catherine's call. Lights glowed in the windows, tourists lingered over dessert on the patio, and the scent of roasted garlic drifted out onto the street. *No bulls, no dirt—just wineglasses and cameras. Easy money.*

As he entered the restaurant, he was greeted by an enthusiastic host who seemed genuinely thrilled to have a "celebrity" in their midst. Jake forced a smile, trying to match the energy, and was soon whisked away for a quick tour of the grounds.

The restaurant gleamed with polished wood and brass. A few tables had been cleared for the shoot, bottles of Graystone wine catching the light like jewels. A photographer crouched near a tripod while an assistant fussed with a stack of linen napkins that looked too fancy to touch.

A woman with a clipboard intercepted him before he could get his bearings. "You must be Jake Rollins. You cut it close."

No sense making excuses. "Sorry," he said, flat.

"Think of it as riding a bull," she joked, adjusting the lighting. "Just without the danger. We plan to start with photos of you alone, both in the restaurant and in the vineyard."

Jake laughed and mumbled, "More likely, a bull in a china shop."

He was introduced to the photographer, a lively woman with an eye for detail, who guided him through each shot with patience and ease. The actual photoshoot was a blur of posed smiles and awkward conversations. Jake did his best to appear comfortable as he held a wineglass with the grace of a bull rider, finally relaxing into his role, the initial awkwardness melting away with each click of the camera.

The woman with the clipboard walked up to the photographer and said, "We're running behind. The female model cancelled, so marketing's sending someone from the winery to stand in." Looking at Jake, she nodded to a table. "Sit here." Her smile was gone.

Jake sank into the chair she indicated, turning a wineglass between his fingers. He'd rather be tightening cinch straps or checking bulls than playing model, but Catherine's voice still echoed in his head: *Read the small print, sweetheart.*

He was halfway through wondering if they'd at least feed him afterward when the door opened.

"I'm just dropping off the updated bottle list for the couple's shoot."

The sound of her voice snapped his attention. Savannah Gray stood by the hostess stand, looking about as excited as he was to be here. She shifted in the red silk, body-fitting dress that hugged every curve and left very little to imagination. As the evening light poured through the doorway behind her, it created a striking silhouette around her figure, as if she were framed there in that moment.

Jake tried to look away, but his body betrayed him faster than he could recover.

Seeing Jake's reaction, the clipboard woman's eyes lit with relief. "Perfect! You'll do."

Savannah blinked. "Do for what? They sent me this dress and said I needed to stand in. I am not a model."

The woman put down her clipboard and with a voice infused with honey said, "Our model cancelled last minute. We just need a few quick shots with Mr. Rollins. Nothing complicated."

Jake, trying to control his eyes, which were no doubt bulging from their sockets, leaned back, fighting a grin. "Small town. Looks like we're in this together." he murmured, standing to hold her chair.

Savannah turned a look on him that could have stopped a charging bull. "This isn't my job."

"Page three, clause nine," he said under his breath.

She folded her arms. "What? I didn't sign anything."

The photographer, oblivious to the tension, motioned them into position. "Let's get you two seated. Think relaxed. Familiar. Maybe a laugh between friends."

Savannah exhaled slowly, took the seat Jake offered, and gave him a glare that said *don't enjoy this.*

He raised his glass. "To the fine print."

"Don't push your luck." She might have sounded harsh, but her pulse was racing under her tone. Jake Rollins, cleaned up and dressed in something other than jeans, with his dark brown hair slicked back, was a lot to take in. She found the blend of her lavender fragrance and his spicy musk unexpectedly intoxicating.

The flash went off. "Perfect," the photographer commented. "Give me more of that chemistry.

Jake's eyes drifted toward the bodice of her dress and, when he looked up, he noticed the sudden blush that rose to her cheeks. Her innocence and discomfort made him want to step in and help. He took her hand and pressed a light kiss on the inside of her wrist. *Snap!* went the camera!

Realizing from his expression that he was willing to meet her halfway, Savannah angled her glass toward Jake's, their fingers brushing as crystal met crystal. There was a subtle warmth in her expression, a hint of something unspoken and profound that drew Jake in, making him feel a sense of connection with this girl he barely knew.

"Got it!" the photographer said. "That's the shot."

Savannah set the glass down, trying to ignore her sudden breathlessness. "Are we done?"

"Almost," the assistant said. "Mr. Rollins, can we get one solo of you pouring?" Jake obliged, steady hand, easy smile. He'd faced worse than a camera lens.

When they finally called, "Wrap," Savannah gathered her shawl. "Well, that was... something."

Jake tipped his hat and couldn't resist taking her hand once again, a subtle spark reigniting between them. "They couldn't have picked a better stand-in." He could feel her quickening pulse and stared into the deep hazel of Savannah's eyes. What he saw in them was a mixture of curiosity and hesitation.

Well, I'll be, he thought, his own curiosity piqued. *Maybe there's more to this winery world than I realized.* He had to admit the experience had been more enjoyable than he could have imagined.

With a new appreciation for the unexpected, Jake headed back to his cabin... Graham's warning already fading further and further away.

CHAPTER 7

R ELIEF washed over Savannah as she finally saw the pale gray light beginning to seep through the curtains. The night had been filled with restless dreams, taunting her with what-ifs and maybes. As she lay there, the images in those dreams began to resurface— the wineglass toast between them, the brush of Jake's fingers, the light kiss at her wrist that shouldn't have felt like anything and somehow felt like everything.

Groaning, she rolled onto her back, reminding herself that the previous day's encounter was nothing more than pleasantries and a photoshoot. That's what she kept telling herself. Just fulfilling his sponsorship duties with a few publicity pictures for the winery, nothing more. But somehow the message did not reach her erratic pulse.

She pushed herself out of bed and crossed to the window. Looking out over the vineyard below, soft and silver in the early light, she tightened her resolve. This was her legacy. Her connection to the land ran deep and she took the responsibilities seriously. Since the accident, she'd been all Duke had to help bear the weight of running the winery. Then why did she feel so off-balance? How could one brief encounter with a rodeo cowboy turn everything upside down?

Her dress from the photoshoot hung over the back of a chair. Reaching for it, Savannah froze, noticing a faint trace of cologne—spicy, warm, a little rough around the edges—still lingering on the fabric. It was not her perfume, but his. She pressed the dress to her nose before quickly dropping it, startled by the intensity of her reaction.

"Get a grip, Savannah," she muttered.

Downstairs, the scent was replaced by that of freshly brewed coffee. The multipurpose espresso machine with a timer was one indulgence she and Duke had agreed upon after her grandmother passed. Lois had always been up before dawn with coffee brewing as she made whatever delectable treats of the day. Whether she was making bread, canning preserves, or baking cookies, the kitchen always smelled divine.

Savannah poured a cup, thinking of her grandmother, and carried it out to the porch, trying to shift her thoughts back to work. The fair would open soon, and there were lists to finalize, vendors to confirm, displays to check. Real things. Manageable things.

But she couldn't hide behind her list of chores. For all her careful composure, something inside her had shifted. Jake Rollins, that impossible, aggravating cowboy, had found a crack in her calm, and she wasn't sure she liked how it felt. The last thing she needed was a passing-by, traveling cowboy.

She sipped her coffee and stared toward the distant hills, where the sun was climbing over the ridge. Somewhere out there, he was probably already working, unaware that he'd managed to upend her sense of order with one look, one laugh, one touch.

The screen door creaked, and Duke stepped out onto the porch, a steaming mug in his hand. "You're up early," he said, settling into the chair beside her.

She managed a small smile, then responded simply, "Couldn't sleep."

Duke studied her, his eyes reflecting years of understanding and a hint of worry about his precious granddaughter. "Fair week'll do that to a person. Too many lists runnin' through your head?" he guessed.

"Something like that." She smiled faintly, her gaze drifting out across the vines. "Just want everything to go right."

With an easy assurance, Duke replied, "It will. You always do a good job, Savvy. Your folks would be proud of what you've kept goin' here. Lois, too."

The mention of her family, so recently lost to them, caught Savannah off guard and brought her emotions close to the surface. "I just... don't want to let you down," she confessed quietly.

Duke gave a small snicker. "You couldn't if you tried. This place runs on heart, and you've got plenty of that."

They sat in comfortable silence, the sort that only years of shared routine could create. The morning light stretched over the hills, illuminating the vines with a golden glow.

Savannah managed a real smile. "Guess I'd better get to work."

As she stood, Duke offered one last bit of advice. "Go easy on yourself. Wine's not the only thing that needs room to breathe. Concentrate on the fair. We have the harvest under control."

***

The excitement was building at the fairgrounds by the time Jake rolled in. The opening was getting closer, and the crisp air smelled of livestock and wood, the kind of morning that usually grounded him. Not today.

Shake it off, Rollins. You're here to get answers, not get distracted by red silk and soft laughter.

The sound of hammers and the chatter of early vendors setting up their tents was a rhythm he'd known most of his life. Work. Noise. Routine. That was exactly what he needed now. He grabbed a coil of rope from the truck bed and started toward the pens, keeping his focus on the tasks in front of him. He needed to check the stock, talk to Graham about the schedule, and, most importantly, avoid thinking about a bunch of set-up photos.

Hell, he'd been around plenty of beautiful women. Whether they were reporters, sponsors, or the occasional thrill seeker, they all seemed to be looking for a cowboy story. But Savannah Gray was different. She didn't seek attention; she deflected it. When she sat across from him, she radiated calm control... until he'd broken through it. He could still feel the tremble in her hand when he kissed her wrist.

What the hell was I thinking? Obviously, I wasn't. Still... she had stirred a curious longing in him that begged to be explored.

Graham's voice snapped him out of his thoughts. "Morning, Rollins. You planning to help, or just stand there lookin' conflicted?"

Jake responded with a dry smile, dropping the coil of rope. "You ever try untangling this mess?"

Graham laughed. "That's why I keep you around, Jake. Now, let's get to it."

They worked side by side for a while, the quiet between them easy and comfortable. Eventually, Graham wandered off to check another section of the grounds, leaving Jake leaning on the fence rail, lost in thought about the real reason he was here.

Across the field, volunteers were busy erecting the bigger vendor tents. A banner fluttered in the wind: **Graystone Winery – Local Flavor, Mountain Heart**. The ad captured the moment he remembered most... Savannah's eyes during the wrist kiss, a mix of fire and vulnerability. Although she'd tried not to meet his gaze and failed, he'd caught that hint of genuine emotion before she shut it away.

Jake scrubbed a hand over his face and forced himself to move away from the fence. "Work," he muttered. "Stick to work." Yet despite his resolve to stick to work and keep his distance, her laugh drifted from the direction of the fair tents... light, familiar, and impossible to ignore.

He turned instinctively toward the sound. Savannah stood near the Graystone banner, sunlight catching the edge of her hair as she leaned to adjust a display. For a moment, everything else at the fairgrounds fell away. She looked up, as if she could feel his penetrating stare, and her eyes reached out with an inevitable pull, a silent current between them that carried no explanation.

CHAPTER 8

THROUGHOUT the fairgrounds, the first hint of color tinged the leaves, a reminder that the grape harvest was imminent. It was the soft opening of the fair for VIPs before the public opening the next day. Savannah moved about the Graystone tent with purpose, stacking bottles and tidying up the counter with practiced precision. The lively chatter of the crowd waiting for a tasting mingled with the soft clink of glassware, renewed the sense of pride she felt each time she poured a glass of Graystone wine.

The only thing rattling her composed exterior was the banner Duke had hung. Each time she glanced up and saw it or a customer remarked on it, recognizing her in the image, she couldn't help but cringe. The intimate image made her uneasy, not because of what it showed, but because it reminded her how easily he could disrupt her careful sense of control.

As the guests wandered by, she welcomed the distraction, letting the motion and noise mask her thoughts. Then, in an unguarded moment, she reached for a heavy crate near the display's edge. It shifted under its own weight, the table wobbling as she struggled to steady it. Before she could react, a strong pair of hands reached in, steady and sure, saving both the crate and her balance.

"Careful." Jake's voice carried quiet concern that slipped past her defenses, washing over her like a soothing balm and sending a shiver down her spine.

"I've got it," she insisted, though the spark was undeniable when his fingers touched hers, drawing them closer in an unspoken dance between longing and restraint.

For a heartbeat, neither of them moved. Savannah felt herself drawn to him, her resolve faltering as she responded to the passion in his eyes. The space between them narrowed... and time itself seemed to hold its breath.

"Savannah!"

The sound of her name interrupted the charged moment like a splash of cold water. Savannah stepped back just as Lizzie appeared, weaving through the crowd with her usual zest, a whirlwind of color and energy.

"There you are!" she exclaimed, breathless with infectious enthusiasm and waving a letter in her hand. "I've been lookin' everywhere for you. I got the mentor I was hopin' for! He is an artist in residence at the San Marco Museum, and he's agreed to work with me. Can you believe it?" Her words tumbled out in a rush as she threw her arms around Savannah, completely unaware of the moment she'd interrupted.

Jake cleared his throat lightly, straightening, the curve of a smile tugging at his lips.

Lizzie froze mid-hug. "Oh! Sorry. I didn't see you there."

"No harm done," Jake said easily, though uncertain whether he was more irritated or relieved.

Savannah forced a breath she didn't realize she'd been holding. "That's incredible, Lizzie." Her friend's mention of Italy and the prospect of new experiences tugged at Savannah's deeply rooted responsibilities here at the winery. "You must be thrilled."

"I am. Can you believe it? Art school in the middle of Tuscany *and* my dream mentor!" Lizzie clasped Savannah's hands, eyes sparkling. "And you must come visit. Or better yet, come with me! Think about it, Sav. The vineyards, the old cellars, the way they make wine like poetry. You've talked about it forever."

Savannah's smile faltered as she stole a glance at Jake. "You know I can't just leave the vineyard. Not now."

Lizzie tilted her head, grinning. "'Not now.' That's always your answer. But maybe 'not now' has turned into 'never,' and you just haven't noticed." Her teasing tone made the words softer, but they landed hard, awakening Savannah's hunger for adventure and self-discovery beyond the limits of her familiar world.

Savannah let the words settle uncomfortably. Before her parents' death, she'd never thought of herself as someone who had avoided life. But standing there, she wondered if this was yet another result of losing them?

Jake's gaze lingered on Savannah, something unreadable in his expression. "Italy, huh?" he said quietly. "That's a long way from Georgia."

Savannah met his eyes, the earlier warmth cooling into something more uncertain. "Sometimes distance is what it takes to see things clearly," she said.

Lizzie looked between them, puzzled by the sudden change in tone. "Well," she said with a laugh, "I'll let you two figure out the meaning of life while I go tell Duke the news!" With that, she disappeared back into the crowd.

The mention of Tuscany stayed with her, unwelcome and persistent. She didn't have time to chase foolish dreams of distant adventures, and she purposely began to reset the tasting glasses.

Jake noticed the momentary sadness in her expression... the faraway dreamlike look in her eyes, a softening of her guarded walls. "Would you consider going?"

Savannah sighed, "I do wonder about a world beyond Blue Ridge. Before my mom died, she often urged me to 'spread my wings and chase the promise of distant dreams.' But I have a responsibility to the winery, and to Duke." Her eyes lingered on his disheveled chestnut hair and his neatly trimmed beard, and she resisted the urge to reach out and touch him. "What about you, roaming from place to place? Girlfriend in each town?"

Jake was about to explain there were no girlfriends, but he spotted Graham waving at him from the far side of the fairgrounds. "Hey, can we continue this later? Meet me at the marina at five o'clock, okay?"

Savannah couldn't help the smile that spread across her face. "Sure, I'll be there."

She turned back to the tent, preparing the bottles for one last tasting before she would secure them for the night. The mention of Italy, of adventure and freedom, had aroused something in her she hadn't wanted to face. Maybe Lizzie was right, and *not now* had quietly turned into *never*. The thought followed her like a whisper in the wind, carrying with it both promise and uncertainty.

CHAPTER 9

THE sun was just beginning to slide behind the ridge when Savannah pulled into the small gravel lot by the marina. The fresh sweetness of pine filled the air around the lake, mingling with the pulsing song of the cicadas... a unique blend so characteristic of the area.

Jake was already there, leaning against a weathered piling next to a wooden bench, hands tucked in his pockets. Savannah's gaze lingered on the bench that held so many memories. Her father used to bring her fishing here at Lake Blue Ridge every Sunday when she was growing up. Afterward, her favorite part was sitting on that bench, with the carved bears on either corner keeping watch as her father spun stories about the real ones roaming these woods.

She shook her focus back to the present.

Jake turned as she walked toward him, that easy half-smile appearing, the one that made her pulse skip even when she told herself it shouldn't.

"I hoped you'd come," he said, voice low and even.

"I almost didn't." She forced a small smile. "Duke was still at the fairgrounds, and I wasn't sure if I should..."

"...Show up?" he finished for her.

She nodded, her eyes drifting toward the lake. The surface mirrored the sky so perfectly that for a moment she couldn't tell where one ended and the other began.

Savannah sank onto the bear bench, and Jake joined her. The water lapped softly against the dock, and the steady shrill of cicadas filled the quiet reflection between them. The first stars began to appear... faint at first, then sharp and brilliant against the darkening blue. Savannah tilted her head back, mesmerized.

"I'd forgotten how many stars you can see out here," she said softly.

Jake followed her gaze. "City lights make it hard to see clearly," he murmured. "But here? You can even see the satellites moving if you watch long enough."

"There," she whispered, pointing as a single dot traced its slow path across the sky. "It almost doesn't seem real."

"Neither does this," he said quietly, his eyes on her rather than the stars.

Her breath caught. For a moment, neither spoke. The world felt suspended... the magic of the cicadas' song, the starlit water, and the pull between them all held time still.

Then Savannah looked away, her voice barely above a whisper. "So... this is what you wanted to talk about?"

Jake smiled faintly. "Not exactly. But it's a good place to start."

Savannah studied him in the dim light, trying to decipher his intentions. There was something intriguing about him... a quiet mystery, the way he looked at her so intently. "You came back here for the rodeo, right?"

Normally a man of few words, he sensed that despite her composed exterior, Savannah Gray carried a restlessness that matched his own. "That's part of it."

"Just part?" she asked, searching for what he wasn't saying.

Jake's gaze drifted toward the water, the reflection of the stars shimmering across gentle waves. "Guess it's just time to get some things figured out," he said finally.

She let the silence sit between them. "And do you always figure things out by drifting from one town to the next?"

He laughed softly, no edge in it. "Maybe. Sometimes it's just easier to move than to stop." There was a hint of wanderlust in his eyes, but something deeper too... a man trying to outrun the weight of his own past.

Savannah turned toward him, wondering what had brought him to this quiet town, what demons he carried, what dreams he was still chasing. "So why here? Why Blue Ridge?"

He met her gaze, an unspoken spark flaring between them. "It's been a while since I was here. Some places just feel right before you can explain them." He paused, staring into her moonlit eyes. "Kind of like people."

Savannah tried to grasp the meaning behind Jake's words. She felt an honest intensity about him... the kind of pull that's hard to name out loud.

"Why me?" she whispered, feeling as though she was teetering on the edge of something important.

Jake reached out and touched her hand. The air between them crackled, the promise of unspoken feelings hanging heavy. As their lips met in a hesitant kiss, the spark ignited a fire that had been smoldering beneath the surface, waiting to be unleashed. The kiss deepened into a moment of reckoning... a haven of solace found in each other's embrace.

The surprise of it awakened a desire they'd both buried beneath layers of caution. When Jake drew back, Savannah felt an unfamiliar surge of emotions wash over her, leaving her breathless and wanting more. The way he looked at her, the warmth of his touch... it all made her heart race in a way it hadn't in a very long time.

Jake traced a thumb along her jaw, the motion uncertain, almost reverent. "Didn't see that comin'," he said quietly.

What was he doing? He'd be gone in a week. Then why did he suddenly find himself drawn to this girl in Blue Ridge?

Thrilled and terrified at the same time, she managed a small smile. "Neither did I."

For a while, they sat there holding hands, lost in their own thoughts. Rational thinking seemed to have left Savannah. *What did that kiss mean? Was it a fleeting moment of passion or the beginning of something deeper?*

Jake was a puzzle she couldn't quite solve. She wanted to unravel the mystery that lay beneath the haunted look in his eyes, the shadow of pain he tried to disguise with his easygoing charm.

He stood and reached out to help her up. When she took his hand, he gently drew her close and kissed her again. "Come on. It's gettin' late."

As she walked to her car, her hand in his, she felt a quiet anticipation about what would happen next. "You'll be at the fairgrounds tomorrow?"

He nodded. "Wouldn't miss it." A pause. "You?"

"Of course. I'll be at the booth."

Jake hesitated, as if there was more he wanted to say, then simply nodded. "Good."

With a final kiss, he turned and started toward his truck, boots thudding softly on the planks. She watched until his taillights disappeared into the night.

Savannah exhaled, the sensation of his touch still tingling on her skin. And as she drove toward Graystone, she sensed that her life might never be the same after that kiss. Perhaps it was insignificant, or maybe it was momentous. Regardless, she felt tomorrow would be different.

CHAPTER 10

J AKE arrived at the fairgrounds early, before the gate had been unlocked. He sat in his truck, feeling restless, taking a swig of coffee from the mug he'd brought along. The night at the marina with Savannah had thrown him off-balance. The moment of intimacy was much more than he'd expected, and he wasn't ready to confront those kinds of feelings yet. Right now, he needed the familiar comfort of being in the saddle and burying himself in the simplicity of his work.

The gatekeeper finally arrived and let Jake in. He headed straight for the barn and his quarter horse, Charro. The horse perked up when he saw Jake coming toward him with an apple from the nearby barrel. Jake leaned forward and whispered words of encouragement to the horse that knew him so well. Their bond was evident every time they competed and performed in perfect tandem. He pulled his hat low and tightened the cinch on his saddle, grateful for the work that required no words or thought... just solitude.

He swung easily into the saddle, letting the leather settle beneath him as Charro shifted, checking his balance. Jake had spent countless hours in the saddle, moving with Charro on instinct after years of practice. Around the arena, a few ranch hands leaned on the rail, trading quiet talk about the day's practice lineup while steam rose from paper cups of coffee. Jake gave a small signal, and the horse lunged forward, hooves striking the packed earth in a steady rhythm.

The motion steadied him. Each turn around the pen was another thought quieted, another memory pushed to the edge of his mind, narrowing his focus to the present moment and the connection he had with the horse beneath him. When Charro finally came to a clean stop, Jake ran a hand along the neck of his loyal companion. "That's it, boy," he murmured. The horse flicked an ear, patient, waiting. Jake rested a moment, the warmth of the animal beneath him grounding him in a way that surpassed any words or gestures.

Across the fairgrounds, Savannah arranged the last row of Graystone bottles with the recently released vintage in the forefront. With her natural eye for detail and talent for organization, she moved with practiced ease, an essential part of the family business—especially during peak season.

Blue Ridge was at its best when the fairgrounds came alive with the annual state fair and rodeo just as apple orchards opened for picking and wineries processed their new harvest. Duke was checking the back inventory, focused as always, while Savannah's eyes kept glancing toward the rodeo arena.

She told herself she wasn't looking for him. But her eyes found the ring anyway. Jake on his horse. Despite her attempts to resist, her gaze repeatedly wandered to him, drawn by his natural skill and confidence in the saddle. His connection with all the rodeo livestock was something Savannah admired from afar, especially the way he moved as one with his horse, and she could see the respect and admiration of those who sat on the rail and watched.

Savannah couldn't help but notice the group of young women gathered, gazing at him with infatuation. Just when she was about to believe the night at the marina never happened, Jake looked her way and winked, suddenly setting her stomach aflutter.

"Someone's got your attention," Lizzie teased, stepping up beside her with a box of tasting glasses.

Savannah blinked. "What? I have no idea what you're talking about. I was just making sure everything's set up."

Lizzie raised an eyebrow at Savannah. "Sure you were." Looking over at Duke, she continued, "I brought an extra box of tasting glasses for you, Duke. And Aunt Natalie asked me to let you know that my cousin, Jeffrey, would be working the Wellington Winery booth. They decided to come from North Carolina this year. She said to stop by before you go back home to check on the harvest."

Duke nodded, clearly trying to look uninterested. "I heard their recent release was fairly noteworthy. Maybe I'll just saunter over there when I have time and have a taste. I'll run back to the winery for a couple of hours and be back in time for our VIP party. Rollins should be here for that around three."

Savannah tried to busy herself with rearranging the banner, but her gaze drifted back to the arena. Jake's focus, the calm authority in the way he rode. She really wanted to see him ride up close.

"Lizzie, would you mind keeping an eye on things here? I'd like to go over to the arena to take a closer look."

Lizzie glanced at her, a hint of surprise in her expression. "Sure thing, take your time."

Jake looked up and spotted Savannah near the edge of the arena. A blush rose on her cheeks as she stepped closer. He pulled the reins and led the horse back to the gate where a cowhand steadied it so Jake could climb down. He was about to walk over to Savannah when Graham stopped him, holding an envelope in his hand.

"Hey, Rollins!" he called, waving it. "Got something for you. Messenger said it came from Mason & Reed Attorneys. Said it was important. You in some kinda trouble?"

The ranch hands around the ring glanced over. The last thing Jake wanted was his business with Mason & Reed to be public knowledge. He took the envelope. His expression didn't change much, not at first. But Savannah noticed the faint edginess in his shoulders, the serious look that replaced his casual smile.

He turned the note over once, twice, before tucking it into his pocket. Whatever it was had unsettled him. The note seemed to cast a shadow over Jake, his usual composure gone. Somehow it raised a flag of concern that Savannah couldn't ignore.

Jake's reaction gave her a sense of foreboding that settled in her gut, hinting at trouble. Jake looked up and hesitated before continuing toward Savannah.

His distraction was obvious when he got closer. "Hi, Savannah. I can't stay and talk. There's something I need to take care of. I'll see you in time for the party."

When Savannah got back to the tent, Lizzie looked at her friend's puzzled face. "What was that all about?"

Savannah shook her head slowly, her stomach tightening. "I don't know," she said softly. "But something tells me it's not good news."

Jake walked away from the arena fence, the sound of hooves and laughter fading behind him. The envelope felt heavier than it should have. He hadn't expected to hear back so quickly. He waited until the noise of the fairgrounds dimmed, then slipped behind one of the storage barns where the distraction gave way to open quiet.

He tore the envelope open and unfolded the single sheet inside.

Jake, I've reviewed the information you left with my clerk. You were right to come looking. There's more to the accident than what you were told. We need to speak face-to-face.

T. Reed, Mason & Reed Attorneys

He read it twice, the words pressing in like the roll of distant thunder. The last thing he'd expected was confirmation that there might be more to that night than he remembered. And yet, here it was, pulling him straight back into a past he'd done his best to forget.

Jake folded the note carefully and slid it back into the envelope. He could hear the sounds again... the distant music, the shouts, the calls from the stock pens... but it all sounded slightly out of tune, as if he were no longer on solid ground.

From across the fairgrounds, he caught sight of Savannah beneath the Graystone tent. Even from here, she stood out... poised, luminous, completely unaware of the storm he'd just stepped into.

He drew a slow breath, settled his hat back on his head, and forced himself toward the noise and color of the fair. Whatever waited with T. Reed, he had a hunch that nothing about what came next would be simple.

CHAPTER 11

THE small law office sat next door to the old post office on Main Street. Jake pushed through the glass door, the familiar bell chiming at his entrance. Inside, the air smelled faintly of paper, ink, and polished oak. He hadn't noticed before, but looking around, it was like time had slowed, a relic from the past that carried decades of legal history within its walls.

The young clerk was not up front. Instead, an elderly receptionist looked up from a ledger, asking his name. Before he could sit down, she motioned toward the half-open door at the back, "Mr. Reed will see you now."

Jake touched the brim of his hat in thanks and stepped inside.

Despite the minimalist setting, the law office carried an air of authority, evident in the well-worn law books lining meticulously organized shelves. Behind a broad mahogany desk sat Mr. Reed, an older man with horn-rim glasses Jake guessed might be in his seventies. He looked distinguished with his silver-gray hair and tailored suit. Jake looked down at his faded jeans and flannel shirt. He squirmed a little, realizing he was being sized up by keen eyes from across the desk.

"You must be Mr. Rollins. I appreciate you coming in."

"Thanks for takin' the time, sir," Jake replied, closing the door behind him. "I got your note today. Wasn't sure if you'd remember an incident from that far back."

Reed gestured to the chair opposite him. "I remember," he said, voice low and deliberate. "We don't often reopen accident files after the initial investigation. I see we sent you a letter from the firm a few months ago. It caught my attention. My file says you were a witness. Can you tell me what you remember?"

The mention of the accident sent a shiver down Jake's spine, unlocking memories and emotions long buried beneath the surface. The chair creaked under his weight as he sat. "It was a few years back." The memory of that night had lingered with him like a stubborn shadow, the echoes of screeching tires and billowing smoke haunted his dreams. Hopefully, Mr. Reed could help.

"I was on my motorcycle up on the Wolfpen Gap Road at a particularly curvy section goin' up a hill. I was behind an old Chevy when another motorcycle came around the bend too fast and crossed the line. The driver of the Chevy couldn't have seen it coming. It all happened so fast. I saw the motorcycle skid by me, but the Chevy went off the road and hit a tree. All I wanted was to help. The motorcycle guy was dead, and I was dragging him out of the middle of the road when I heard screaming coming from the car. I don't remember what all happened. I think I was able to break a window, but then there was an explosion. The next thing I knew, I woke up in the hospital."

He could still feel the blast in his chest, hear the ringing in his ears. He thought he remembered pulling someone from the wreckage just moments before the fire took it all, but he'd never found out what happened, and the incident had haunted him ever since.

Reed listened, face unreadable. "Tragic business," he said, scanning the first page. "You were treated afterward?"

"They kept me overnight," Jake said. "Checked myself out as quick as they'd let me. Didn't see much point stickin' around. The nurse said everyone died. I figured there wasn't anything left I could do."

Reed adjusted his glasses. "There were inconsistencies from the start. Duplicate records, conflicting medical reports. One report mentioned someone being pulled from the wreck before the responders arrived. The details were incomplete. The family involved handled things privately afterward."

Jake's brow furrowed. "So... someone lived? I keep having these nightmares that someone crawled out the window."

Reed's gaze lifted, calm but scrutinizing. "There were indications, yes. That's all I can say." He closed the folder gently. "At the time, my firm received instructions to locate the man who stopped to help. A gesture of gratitude was intended. You had already checked yourself out of the hospital, leaving no forwarding address. Took some time, but we eventually tracked you down."

Jake blinked, the words landing heavier than he expected. "They wanted to thank me?"

"That was the intent," Reed said, a trace of weariness in his tone. "Sometimes people who've experienced a tragic loss find it comforting to think someone tried to help their loved ones. I kept the file active, thinking one day you might show back up."

Jake stared at the closed folder, the faint whir of the ceiling fan the only sound. "You don't have a name?"

Reed met his eyes. "I'm afraid I can't disclose more. However, I can let them know you are in town."

Jake stood, steadying himself, more confused than before. "I appreciate your time, Mr. Reed."

Reed nodded once. "Mr. Rollins... whatever brought you back here, I hope you find what you're looking for."

Jake left the office, the word *Wellington* circling through his mind. He'd seen the name "Wellington" on the tab of the folder.

***

Savannah couldn't shake her curiosity about the note Jake received. Even after what had happened between them the night before, she hardly knew him. Watching Jake walk away, the sudden slump in his shoulders told her more than words could.

Lizzie stepped beside her, wiping her hands on a napkin. "Jake looked distracted," she said quietly.

Savannah nodded, forcing a small smile. "Probably just tired. It's been a long day for everyone." But the feeling that something wasn't right refused to fade.

Duke returned then, carrying a box of brochures under one arm. "You two about finished settin' up? It's near time for the VIP crowd."

"We're ready," Savannah said, adjusting the banner again. She couldn't help pausing to look at it closer.

Duke set the box down, his expression softening as he looked around the bustling fairgrounds. "Your folks would've loved this, you know. They always did say the fair brought out the best in people."

Savannah's throat tightened. Memories of their unwavering support and love lingered in the air, bittersweet and tender. "Yeah," she whispered. "They really would have."

Beside her, Lizzie went still, her hand smoothing a wrinkle in the tablecloth that didn't exist. "They'd surely be proud," she murmured, voice low and careful.

Savannah glanced at her friend, smiling through the ache that welled up. "They'd be proud of both of us."

Lizzie's eyes glistened, the words settling deeper than Savannah had expected.

Duke patted Savannah's shoulder and gave Lizzie a sympathetic nod before moving off toward another tent, leaving the two women standing in the soft, cooling light.

Savannah looked toward the horizon, where mysteries lurked. Somewhere out there, Jake Rollins carried a secret, and somehow she knew it would find its way back to them before long.

CHAPTER 12

THE final preparations were underway for the official party that would mark the opening of the fair that afternoon. The gates were already gathering an enthusiastic crowd ready to enjoy all the fair had to offer, and the sold-out rodeo would round out the week as the finale. In the meantime, there would be livestock shows and practice rounds to keep the arena busy when the cowboys weren't practicing.

Lizzie returned with Duke pulling a cart with a wide assortment of homemade baked goods, relishes, preserves, and various flavors of beef jerky smoked right there in Blue Ridge. Savannah had overseen some of the baking, but most came from local farmers.

She had loved watching her mother and grandmother bake pies, cakes, and cookies for the fair, using some of the Italian recipes passed down by her great-grandmother. All those homemade goods would be proudly displayed, surrounding the featured vintage of the year. After the first year at the fair without her mother and grandmother, Savannah quickly learned baking and canning were not her strongest assets. Fortunately, Lizzie had located a great local substitute.

The Graystone booth had been a mainstay at the fair for generations, serving their finest wines to eager customers year after year. Growing up among the sprawling vineyards and cozy tasting rooms, Savannah had been fascinated by every aspect of the trade, even as a young girl following her father, who instilled in her a deep appreciation for cultivating products from the land. Her father often told her stories about the vineyard's oldest vines... how her great-grandfather had traveled to Italy to bring home vintage cuttings and had remarkable success in adapting them to the soil at the winery.

This year's showcase wine was a beautifully crafted cabernet-franc blend, aged five years to allow the complex flavors to emerge. Duke and Savannah knew their customers would love it. Savannah stood back and watched Lizzie, with her infectious enthusiasm, pair the wines with the baked goods to make an impressive display. There was no question that Lizzie had become a vital part of the Graystone team, and knowing she'd soon leave for Italy made the day's excitement bittersweet.

The thought of Italy once again brought a wave of wistfulness. Though her demeanor remained composed, she knew there was a hint of anticipation in her subtle glances toward the gravel lot, where Jake Rollins was expected to arrive for his sponsorship duties. She was curious whether his earlier mood would carry over. Graystone needed his easy charm, sincere smiles, and steady confidence to draw people in.

She tentatively looked over at the giant poster of the two of them at the photoshoot dinner with a bottle of their featured wine between them. Savannah had to admit that the photographer knew her business. She'd caught them at an off-guard moment; the photo perfectly conveyed the electric spark exchanged between them.

Lizzie backed away from the booth to stand next to Savannah, both assessing every detail. "Shouldn't Jake be here by now? When I was coming out of the bakery, I saw him go into Mason & Reed's law office. Maybe he got held up in a meeting."

Duke's attention shot to Lizzie. "Jake was down at the lawyer's office? Must've had a last-minute permit issue. But meeting or no meeting, he made a commitment, and I expect him to honor it."

Savannah intervened. "No reason to make a fuss, Duke. There he is now, parking his truck. We will get things set up here. Why don't you go check out the Wellington Winery booth. I think it would mean a lot to Natalie. It's their first time here, and Jeffrey's in charge."

Duke rolled his eyes but relented. "All right, but you be sure that boy toes the line. I'll be back after I try what Wellington's offerin'." Then, muttering to himself, "Wonder where Earl Wellington might be?"

Savannah and Lizzie watched him saunter off. As he moved through the fairgrounds, interacting with vendors and customers alike, his charisma was undeniable. Duke had a way with words, effortlessly making connections and leaving a lasting impression wherever he went.

Savannah exhaled and turned back to the booth, unaware that Duke's visit to the Wellington booth would stir more than old rivalries.

***

Jeffrey Maxwell had been waiting for this moment. Against his mother's pleas to stay quiet, he was determined to face Duke Gray himself. He knew their current release of Wellington's cabernet had exceeded expectations, and he wanted Duke Gray to try it firsthand. This was Jeffrey's first vintage since Earl had stepped away from running the winery full time.

As Duke approached, Jeffrey busied himself with the appearance of nonchalance. Despite his success, Duke had always remained grounded and approachable, earning him respect and admiration across the community, and he was known for fostering a sense of unity and camaraderie. But the Gray family's history was not without its scars. A long-standing rivalry with the Wellingtons—stemming from a bitter dispute years ago over a piece of land—had divided the two families for generations. The land had long since changed hands, yet the tension lingered.

Duke was not one to shy away from a challenge. As he approached the Wellington booth, he saw an opportunity to extend an olive branch.

Jeffrey inwardly cursed as his mother walked toward Duke. He didn't want her interference; he wanted Duke's approval on his own merit.

Duke tipped his hat politely to Natalie as she approached, though his eyes were on the man at the booth, studying him closely. Jeffrey flinched under Duke's piercing scrutiny but quickly regained his composure. He'd rehearsed a dozen ways to greet Duke Gray, none of which seemed quite right now. Still, this was the moment. He straightened his collar and reached for the bottle resting on the tasting counter.

"Mr. Gray," Jeffrey said, his voice steady though his pulse quickened. "An honor, sir. Would you care to try our new cabernet?"

Duke smiled... that calm, measured look that never revealed more than he intended. "Call me Duke. Everyone does. Your mama here has been tellin' me good things about what you're doin' over there at Wellington's. Let's see if it lives up to all the talk."

Jeffrey poured a sample, his heart racing as he searched for Duke's approval. Duke accepted the glass, swirling it lightly before bringing it to his lips. Around them, the crowd seemed to fade... just the sound of the glass turning, the quiet breath between the taste and the verdict.

Natalie stood a few steps back, hands clasped tightly, unable to look away from Duke's expression. He took another sip and nodded once, the gesture offering praise that was both genuine and measured. "You've done fine work here, son. A strong wine. Confident but not overdone."

Jeffrey exhaled, his relief almost imperceptible. "Thank you, sir. That means a great deal to us."

It was a small exchange, courteous and professional, but to Natalie, it was a relief. For the first time in years, the Gray and Wellington names had met in public without bitterness or pretense. Yet beneath her gratitude, she felt the smallest tremor of unease. Thankfully, he had not asked about Earl.

***

Jake stepped through the crowd, noting the way the late-afternoon light caused a glow on the Graystone banner. He slowed when he saw the poster standing tall beside the tasting table.

He remembered that moment during the evening: the laughter, the photographer's easy chatter, Savannah's hand brushing his as she reached for the bottle. But in the photo, frozen between smiles and shadows, there was something he hadn't noticed before—something that felt too real for a promotional shot.

His gaze drifted from the image to the woman herself, only a few feet away, opening a bottle of the new vintage. The resemblance was uncanny, but what caught him wasn't the likeness... it was the warmth in her eyes when she glanced up and caught him watching.

For a second, neither of them moved, mirroring each other's hesitation. It wasn't a smile, not exactly. But the way her eyes held his, steady and certain, said more than a smile could. He'd come to the rodeo out of obligation and to search for answers to an accident that haunted him. Yet the unexpected connection he felt in this singular instant left him questioning everything.

CHAPTER 13

DURING social events, Savannah felt the loss of David and Margaret most acutely. That grief had only deepened when her grandmother, Lois, died months later. She and Duke had been devastated. At the winery, work helped. But in public, surrounded by sympathy, it was harder to bear.

She took a deep breath, knowing what was expected of her. Admittedly, it had become easier with strangers and her interactions with the visitors were marked by a genuine interest and a friendly demeanor that made them feel welcome and appreciated. Even when the booth was crowded, Savannah maintained a poised composure that Jake couldn't help but notice. He found himself drawn not only to Savannah's energy and efficiency but also the occasional look of vulnerability she had when she glanced in his direction.

"You handled the crowd like a pro," he said finally, his voice low, during a quiet break in the activity. He looked at the number of empty wine cases and added, "It looks like today was a big success."

The day's success had lightened her mood and, with a twinkle in her eyes, Savannah smiled. "Mr. Rollins, I think you might've had something to do with that. Your fame precedes you, sir, and I do think the entire town of Blue Ridge wanted to come out and meet you. Duke was smart in sponsoring you."

Duke chuckled at her compliment, stacking the empty boxes. "Between his being here and that poster—the crowds were definitely drawn."

Looking at Lizzie, busy tallying the register receipts, Duke asked how they'd done.

Lizzie was beaming. "This is the largest sales day Graystone has had since I started tendin' the register on fair days."

Duke looked at Jake with appreciation. "Nicely done, Rollins." Then, putting an affectionate arm around Savannah, he bragged, "And you, little lady, were the star of the show. Your mama and daddy would be so proud of you. But not half as much as I am."

Jake lingered nearby, pretending to help, though his attention never strayed far from Savannah. His easy smile and playful banter hinted at a connection that simmered beneath the surface. Their shared laughter and meaningful glances added a layer of unspoken understanding about how comfortable they were becoming around each other.

The gentle sway of the poster from the photoshoot mirrored the delicate balance of emotions between Savannah and Jake. Lizzie looked at them and smiled to herself, certain there was a story there waiting to unfold. Neither Jake nor Savannah noticed.

"How about a change of scenery? Maybe dinner, somewhere with real plates instead of paper ones?" Jake's grin deepened. "We could revisit that restaurant from the photoshoot. No camera this time, just dinner."

Savannah's curiosity was piqued. For a fleeting second, as she reached to close a box and he steadied it with his hand, a small, electric moment passed between them. The idea of a quiet evening with Jake sparked a promise of something more profound, a hint of more to be discovered.

Duke saw the exchange between them and scooted them off. "Go on to dinner, you two. Lizzie and I've got this. We'll lock up."

As Savannah and Jake left the fairgrounds behind, Lizzie winked at Duke. "I think our girl's falling for that cowboy!"

Duke gazed after them and reflected. "Love's like fine wine—it needs time to mature and refine. Jake will be leavin' soon... not much time for refinin'."

***

Blue Ridge had its share of fine restaurants, thanks to its steady influx of tourists. The Southern-style restaurant that was the location for the photoshoot was softly lit, the aroma of fried chicken and warm biscuits easily whetting their appetite. A candle glimmered between them, its glow catching the deep amber of the wine in Savannah's glass. Outside, Blue Ridge had quieted, but inside, the evening still carried a hint of celebration from the fair.

Savannah spread warm apple butter on a biscuit, finally relaxed after the long day. "I'd forgotten how good this place is," she said, glancing around the room. "It feels different without all the cameras and lights."

Jake smiled faintly. "Less pressure to perform." He met her eyes across the table. "You were a natural back there with all those customers... like you'd done it a hundred times."

She laughed softly. "I probably have, but today it was the company. We made a pretty good combination with all the locals lining up to meet you, then me sweeping in to get them to taste our wine."

The easy banter between them returned. During dinner, the day's fatigue melted into something gentler... a quiet contentment new to them both. Savannah sensed something in Jake beneath the devil-may-care rodeo cowboy, particularly when he'd received the note from the attorney... a vulnerability that he tried to conceal, as if he was still proving something to himself and the world.

As the waiter refilled their glasses, Savannah's curiosity enticed her to probe gently into what had happened earlier that day. "Jake," she said carefully, "that note you received at the arena... I've been meaning to ask about it. Was it bad news?"

Jake's fingers tightened around the stem of his glass. "Nothing I wasn't expecting," he said after a moment. "Just some old business that needed tendin' to."

But even as he said it, the name he saw on the file at the lawyer's office circled back through his mind.

Wellington. He had noticed the other winery booth with the Wellington banner today at the fair.

Something in the way he said "business" made her hesitate, but she let it go. The pause stretched between them... questions left unasked.

Finally, eager to change the subject, Jake drew from the comments he had heard Duke make earlier. "Tell me about your family," he said quietly. "I know Duke's rightfully proud of you, but what about your parents? Were they involved in the family wine business?"

Savannah rested her elbows lightly on the table and took a deep breath, suddenly wanting to share her loss with Jake. Her fingers delicately circled the base of her wineglass, a subtle habit honed from countless tastings and intimate knowledge of the world of wine. Her eyes held a mixture of fond reminiscence and quiet sorrow. Jake squeezed her hand, his touch bringing her a moment of solace, realizing how hard this must be for her. "Tell me whatever you're comfortable with. I'm genuinely interested."

"My great-grandparents migrated to this area from Italy. Their family had been in the wine business for generations, and they brought the rich tradition of their winemaking process with them. They faced hardships and struggles as they tried repeatedly to adapt their Old World vines to the acidic soil of North Georgia. But they refused to give up. They kept working the local soil, learning the nuances of the land until they could find a formula that would give their vines, which were used to a softer, more alkaline earth back in Italy, a chance to thrive. This adaptation was the beginning of the unique blends that allow Graystone to stand out among its peers."

Jake was fascinated by her family's resilience and determination. "They must have loved it here. It sounds like it was not just a business; it was a labor of love. They obviously figured it out. Is that why you want to go to Italy?"

Savannah, lost in her family nostalgia, nodded, then continued. "Once they found ways to compensate and knew the varietals that would prosper here, they returned to Italy for more vines. Duke was a small boy then, but he still remembers that trip. His father instilled in him a love for the business and particularly for creating innovative blends. He's always had a nose for the right minerals or fruits to bring out in a vintage. It is an art to know exactly how long a barrel should be aged. My father learned from Duke and became a skilled winemaker who poured his heart and soul into making exquisite vintages that enchanted the palate, and he began receiving awards. He was the creator of the vintage we were selling at the booth today."

A tear fell from Savannah's eye. "The vineyard was not just a business to my family; it was a manifestation of their dreams and hard work. My mother thrived on the bustling energy that surrounded the winery. She loved the guests, greeting each one with an abundance of Southern hospitality. My father was happiest out among the rows at sunrise. Everyone worked hard, but they loved what they'd built."

A soft smile of remembrance touched her lips, then faded. "It was good for a long time. Until the accident."

Jake listened, his fingers tightening around his glass. "Accident?"

She swallowed, trying to speak around the lump that had formed in her throat. "It was fall... three years ago. I was a senior in college. My parents had promised to take me to Italy when I graduated, and I had doubled up on my classes to graduate early by the end of the fall semester. They were driving home late from a delivery. A storm was threatening through the mountains. A motorcycle came around a curve too fast." With a deep swallow, she continued. "The police say my father tried to avoid him and drove off the cliff into a tree. Neither of my parents survived the explosion."

The candle flickered, catching the faint tremor in her voice.

Jake stared at the flame, his pulse beating hard in his throat. A mountain road. A motorcycle. An explosion. Three years ago. *Oh my God.*

The memory came rushing back... the motorcycle running into their lane, the screech of tires, the sound he could never forget. Surely it was a coincidence. He forced his voice to be steady. "Savannah, I am so sorry. That must've been devastating to lose them both like that. I guess no one could survive an explosion like that."

Savannah took the handkerchief Jake offered her and dabbed at her tears. "The sudden loss shook us to the core. I came home from school and couldn't go back. Eventually, I finished my classes online, but there was no way I would leave Duke, and especially my grandmother. She wouldn't eat. She hardly came out of her room. She was just crushed. That left Duke and me trying to deal with the grief while carrying on with business. Those were some really dark days."

Jake took her hands across the table. "I can't imagine."

"Then, before we'd had a chance to heal from the loss of my parents, another blow hit us with the sudden death of Grandma. She had a heart attack and Duke was convinced she died of a broken heart after losing her son and her daughter-in-law."

Savannah smiled softly then, her hand gently squeezing his back. "Thank you for listening, Jake. I haven't shared this with many people. You've got a way of making the hard stuff easier to talk about."

Jake's thumb grazed her fingers, the instinct to hold on to her fighting against everything he now realized. He pulled back slowly, forcing a small smile. She mistook his hesitation for tenderness, her expression warm and open. "You're a good man, Jake Rollins."

He looked away, his jaw tight. *If she only knew.*

Jake tried to answer, but the name from Mr. Reed's folder landed in his mind again, Wellington. Reed hadn't said anything about the Grays. But they were speaking of the survivor, not the deceased.

Outside the restaurant, Savannah hesitated beside her car, sensing something in Jake—a distance she hadn't felt before. She offered a questioning smile, wanting to ask if she had ruined the evening. But, instead, she kept quiet, then drove off beneath gathering clouds, the uneasiness following her all the way home.

CHAPTER 14

J AKE sat alone in the dark on the porch of his rental cabin, taking the occasional sip of whiskey. The night seemed to close in around him, thick and stifling. He felt trapped by the haunting memories. What a tragic twist of fate that the echoes of that night might hit closer than he could have imagined.

Thoughts of Savannah pierced his heart. He hadn't meant for the evening to end the way it had. He'd planned a quiet dinner, maybe a few laughs. How could he have known that the same accident that plagued his dreams had taken her parents and changed her life? In his mind, he replayed every word she'd said, every image her voice had painted... her pride in her family and their vineyard, and then the horror of the accident that killed her parents and subsequently her grandmother.

Now, three years later, the past had come back to confront him. A motorcycle. An explosion. The same night. The same road. How could he face the daughter of the couple he had failed to save?

The letter from Mr. Reed lay on the counter where he'd dropped it earlier. It had been waiting for him at the cabin. He unfolded it again, though he could recite every word by heart. The lines were few, but the weight behind them had deepened:

Mr. Rollins,

You were correct about a survivor. I have been in touch with the estate, and they have requested your discretion until the sealed documentation can be reviewed. We would appreciate your speaking only to me about this.

Attorney Tyler Reed

Jake stared at the paper until the letters blurred. There had been no mention of the name *Wellington*. Still, the possibility that a survivor existed—someone who might hold the answers to what truly happened that night—tightened Jake's chest with anxiety. The thought that someone could be out there carrying the truth he'd questioned for so long, while Duke and Savannah remained completely unaware, was almost too much to bear. Each unanswered question seemed to multiply, making the silence around the accident, with the mention of compensation and sealed documents, tainted with secrets hidden beneath the surface.

He knew one thing for certain. The past was not done with him yet. What were the odds that he might be falling for the one person who represented everything he'd failed to protect?

***

Savannah sat at her vanity, the lamplight soft against the framed photo of her parents that always seemed to watch over her. The evening replayed in her mind. Jake's quiet pauses, the way his gaze had drifted when she mentioned the accident. She'd told herself it was nothing, that he was tired from the fair, but doubt had a way of undermining even the best memories.

She traced a fingertip along the edge of the photo, following the familiar curve of her mother's smile. *Did I say too much? Was I wrong to bring it up?* The questions came one after another, uninvited and unkind.

Savannah wanted to allow herself to be vulnerable and feel things she had long held beneath layers of protection, but her fear of being hurt was real. Maybe he was just having an off night. It was the first time in a long while she had developed romantic thoughts about someone. *What if he didn't feel the same way?* As thunder rolled in the distance, she couldn't help but wonder if maybe, just maybe, it was time to lower her defenses and let someone in. If only her mother were here, she thought wistfully, perhaps she would have the courage to take a leap of faith.

By the time she turned off the light, the photo on the dresser caught the faintest reflection of lightning, and for a moment she could almost believe her parents were trying to tell her something she couldn't quite hear.

She drew a steady breath. The rodeo was only a week away. Whatever Jake was holding back, she needed to understand before he left... while there was still time to ask.

***

Jake woke before dawn, his face etched with lines of exhaustion and worry. The weight of Mr. Reed's letter bore down on him, clouding his thoughts and haunting his sleepless night. *What was all the secrecy about?* Savannah had never mentioned a survivor. *If someone was in the car with her parents and lived, how could Duke and Savannah not know?*

He stepped onto the porch, watching the sun rise over the mist-covered foothills. His gut told him the survivor did not want anyone to know they had been in the car that night. But how could something like that be kept quiet? Jake racked his brain trying to remember that night. Was the window he broke in the front seat or the back? Who was it that crawled out?

He made coffee out of habit and stood at the counter staring into the steam, the letter still lying folded but not far from reach. The mandate of silence weighed heavily on him. He felt like a puppet in a grander scheme, expected to dance to someone else's tune. Somehow he knew breaking his word to Reed would make everything worse, especially if the survivor was tied to Savannah's family in ways no one had revealed.

As if on cue, his phone buzzed with a text message from Reed:

Appreciate your cooperation, Mr. Rollins. The estate is proceeding cautiously. Please avoid further discussion of the matter until instructed.

The message only deepened his turmoil, the word *cooperation* ringing hollow in his ears. How long could he keep the truth from Savannah? Honesty had always been a guiding principle for him, yet the repercussions of defying Reed's instructions were too daunting to ignore.

Jake gazed out over the ridge. Somewhere beyond the trees lay the fairgrounds, where Savannah was moving through her day as if nothing had changed. He couldn't bear the thought of her going about it unaware of the secrets that surrounded her.

Jake clenched his jaw. What was the connection between the survivor and Savannah's family? Would the truth hurt her? How could he know?

One thing was clear. Jake Rollins needed answers about what really happened that night, and he was determined to find them.

He just hoped that finding the truth wouldn't cost him the trust of the one person who was beginning to matter most.

CHAPTER 15

NATALIE Maxwell paced the floor of her living room while Jeffrey poured the last of the bottle of cabernet. There was a steely resolve on Natalie's face... her every decision weighed down by the burden of protecting those she held dear. Propelled by a fierce sense of loyalty, she found herself navigating the treacherous waters of secrets, sacrifice, and half-truths.

Her gray-streaked hair and the lines of her face hinted at wisdom and experience. To the world, she appeared poised and composed. But when Jeffrey handed her a glass and her features softened slightly, he could see the sadness in her eyes that he knew she kept carefully concealed.

The first day of the fair had gone better than either of them had expected. Duke's visit to the Wellington booth had been anticipated. When he stopped by to taste their new vintage, Jeffrey found it stirred up old doubts and insecurities.

"Duke didn't stay long. He was polite... even seemed to approve of the wine. He said it was 'confident but not overdone.' What does that even mean?"

Natalie smiled faintly. "That sounds like Duke. Considering the history between the Wellingtons and the Grays, I'd consider that a positive response."

He nodded, then frowned. "Do you think he suspected anything?"

"About what?"

"About... us being at the fair. Me manning the booth. About any of it."

Before she could answer, the phone rang—a sharp, old-fashioned sound that cut through the stillness. Natalie's hand froze halfway to her glass. "Who would be calling at this hour?" For an instant, she didn't move.

Jeffrey started to rise, but she was faster. "I'll get it," she said quickly and lifted the receiver. "Hello?"

A pause. Her posture stiffened. "... Yes." Another pause. "Yes, he came by."

Her voice lowered. "No. There was no scene. Everything went as well as could be expected."

Her fingers tightened on the receiver. "I asked you not to call tonight."

A long silence followed, broken only by the clock's tick. "No, he doesn't know. None of them do. And it needs to stay that way. Why on earth would you get Jake Rollins involved?"

She listened for a moment longer, then whispered, "Please, just don't make it harder," before hanging up.

A heavy silence settled over the room, the unease from the call still hanging in the air. Jeffrey stared at her. "Was that who I think it was?"

She met Jeffrey's questioning gaze with a flash of something unreadable in her eyes... a silent warning not to probe further. "Let's leave it alone, Jeff. For everyone's sake."

With a shared look, they both understood the unspoken agreement between them. There were some truths better left alone, some questions best left unanswered.

Natalie stood for a long time, staring at the silent receiver. She held the pieces of a delicate puzzle in her hands... a puzzle that threatened to shatter at any moment.

Jeffrey spoke softly, careful not to startle her. "You hate this as much as I do, don't you?"

She turned toward him, the mask of composure slipping just enough for him to see the truth underneath. Jeffrey's discovery had forced her to face the consequences of keeping secrets since the accident.

"I hate all of it," she admitted. "Every lie. Every time I look at them and can't say what I know." Her loyalty, unwavering and fierce, was her greatest strength and her heaviest chain.

He hesitated. "Then why keep doing it?"

"Because, after all this time, stopping would destroy people I care about." She sank into the chair across from him, her voice breaking just slightly. "Duke... Savannah... even you. None of you deserve the wreckage that would come from this. And now Tyler

Reed and his law office have stirred everything up by seeking out the man at the scene of the accident that night. Those records are supposed to be sealed."

Her gaze drifted to the window, reflecting. Some promises, she thought, were never meant to be broken, or sometimes even remembered. The past had already claimed so much, and to uncover it now would only take more from them.

Natalie gave him a small, bitter smile. "That's the part I didn't think through." She looked down at her gloveless hands twisting the stem of her wineglass. "Your uncle made mistakes. So did I. This could all have been handled differently. But we can't undo what's been done. All we can do is try not to make it worse."

He wanted to press her, to demand more, but the defeat in her eyes stopped him.

"I know you think I'm protecting him," she said, her tone low. "But I'm protecting everyone else from the truth about him."

Jeffrey nodded slowly. "And if Duke ever finds out?"

Her voice went barely above a whisper. "Then that's the day everything ends."

***

Natalie and Jeffrey were sharing a quick breakfast before heading back to the fairgrounds for the day when an unexpected rap on the door took them by surprise. Jeffrey looked up from his newspaper, the edge of fatigue still in his eyes.

When Natalie opened the door to find her niece, Lizzie's smile met her like sunlight after rain.

"Aunt Nat! I just had to stop by for a minute... everyone's talking about the fair!"

Natalie stepped aside. "Come in, sweetheart."

Lizzie breezed through the doorway with all the effervescent energy of youth, dropping her jacket over the chair and talking before she'd even sat down. "The Graystone booth was amazing yesterday! I don't think we've ever sold so much wine in one day." With a grin, she added, "Of course, half the crowd came because of Jake Rollins. People were lined up just to meet him, and while they waited, they bought bottles... dozens of them! Savannah had the crowd in the palm of her hand, and I could barely keep up at the register."

Jeffrey's mouth curved, but not in amusement. "Well," he said, turning the page of his newspaper, "it helps when you have a celebrity working your tent. Hard to compete with a rodeo poster boy. You know, we tried to sponsor him, but Duke had already set his eyes on him."

Lizzie laughed, missing the edge in his tone. "Oh, come on, Jeffrey. You'd have liked him. He was so gracious, signin' autographs, talkin' about the vineyard—like he'd been one of us for years."

The old rivalry still simmered beneath his composure, remnants of past conflicts.

Lizzie went on, bright as ever. "And Savannah... well, let's just say she couldn't stop smilin'. I think she might be fallin' for him."

The words landed like stones in the quiet room. Natalie felt the air shift, heavy again.

A relationship between Savannah and Jake Rollins might set in motion a chain of events that would ruin the delicate balance she had worked so hard to maintain. She caught Jeffrey's glance and knew he, too, understood the peril. Jake slipping information to Savannah could reopen old wounds they had both fought to keep closed.

Lizzie noticed nothing, gathering her bag. "Anyway, I just wanted to share the good news. Duke did tell us he thought the Wellington cabernet was excellent."

"That's good news, dear," Natalie said softly. "We need to get to the fairgrounds. See you there?"

Lizzie smiled and nodded, unaware of the effects of her visit. When the door closed behind her, the silence returned. Thicker now, almost tangible. Jeffrey set his paper down without speaking. Natalie stared out the window, a wave of foreboding sweeping over her... a feeling that the past had started to unravel, no matter how carefully she'd tried to keep it buried.

CHAPTER 16

J AKE couldn't shake the feeling that the accident was more complicated than it appeared... that there was a part of the night he should remember. Determined to uncover the truth, he turned to the local library, hoping to find answers in the archives. Jake was not only seeking closure but also a sense of justice. Maybe that's why his subconscious never let go of that night.

He scrolled through article after article, his mind racing with possibilities, each one repeating the same sparse account of the accident that had taken Savannah's parents. When he saw the date, he knew. It was the same night.

"Local couple, David and Margaret Gray, and motorcyclist Randy Townsend of North Carolina, were tragically killed in a crash on SR-180. From the position of the motorcycle and the skid marks, the accident was deemed the fault of Mr. Townsend. No

witness came forward to make a statement. Investigation closed."

No witness came forward. The words lodged in his chest. Mr. Reed had said they came by his hospital room for a statement, but he'd already checked himself out. *Why didn't I go to the police? Why can't I remember more about that night?* Nowhere could he find anything about someone surviving.

He leaned back, rubbing his neck in frustration. Reed had said the files were sealed. What struck Jake now wasn't what was written; it was what wasn't. He had pored over reports and faded photographs. The absence of the Wellington name in any official records raised red flags in his mind. Someone had buried the connection, and that knowledge sparked a relentless determination in him to uncover it.

He searched through the archives again. Wellington Winery, Asheville, North Carolina. The motorcyclist had been from North Carolina. There was no related information regarding Randy Townsend, other than that he left a grieving family in Fayetteville... nowhere near Asheville. *Where had he heard the name Wellington before?*

Then he remembered. Wellington Winery had reached out to his agent before the rodeo, offering to sponsor him. She had declined since Graystone already had him. He'd heard the name again at Duke's sponsor meeting, when Duke had mentioned in passing that Wellington had wanted Jake too. At the time, it felt like small talk. Now it didn't.

At dinner the night before, Savannah had spoken about her parents and seemed to be unaware of any survivor. If she didn't know about any of this, then every new piece he uncovered might risk hurting the only person who made him think about staying in Blue Ridge.

He stared at the headline on the screen, his reflection faint in the glass. A line of thought was forming, unwelcome but relentless. The missing survivor. The sealed files. The Wellington connection that everyone seemed to avoid mentioning.

Outside, a siren wailed faintly down Main Street, fading into silence. Jake gathered the stack of printed clippings, sliding them into a manila folder from the desk. He wasn't sure what he was looking for yet, but he knew one thing for certain: Savannah didn't know the whole story, and someone wanted to keep it that way.

He rose, the folder tucked beneath his arm, a fleeting memory of her smile in his mind... open, trusting. Whatever the truth was, he'd find it quietly. She deserved that much.

When Jake made his way back to the fairgrounds, Graham was waiting for him. "Jake, you've seemed distracted the last few days. You know, cattle roping is the first event of the rodeo. Why don't you get in some practice?"

With a subtle glance toward the Graystone booth, he nodded with a practiced smile. "Yeah, those cows have been a mite frisky lately. I'll go check out the practice ring."

Graham patted him on the back. "We're expecting big things from you, son. The rodeo here in Blue Ridge is completely sold out."

Jake headed to the ring and grabbed a lasso from one of the cattle hands. From an early age, he'd shown a natural talent for roping, and he normally loved nothing more than to spend hours practicing in the dusty ring behind the barn, his rope moving with precision and grace. Despite his usual enjoyment of the sport, this time each throw of the rope, looping it again and again around a battered post, felt forced without his full concentration.

Sweat darkened the brim of his hat and dust clung to his jeans, but nothing eased the restlessness left from the library that morning. The idea that there was more to the accident than Savannah was aware of caused a knot to form in the pit of his stomach. His instinct told him if something was being hidden, it couldn't be good.

When he finally stopped to coil the rope, his gaze drifted across the fairgrounds. Beyond the rows of vendor tents and fluttering banners, the Graystone booth stood out in familiar colors. Savannah was there, moving with confidence, pouring samples, and chatting with guests... clearly in her element. The late-afternoon sun caught the highlights in her hair, adding a radiant glow that seemed to match her personality.

Jake hesitated, the rope still in his hands. He could have walked the other way, blended into the crowd, but he couldn't stop thinking about her. He wanted to know the truth about that night, but at what cost?

As hard as he tried to resist, he slung the rope over the fence, dusted his hands, and started toward the booth.

Duke spotted him first, lifting a hand in greeting. "Well, look who decided to make an appearance. You're still drawing customers, Rollins. We should've put your picture on the wine labels."

Lizzie laughed. "People keep asking when you're signing autographs again."

Jake dismissed the compliments and smiled faintly. To be honest, he felt comfortable around Duke's joking banter and Lizzie's easy laughter. "Guess I owe you a few more handshakes, then."

Savannah turned, surprise brightening her expression. "Didn't expect you back so soon."

Jake could see in her eyes that he hadn't handled the end of their dinner together well. "Finished practice early," he said, pushing his hat back, intent on making things right between them. "Figured I'd check in on y'all."

Duke gave Savannah an approving nod. "She's been running this place like she owns it. You might want to steal her away before I work her to death."

Jake met her eyes. "He's right. You look like you could use a break. Care to walk with me?"

Savannah hesitated only a moment before turning to Lizzie. "Can you handle things for a bit?"

"Go," Lizzie said, smiling. "You've earned it. Duke and I will be fine."

As Jake and Savannah stepped away from the booth, they each carried thoughts they weren't ready to share. Then, with gentle intention, Jake reached for Savannah's hand. The simple act dissolved the tension that had built between them, and Savannah's answering squeeze offered Jake reassurance and a quiet sense of hope.

Jake sighed, wondering where to begin. "I know I seemed distracted last night. It wasn't you. I promise."

Savannah tucked a loose strand of hair behind her ear. "I wondered if I had done anything to upset you." She paused, then added, "The preparation for the rodeo must be intense. You ever think about leaving all this behind? The traveling, the constantly being on display, the never-ending pressure to prove yourself?"

Jake's expression was thoughtful. "Sometimes. But it's hard to leave the past behind when it still feels unfinished."

She looked up at him then, her expression softening. "You don't strike me as the running type."

Her insight offered Jake a glimpse of something he'd been missing. Was it possible that she would see beyond the image he presented to the world? "You'd be surprised," he said, willing her to understand the complexity of his inner turmoil.

The wind shifted, carrying the distant sound of laughter and carousel music. She wanted to ask what he meant but didn't. Something in his voice told her he wasn't ready to explain.

Instead, she smiled gently. "Thanks for the walk."

"Anytime," he said. "You needed it." He turned her to face him, then pulled her into an embrace.

They locked eyes. Savannah whispered, "Maybe you did too."

That caught him off guard. He looked down at her, the corner of his mouth lifting despite himself. "Yeah," he admitted quietly. "Maybe I did." His eyes drifted to her lips, and all he wanted was to quiet the small tremble he saw there. She came to him willingly, wrapping her arms around his neck.

They finally turned back toward the fair, walking in easy silence, a sharp contrast to the tension felt at the beginning of the walk. When they reached the booth, Savannah paused, her hand resting on the edge of the table as if anchoring herself.

"See you tomorrow?" she asked, trying to sound casual.

Jake nodded with a smile that began in his eyes. "Count on it."

He started to step away, then hesitated. "Savannah…"

She looked up.

He wanted to tell her everything… the truth, the past, the reason he couldn't sleep… but the words never came. Instead, he offered her a simple reassurance, "You did good today."

Her response was slow and warm, her smile hinting that she understood he wasn't just talking about the fair. She met his gaze, her voice gentle. "So did you."

He tipped his hat, then walked away, the sound of her laughter trailing behind him... bright, unguarded, and almost enough to make him forget what lurked in the shadows.

CHAPTER 17

JAKE Rollins had earned his rodeo reputation through hard work and dedication. He knew how to bring on the charm and please a crowd. But outside of the public eye, his introspective nature preferred a more solitary life. The quiet hills surrounding his rental cabin suited him. As he drove back to his cabin with the windows down, enjoying the cool night air, he suddenly saw a doe and her fawn standing on the side of the road. He lowered his speed to almost a standstill to marvel at nature so close to his doorstep. Careful not to startle them into dashing in front of his truck, Jake found himself wishing he could share the moment with Savannah.

Once his mind turned to Savannah, he smiled inwardly at the way her hand felt in his and the warmth of her smile. It had been a long time since anything with a woman had felt that simple, stirring feelings long dormant within him.

The porch light was still on when he pulled up. He didn't notice the envelope until he stepped onto the top stair. It was tucked under the doorframe, the corner fluttering slightly in the breeze. The formal envelope, with his name typed across the front, gave him an eerie premonition. Who would have hand-delivered all the way to his cabin?

Inside was a folded sheet of letterhead from Mason & Reed Attorneys, and a sizable check. He stared at it, the implications sending a chill through his veins. Slowly unfolding the letter, he read:

Mr. Rollins,

Our client appreciates your continued discretion regarding the events of October 26th. If the matter remains undiscussed, an equal amount will be forwarded in thirty days. Please understand, it is imperative that the Grays remain unaware of this correspondence.

—T. Reed

The implication that his silence about the night of the accident was being bought with a sizeable sum of money presented him with a moral dilemma, a choice between silence for a hefty sum or seeking the truth at the risk of stirring unknown shadows. He let out a low breath, more disbelief than anger, and sank into the chair by the window. He was not one to be bought, especially not when the price was secrecy and a warning to keep the Grays—a family that had shown him nothing but kindness—unaware.

He rubbed a hand over his face, a chord striking deep within his moral code. He hadn't asked for this. He hadn't told anyone what he remembered... or what he still couldn't. And yet someone—Reed, or whoever was behind him—clearly assumed that silence had a price, a bribe disguised as gratitude.

The mention of the Grays lit a fire within him, a determination to protect them from the shadows lurking due to that fateful night. What had he seen? What had he stumbled upon? The memory refused to surface, leaving only fragments of unease and a lingering sense of unfinished truth.

Why keep them out of it? Unless someone feared what they might discover...

He folded the check back into the envelope and tossed it onto the table like it burned. His resolve hardening, Jake made a decision, refusing to be a puppet in someone else's game... a pawn in some power struggle behind closed doors.

He glanced toward the distant glow of town lights. Reason told him the law office would be dark at this hour, but that didn't matter. Someone had crossed a line, and Jake needed answers now.

The only fleeting thought that interrupted his focus on the drive to town was to look for the deer and her fawn. However, as hard as he looked, they were nowhere to be found.

As he suspected, the street was quiet and the office windows at Mason & Reed were dark, the front door locked. Standing tall in the darkness, Jake clutched the envelope, a tangible symbol of the choice he'd made and the consequences he was willing to face.

Then, without hesitation, he shoved it through the mail slot—the check, the letter, the insult—all of it. A defiant reflection of the principles he refused to compromise.

He started the engine of his truck, his anger cooling into something steadier: determination. There was only one person he trusted to hear the truth, even if he didn't yet have all the pieces. Savannah deserved to know what was happening. Whatever this was, it involved her family, and he couldn't keep the burden to himself any longer.

He had no idea what he'd say when he saw her or how he would explain about that night. But wherever the path to truth might lead, he had to follow it... for himself, for Savannah, for Duke, and for the truth waiting to be uncovered.

CHAPTER 18

SAVANNAH checked her watch. It was late, the kind of quiet that made every sound sharper. She had been lost in a captivating book on the sofa when the rumble of a truck cut through the quiet and stopped outside. Headlights swept across the window, and her heart skipped a beat even before the knock on the door. She hesitated, caught between relief and confusion at Jake's unexpected late-night visit. She'd wondered whether she'd see him that evening, staying up just in case. But as the hours wore on, her hope had dwindled.

Opening the door, Savannah found Jake standing there beneath the porch light, hat in hand, his jaw set and exhaustion shadowing his eyes. The tension in him was unmistakable, evidence this visit was more than just a social call. He reached up, gently cupping her face. As if words might fail him otherwise, he kissed her. It wasn't gentle or exploratory like before; it was filled with urgency, a silent plea for understanding. The kiss left her breathless, and she leaned into it, offering him a physical assurance that his presence in her life felt both inevitable and surprising, like a key finally fitting into a long-forgotten lock.

As he pulled back, his voice was a mere whisper. "You asked why I was here," he said, "and if I'd stay." Another heartbeat passed before he continued, "There's something I need to tell you... the real reason I came to Blue Ridge."

Savannah stepped aside, opening the door wider to reveal the firelit room behind her. "Then you'd better come in."

They entered, and the warmth from the fire cut through the chill that clung to his coat. Savannah moved toward the kitchen, her Southern hospitality surfacing instinctively. "Can I get you something?"

He shook his head. "No, thanks."

His reply sounded distracted, more weary than dismissive. She paused, then gestured toward the sofa. "Sit down, Jake."

Jake sat with his elbows on his knees, staring into the fire. The firelight danced across his features, revealing a vulnerability she hadn't noticed before. Savannah settled beside him, her legs tucked under her, close enough to catch the faint scent of his cologne... that masculine blend of musk and earth that pulled her closer.

She sat quietly, allowing him to gather his thoughts. He didn't speak immediately, and she didn't press. The silence stretched between them, full yet not uncomfortable.

Finally, he looked at her, his expression caught between resolve and regret, struggling with a truth he could no longer avoid. "There's something I should've told you sooner."

Her stomach tightened, bracing for the news there was a wife or girlfriend tucked away somewhere. But she pushed the notion aside and kept her voice even. "All right, Jake. Tell me."

Jake's confession unfolded slowly, each word heavy with memory. "I honestly don't know whether I should tell you this, but it has gotten to a point that I feel I have to. About a month ago, I got a letter," he said, gaze fixed on the fire, "from a law firm here in town. Mason & Reed. They said my name came up in connection with an accident that happened around here a few years back."

She frowned slightly, curious. "An accident? Are you in trouble?"

"No. They didn't give details, simply that I'd been listed as a witness. They wanted to meet with me." He took a steadying breath, each word heavier than the last. "The thing is, I don't remember much from that night. It was terrible—just flashes." He rubbed his hands together as if trying to clear away memories.

"It all happened so fast. A motorcycle took the curve too fast... the screech of tires, the motorcycle lying broken on the side of the road, a figure sprawled on the ground." He shook his head, the fire reflecting in his eyes. "After that, I heard shouting from the car. I remember running toward it, and after that... it's fragments. Just pieces of memories." The fire crackled softly, filling the pause that followed.

Savannah's empathy swelled as she watched him struggle through the memories, his vulnerability laid bare. A quiet resolve settled in her... she wasn't going to let him carry this alone.

Jake's voice was filled with sorrow and deep regret. "I went to the law office seeking answers soon after I arrived. Figured if anyone still had the file, it'd be them. I just wanted to see what was on record, maybe understand what really happened that night."

Savannah turned slightly toward him. "Did you ever talk to the police?"

He hesitated before answering. "No, I should have. That's what eats at me. I was in shock, banged up, and I just... left. I wasn't thinkin' straight. Checked out of the hospital, got on my bike, and kept goin'."

"You didn't give a statement?" she asked.

He shook his head, shame settling in his features. "No. It was all over the news for a while, but by the time I was thinkin' straight, I figured they'd already pieced it together. I told myself I was just a bystander, that I couldn't add anything, but that was a lie. I just couldn't face it."

Savannah's heart ached at the quiet remorse in his voice. "You must've felt completely alone afterward."

The weight of that night hung heavily between them. "In a way, I did. Guilty for surviving. Still do," he said. "I keep thinkin' if I'd stayed, if I'd talked to someone, it might've helped the families understand what happened. Maybe even find out who survived."

She leaned in slightly. "There was a survivor?"

"Reed said the records never matched. Different reports... a survivor pulled from the wreck before responders got there. The rest was handled quietly."

Savannah tried to piece it together. "I don't remember anyone around here surviving a bad accident. Did it happen nearby?"

"Not too far," he said. "Up on Wolfpen Gap. Twistin' road, no lights, no time to react."

Savannah nodded slowly. "Wolfpen Gap... I know that road." Something faint and uneasy stirred at the edge of her memory. Almost to herself, she murmured, "That road is hard to navigate any time." Then, quieter, "You never found out who lived?"

He met her eyes. "No. I ran instead of facing it, and I've regretted it ever since."

Jake hesitated, his voice dropping lower. "Savannah, there's more."

She watched him, waiting.

"Someone tried to bribe me not to talk about any of this to you or Duke. It might be bad, but you and your grandfather have been great to me. I can't just take money to keep quiet. And, Savannah, when I was in the law office, I saw a name on the file. It was Wellington."

Savannah froze. "*Wellington*?" The word barely formed. "As in the *winery*?"

Jake nodded.

Savannah's breath caught as shock rippled through her. Someone from the Wellington family was involved in a deadly accident, and she had never known? She pushed to her feet, pulse racing.

"I need to wake up Duke."

CHAPTER 19

DUKE Gray was no stranger to solving difficult situations. Despite being abruptly awakened and groggy, he descended the stairs with a natural air of authority. Halfway down, he stopped, noticing Savannah standing rigidly by the sofa with Jake pale and silent beside her. His sharp eyes took in the tense atmosphere in their troubled expressions.

"What's going on?" he asked, his voice still rough with sleep.

Savannah glanced at Jake, then back at Duke. "We wouldn't wake you unless it was important."

Duke blinked, struggling to focus. "Is someone hurt? Somethin' happen at the winery?"

"No," Savannah replied quickly. "Nothing like that."

Relief flashed briefly across Duke's face, but only for a moment. It vanished as he noted the stiffness in his granddaughter's posture and Jake's inability to meet his gaze.

As Duke sat in his favorite recliner, his demeanor moved from confusion to unwavering focus. "All right," he said carefully. "Let's have it."

Savannah didn't repeat everything Jake had shared. She summarized… the accident, the letter from the law office, a potential survivor, the bribe, and the connection of the surname Wellington.

Duke listened intently, absorbing the information with a quiet intensity. When she said the name Wellington, something in his expression shifted, his brow furrowing as he absorbed the implication.

Jake, head still lowered, added, "I swear I never connected any of this until tonight. I found the letter from Reed with the check attached when I returned to my cabin. Sir, it mentioned your family's name and that I should not say any of this. I honestly don't know why the secrecy, but I knew I wasn't goin' to take some kind of hush money."

Visibly miserable, Jake added, "I don't want to hurt anyone. But Duke, you and Savannah have been nothin' but good to me and there was no way I was gonna keep things from you."

Duke raised a hand, not in accusation but deep in thought. "May I see the letter, Jake?"

Jake's eyes widened with alarm, suddenly realizing he might have made a mistake. "I went by Reed's office first. I didn't want to keep the check and wanted him to know I couldn't be bought." He lowered his head in frustration. "I shoved the letter and check through the mail slot."

"So let me get this straight," he said slowly. "You were involved in an accident three years ago. Someone survived. And the name you saw connected was Wellington."

Jake nodded, throat tight. "Yes, sir."

Duke's gaze hardened with determination. Then, as if connecting the pieces, he said, "And now someone is trying to pay you to keep the events of that night away from my family."

With Jake's answering nod, the implications of someone attempting to buy silence regarding a past tragedy involving his family fueled a fire within Duke.

He took one slow breath, the kind a man takes before stepping into a memory he doesn't want but can't avoid.

Savannah moved toward him, uneasy. "Duke?"

He didn't look at her. His expression became a mix of disbelief, grief, and controlled anger.

"Duke?" she whispered again.

He finally raised his head, looking at Jake with a calm so controlled, it bordered on frightening.

"There's one thing I need to know," he said. He already knew in his gut, but he had to ask.

Jake straightened. "Anything, sir."

Duke held his gaze. "What was the date of the accident you were in?"

Jake took a deep breath. This was the moment of confirmation, from what he'd learned at the library, when everything would come crashing down. "Three years ago. October twenty-sixth." He waited for the re-action but both Duke and Savannah went perfectly still, the date sending shockwaves through them that Jake was present the night of their biggest family tragedy. And that a survivor might have been hidden from them all this time.

Savannah was the first to speak. Her voice cracked. "Duke, that's the night..."

"I know," he replied sharply, hollowly, stripped down to raw emotion.

"My parents," Savannah whispered. "That's the night they died."

"My boy, David," Duke said, voice tight. "My son and my daughter-in-law, Margaret."

Jake saw their pain, horrified he was the cause. "No... no, I didn't want it to be true. When Savannah told me about her parents' accident, it sounded the same. But when she didn't mention a survivor, I thought it must be a different accident." Jake's eyes filled with tears. "I saw the dates were the same when I went to the library. Oh my God. I couldn't save them. I should have done more..."

Duke, tears in his own eyes, lifted a hand, stopping him. "Jake, Savannah said you ran toward the burning car, risking your own life. The explosion caused the car to be destroyed beyond recognition. No one indicated there was an eyewitness, much less a survivor." His voice trembled. "But someone else knew. Someone pulled a survivor out of that wreck, then kept him or her hidden. And that someone let us believe everyone died."

Savannah stared at him, crying, disbelief splintering through her. "Do you think a Wellington survived... and nobody ever told us? How is that possible?"

Jake's voice was barely a whisper. "Savannah, I never meant..."

She looked at him through tear-soaked eyes. "I know. This wasn't you. This was someone who made a choice."

With a plan taking shape in his mind, Duke inhaled slowly, his shoulders rising with a controlled breath, then turned toward the door. "Savannah," he said, "get your coat. You too, Jake."

She blinked. "It's after midnight. Where are we...?"

"To get answers."

His jaw set with determination, he grabbed his jacket,. But as he opened the door, he froze.

Savannah stepped closer, confused. "Duke?"

A plain white envelope was taped neatly to the outside of the door... centered, deliberate, waiting. No stamp. No name. Typewritten.

Duke snatched the envelope down. His hands, usually steady and sure, trembled now for the first time all night. He opened the envelope, unfolded the single sheet inside, and read it without a word. Then he handed it to Savannah.

Her lips moved silently as she read the entire unsettling threat disguised as a cryptic message:

"Walk away from October 26. Some truths aren't meant to surface. We told him not to involve the Grays. You have no idea what you've stepped into. Turn back now."

Savannah's breath caught. "Duke, who would...?"

Jake watched him, throat tight. "They did warn me. I should have never come here."

A sense of grim resolve settled over Duke. He was not one to back down easily. To Jake, he said. "It seems as though we think alike, son. I'll be damned if I'll cower in fear. You're part of this now. We'll face whatever challenges come our way together."

Savannah felt the floor tilt under her. "Duke... this was left tonight. Someone knows Jake is here and that he must have told us."

Jake stepped back, feeling like the walls were closing in. "Savannah, I swear..."

She shook her head sharply. "Jake, this isn't you. Someone is watching us. Right now."

With a calm but resolute demeanor, Duke made a quick decision, guiding Savannah and Jake with a protective hand and a steely resolve. He folded the letter with careful, deliberate movements, then slipped it into his jacket pocket and looked at both of them.

With a firm but gentle hand upon Savannah's shoulder, Duke tried to reassure them both. "We're not going anywhere tonight," he said, voice low and firm. "Not with someone circlin' this house."

Duke continued, "Natalie Maxwell is a Wellington. That's where we'll start. We'll confront her and that son of hers, Jeffrey, in the morning at first light when we're not walkin' into some trap."

Savannah nodded, wiping tears from her face, reaching to hug her grandfather who was her rock of security even as their world seemed to crumble.

Jake looked between them, guilt carved across every line of his expression, the weight of his disclosure bearing down on him. "I'm so sorry. I never meant to bring a threat to your doorstep. I will do whatever it takes to make things right," he vowed, his voice edged with determination.

Duke stepped closer, placing a steady hand on Jake's shoulder. "Jake... you didn't bring the threat. Evidently, it was already here. You just exposed it."

Duke locked the door with a decisive turn, then pulled down the shade as if shielding them from a world that had suddenly grown far too close. Savannah stood frozen where she was, searching her mind for answers. She questioned aloud, "If Natalie is involved, wouldn't Lizzie know something? She's her niece, but she's dedicated to us. Surely, I would know if something dire happened that night. Lizzie has never been able to keep a secret from me."

Seeing Savannah's distress, Jake swallowed hard. "Sir, I'm not goin' back to my cabin tonight," he said quietly.

Duke stood tall, solidifying his position as protector. "It's late. You're stayin' here, Jake. No arguments."

Savannah looked at the man she had so recently met and nodded, though her voice was barely steady. "I'll get you a blanket and a pillow."

Jake shook his head. "I won't be sleepin'."

Duke glanced at him, really looked at him, and gave a single, heavy nod. "None of us will."

Duke fixed a pot of coffee, his mind turning toward the challenges ahead. Jake silently took the cup offered, feeling a deep push toward justice now... a desire to uncover the truth, whatever the cost. When Savannah joined them and took a sip of her coffee, Jake took her hand and, mindful of Duke, quietly grazed the inside of her wrist with a brush of his lips. That gentle gesture, and the comfort of Jake and Duke nearby, was all it took for Savannah to find the courage that ran deep, a resilient determination to uncover the truth surrounding her parents' accident.

Savannah took Duke's hand, her voice raw. "I can't believe Natalie would be involved."

Duke didn't answer at first, his sharp mind working to stay one step ahead of whoever was seeking to deceive them. "We'll get answers," he said finally, voice low and full of steel. "But we're doin' it in daylight."

He looked at them both... Savannah's grief-stricken face and Jake's tortured guilt. He stiffened his commitment to unravel the mysteries of that night and face the challenges awaiting together.

"Try to rest," he said. "Morning's comin' soon enough."

CHAPTER 20

THE early-morning air was crisp, carrying with it a sense of anticipation and foreboding as Savannah, Duke, and Jake prepared to face a day that promised to unravel long-held secrets. Savannah, nerves on edge, clutched her jacket tighter, seeking both warmth and protection from whatever the day might bring.

"Which truck are we taking?" she asked quietly.

Duke seemed poised for a confrontation. "You two take Jake's truck. I'll be right behind you."

No one objected. Jake held the door for Savannah, his glance carrying a silent promise that he wasn't going anywhere. In the truck beside her, he exuded a fierce protectiveness, his eyes a mirror of the unspoken bond that had formed between them. Overnight, they had become kindred spirits, carrying a shared history of pain and unanswered questions. Behind the wheel, Jake's every muscle seemed taut with anticipation, his focus straight ahead as though bracing for an impending storm. Savannah sat close beside him, realizing they were undeniably in this together.

In the truck behind them, Duke drove with a determination that reflected his inner turmoil. As they turned onto the gravel road leading toward the fairgrounds, the early-morning quiet felt almost eerie. The lights were on, but muted... a stark contrast to the previous day's laughter and noise. Vendors were beginning to unzip tents, the clink of metal poles echoing across the stillness.

After parking, Savannah whispered anxiously, "You think she'll be here this early?" Her heart pounded. She couldn't believe Natalie had anything to do with this.

Duke didn't answer immediately, still shocked over the possibility of Natalie's involvement. He stared straight ahead, thinking of all the times when Lois was still alive that they'd gone out together as couples. He said confidently, his voice carrying something Savannah had never heard in it before. "Natalie won't miss fair days. She's steady. Reliable. Always has been." He drew a steady breath. "That's why we'll check here first."

Jake stood beside them, scanning the grounds with the same wariness Savannah had seen the night of the bench confession. Out of habit, he shot a glance toward the arena where he'd play a major role in the upcoming rodeo. Was he prepared for whatever upheaval would happen between now and then?

"Somethin' doesn't feel right," he murmured.

Duke shot him a look. "Yeah, it's that prickle you feel when you don't know what's comin'."

Savannah swallowed hard. The Wellington tent was only a short walk away, its blue banner fluttering in the morning breeze. But it wasn't just the tent. It was the feeling that her entire understanding of the accident was about to unravel.

Beside her, Jake lightly touched the small of her back. "I'm right here," he said simply.

She nodded. It was all she could manage. With a final glance exchanged between them, they crossed the empty fairway toward the Wellington tent, where answers awaited, and where truth would demand its due.

Jeffrey was setting up his display when he spotted the three of them walking with a sense of purpose toward him. His eyes darted nervously from one to the next. Although he struggled to maintain composure, he did not seem surprised at their arrival. In his heart, he was well aware of the tensions that simmered between Wellington and Graystone. Jeffrey had hoped that somehow by coming to Blue Ridge for the fair, that the wounds between the two wineries could be mended. But now, staying at his mother's house, he had learned the unthinkable. There was a conflict within him, a desire to speak the truth but also a deep-seated fear of the consequences.

"Mr. Gray—Duke..." Jeffrey started, voice catching.

Before Duke could answer, the back flap of the tent lifted. Tom Maxwell stepped out into the morning light, one hand still holding the canvas aside, the other braced loosely on his hip. He took in the three of them in a single measured sweep... Duke's hard-set jaw, Savannah's strained expression, Jake's guarded posture at her side.

"Duke," Tom said quietly, the word heavy with history.

Duke stopped a few feet short of the tent, his boots set firm in the grass. "Tom," he acknowledged, his tone flat and controlled. "Didn't expect to see you here."

Tom nodded toward Jeffrey. "Figured my boy could use a hand at the fair." His gaze shifted back to Duke. "Looks like I was right."

Jeffrey opened his mouth, then closed it again, quickly silenced by the authoritative glare of his father. He wanted to intervene, to somehow diffuse the tense situation, but he quickly realized, watching the dynamic between these two men, that he was out of his depth.

Tom lifted a hand, not unkindly, but firm. "Jeff, why don't you check on that case in the truck for a minute?"

Flushed with embarrassment at being dismissed, he started, "Dad, I…"

"Now, son."

Jeffrey, torn between loyalty to his family and curiosity about the unfolding drama, bristled at being shut out, but reluctantly obeyed his father's orders and retreated to the sidelines. A lingering glance back at the trio displayed a silent regret for his inability to stand his ground.

The moment he was out of earshot, Duke folded his arms across his chest in a stance of quiet strength and restrained anger, bottled up beneath a controlled exterior. "Why are you here, Tom? Where's Natalie?" he asked, voice low.

Tom Maxwell, a man of authority in his own right, chose his words carefully. "Duke, you and I go back a long way. Our wives were best friends. We were too. The tension between the Grays and the Wellingtons goes back decades. With Jeff working at Wellington, I sent him away because whatever we say next doesn't belong in front of him... or half the county." He glanced around at the slowly waking fairgrounds, then jerked his chin toward the side of the tent. "Let's step back here a minute."

Duke didn't move. "If Natalie's somehow mixed up in this, I'm in no mood for sidesteps, Tom."

Savannah could feel Jake tense beside her.

Tom held Duke's stare. "Neither am I," he said. "But you came for answers, and I aim to give you what I can. I'm just not doin' it center stage." He nodded at Savannah, his expression softening. "We don't all need to be on display for the gossipers."

Savannah felt caught in a storm she hadn't seen coming. She looked at Duke, determined to assure him she would remain steadfast.

That was enough. Duke gave a single, clipped nod. "All right. Make it quick."

Tom led them around the side of the tent, away from the foot traffic. The canvas muffled the fairground noises. The air felt tighter back here, boxed in.

"Natalie's not here," Tom said. "Hasn't been since last night."

Savannah's stomach dropped. "Where did she go?"

Tom's jaw worked for a moment. "Gone to North Carolina."

"North Carolina?" Duke repeated. "For what?"

"She left you a note," Tom said, looking straight at Duke. "At the house. Said she couldn't keep hiding what she's been carrying. That it was time the truth came out." He paused. "And that she had to tell it to someone face-to-face first."

Duke was not a man to be trifled with, and they all knew it. His eyes sharpened. "What do you mean, face-to-face? Who is she meeting? My family, Tom. Are there hidden secrets about my family?" His gaze never wavered as he demanded answers.

Tom knew Duke well enough to recognize a loose cannon when he saw one and kept silent.

Duke took a step forward. "Tom, I'm askin' you straight. Is someone keepin' somethin' from me about that accident?" His jaw flexed. "That accident left scars, as you well know. And if Natalie left in the middle of the night to spill secrets she's held for years, I deserve to know why."

He took a steady breath. "And not just me, Tom. Savannah deserves to know. And Jake was at the damn scene, carryin' the weight of it ever since. We're not leaving without answers."

Jake's clenched fists and tense demeanor mirrored the gravity of the situation. The unspoken agreement between him and Duke was clear—they would get to the truth, no matter what the cost.

Duke pressed on, voice unwavering. "Whoever's been trying to keep this from me, including Natalie...

there'll be hell to pay. I'm not sittin' back waiting for someone else to tell me what happened. I'll find the truth myself."

Tom exhaled slowly, like he'd been bracing for this. "Duke... I know you're angry."

"I'm beyond angry," Duke snapped. "Those attorney letters got Jake involved. The money, the order to back away from the accident, and keep the Grays out of it. And now Natalie vanishin' the same night?" His eyes burned into Tom's. "That's no coincidence. That's a pattern."

Savannah's eyes blazed with determination. Jake's fists tightened once again.

"And I'm done with people hidin' pieces of that night from me," Duke finished quietly. "Whatever Natalie thinks she needs to say face-to-face in North Carolina, it damn well better come to me next."

Tom swallowed. "Duke..."

"No." Duke cut him off. "If you know somethin', say it. If you don't, then stay out of my way."

CHAPTER 21

DUKE didn't wait for Tom's response. He pivoted sharply, boots slicing through the damp grass as he headed back toward the fairgrounds' entrance. The sheer magnitude of Duke's authority was enough to make Savannah and Jake fall in line behind him without hesitation.

The fair was stirring into motion, life moving forward despite the truth that needed to be uncovered. With determination and purpose, Duke laid out a plan. "We can't just stand here," he said quietly. "Everybody's expectin' us."

He was right. Savannah was never one to shrug off responsibility. They had obligations. Lizzie would already be at the Graystone tent, setting out pastries and wiping down the tasting counter, wondering why Savannah and Duke hadn't shown up. The fair would be in full swing shortly. Jake was expected at the arena, and Graham wouldn't take kindly to his tardiness.

Life hadn't stopped because they had discovered a tangled web of deceit and betrayal around them. Duke's keen intuition led him to suspect Reed and Natalie were at the center of the mystery. He was about to voice his thoughts when Jake stepped forward.

"Duke… you're thinkin' Reed is the next move, aren't you?"

"Jake, that's exactly what I'm thinkin'." With emphasis, he added, "And I'm not lettin' another day go by without answers."

Savannah listened intently, her own determination matching Duke's. "I agree. So, what do we do first?" Jake couldn't stop a grin at her assertiveness.

It was one of the things about Savannah that Duke was most proud of. He nodded and answered Savannah with, "You and Lizzie are always together. She's Natalie's niece. Have you noticed anything unusual about her lately? Someone needs to get to the Graystone booth. It makes sense that it would be you."

Savannah nodded. "I'm the logical choice," she said softly. "Lizzie's probably worried sick that we're not already there. But to answer your question, I haven't noticed anything different, but I admit I wasn't really looking." She hesitated, then continued, "There is one thing I need to ask her. Something about the other morning. It's probably nothing, but right now, everything seems suspicious."

Jake's eyes narrowed with understanding. Duke gave a short, approving nod.

Jake turned to Duke and spoke up. "If you're planning to track down Reed, I'm goin' with you. I'm knee-deep in all this and just as determined to find out about that night." He shot a quick glance at Savannah before continuing, "I'll swing by the arena. Graham's expectin' me. I can't leave him hangin'. I'll tell him I've got somethin' to take care of in town with my sponsor before I get to practice. That should buy me some time."

Duke's gaze settled on him, studying the young man in front of him. "All right then, meet me back by the truck as soon as you're done. We're goin' to see Tyler Reed."

Jake nodded, his jaw tightening. "I'll be there."

Savannah reached out, lightly brushing her fingertips against Jake's arm. "Be careful."

His eyes softened just a fraction. "You too."

Jake jogged toward the arena, cutting across the fairgrounds, while Savannah turned toward the winery tent, trying not to let her eyes wander toward the Wellington tent where she could feel Jeffrey's gaze.

Duke, alone for a moment, allowed himself to open the door to his grief and see his son and his beautiful daughter-in-law. Putting his head in his hands, he made a silent vow and a plea. *Whatever happened that night, I'm your father and I want to know. God, I miss you every day that goes by. Why have I been kept in the dark?*

His shoulders filled with purpose, Duke walked to his truck, already bracing for the confrontation to come. He had known Tyler Reed since college and considered Tom Maxwell a good friend. Just how deep did this mystery go? By damn, he was going to find out.

***

The bell over the door gave a dull chime as Duke entered the Mason & Reed office with Jake close behind. The lobby was quiet, the receptionist absorbed in her paperwork. She looked up at the sound of the bell, only to encounter Duke Gray's commanding presence.

"Is Reed in, Gracie? It's important."

Before she could answer, the door to Tyler Reed's office swung open. The attorney took one look at Duke, and it was clear he wouldn't let up until he had every detail.

Duke didn't bother with pleasantries. "Tyler," he said, voice low, edged. "Looks like you were expecting us. Figured retirement was supposed to keep you away from places like this."

"I had a feelin' you'd be comin', Duke. Please, come into the office." As they entered, he shot a glare at Jake, as if blaming him for not keeping quiet.

Jake shifted, the old burden pressing on him again. The guilt and confusion surrounding that night had aged him. A hardness etched across his features… his resolve and refusal to be manipulated firmly rooted.

Duke narrowed his eyes. "And why's that, Tyler?"

As Duke pressed, Tyler hesitated, his jaw tightening. "Duke, it's not that simple."

Duke's glare was unwavering. "Then make it simple, Tyler."

Tyler exhaled. "Tom Maxwell called earlier. Said you've been askin' questions… he sounded shaken."

Duke stepped forward, boots landing with purpose. "Oh, I've only just begun."

Duke didn't waste another heartbeat. "Jake said you told him someone survived that accident that killed my kids. How is that possible? No one else was found at the scene other than Jake and the kid on the motorcycle."

Tyler didn't answer immediately. His eyes dropped to the desk, then slowly lifted to meet Duke's stare. The attorney's weariness—and the regret in his gaze—betrayed his involvement in difficult choices and the consequences of keeping dangerous secrets hidden.

"Duke..." he said, voice roughened by too many years and too many secrets, "that night wasn't as simple as you were led to believe."

Jake felt the floor tilt under him. "So, it's true," he said quietly.

Tyler didn't look at Jake... not yet.

Duke's shoulders squared, his voice dropping to the tone he used when he already knew he was right. "Tell me who survived. Why is there no evidence or report?"

Tyler had no choice but to resume his legal role. Ethically, he faced the moral dilemma between his oath to his client versus revealing the truth to his friend. When he spoke, his voice was resigned. "Duke, you're asking questions that should have been left alone."

With Tyler's words hanging heavy in the air, Duke braced himself for the truth that had been waiting for him all along. A muscle in Duke's jaw twitched. "Just tell me straight, Tyler. Someone survived out there on that road other than Jake."

Tyler hesitated, stopping to look at Jake. His office should never have tracked Jake down. If only they had known the cowboy hadn't remembered a survivor. Now, it was too late to go back. Then he nodded at Duke, slow and grim, bearing news that he knew could shatter lives.

Jake whispered the name he'd seen on the folder. "Wellington."

Tyler realized his mistake, looking down at the name on his file, something hollow settling in his eyes. He had carried the burden of the Wellington survivor's secret. "I assure you, Duke, the primary reason for the secrecy has been to protect you and Savannah. Earl Wellington's been living in the shadows since the accident. And now... he's resurfaced and is on his way to the fairgrounds to find you."

Jake's pulse spiked. "Savannah!" he breathed, the gravity of the situation setting upon him like a crushing weight. "She doesn't know."

A sharp alarm of fear crossed Duke's face—gone just as fast, replaced by a grandfather's steel. "She's standin' in that tent with no warnin' at all."

Jake was already moving toward the door. "We've gotta get back, Duke. Now."

Tyler spoke up. "I am so sorry, Duke. I shouldn't have agreed to keep this from you. Maybe I should go with you. Diffuse things a little."

Duke looked at the lawyer with steel in his eye. "You should have thought of that a long time ago. Your services are no longer required."

Tyler watched them go, a man haunted by the secrets he chose to keep, knowing that the time for hiding was over and the time for reckoning had arrived.

126

CHAPTER 22

S AVANNAH walked across the gravel toward the Graystone booth, her steps overshadowed by a growing sense of unease. Normally, the aroma of kettle corn and fresh coffee at the fairgrounds filled her with delight, but not today... not with the turmoil brewing inside her. She tried to steady her thoughts, determined to maintain her composure despite the chaos of the last twenty-four hours.

Learning of Jake's presence at her parents' accident and his unsettling revelation about a possible survivor, combined with Duke's fierce determination to get to the truth, made her feel as if she'd been drawn into a web of secrets and revelations that challenged everything she thought she knew about her parents' death.

Despite the restless night she endured, she had taken in every word last night and this morning...quietly, carefully. One thought kept nagging at her. *If a survivor left the scene of the accident, did that mean my parents' deaths might have been avoided?* A pang of pain hit her hard and she tried to will the unwanted thought away.

For now, the day demanded her attention, with responsibilities waiting. She had to pull herself together.

Inside the booth, Lizzie was setting up freshly cleaned tasting glasses. She looked up with relief when she spotted Savannah. "There you are! I was beginnin' to think you'd run off with Jake Rollins."

Savannah managed a soft laugh that didn't quite reach her eyes. "Very funny." She stepped inside, trying to appear casual, aiming for normalcy. "Hey... quick question." She kept her tone light, appearing to discuss nothing more than trivial gossip. "Did you know Natalie left in the middle of the night?"

Lizzie blinked in surprise, a napkin dangling from her fingertips. "What? Left? Where'd she go?"

"I heard she drove up to North Carolina," Savannah said, still trying for breezy. "Tom mentioned it. He is over at the Wellington booth helping Jeffrey. I just figured maybe they told you."

Lizzie shook her head slowly. "That's odd. I didn't know Uncle Tom had arrived in town from Murphy. Natalie didn't say anything to me." She frowned, genuinely puzzled. "Weird... she *just* asked me yesterday to pick up another pair of gloves at Mountain Ridge Outfitters. Said hers were wearing thin."

Savannah paused, something in that detail tugging at her thoughts. "Gloves? I don't think I've ever asked why she wears those all the time."

"Oh, she burned her hands years ago and..." Lizzie stopped mid-sentence.

Her expression changed suddenly as Lizzie looked past Savannah. Curious, Savannah turned, torn between curiosity and alarm. A man was approaching the booth. There was something haunting about him, something in the way he moved... slow, determined, limping, that set off alarm bells in her mind. As he drew closer, Savannah's instinct screamed at her to stay alert, given everything that was going on outside of this booth. She exchanged a glance with Lizzie, seeing the same mix of fear and curiosity reflected in her friend's eyes.

His posture was bent, his face shadowed, and his clothing didn't fit quite right. His skin, hardened and mottled by burns, contrasted with the unsettling certainty in his eyes, sparking a sense of imminent confrontation. He wasn't hurrying, but he wasn't wavering either, as if he had crossed miles just to reach this exact spot.

Savannah's instinct told her something was about to break open. Beside her, Lizzie whispered, barely audible, "Who... who is that?"

Savannah stood immobilized. It was hard not to stare at the man's disfigurement, but what had her mind racing was that he was staring directly back at her. There was something unsettling about his purposeful movements... slow and deliberate. As she tried to comprehend the scene unfolding in front of her, the way he locked eyes with her sent a shiver down her spine. This was no ordinary stranger.

Lizzie gasped beside her. "Savannah... look." Her voice was barely a whisper.

Savannah followed Lizzie's gaze past the stranger's shoulder and froze. "What...?"

Just behind him, partially obscured by the morning glare, Natalie stood very still. Her stance was tense, almost protective, one gloved hand hovering just behind the mysterious man's back. She looked like she was guiding him... or ensuring he didn't fall. Her face was pale and strained, her eyes darting between the man and the girls as though she were walking straight into a confrontation.

Natalie's sudden appearance sent a shockwave through Savannah, stirring up every question they'd spent the morning trying to untangle. Lizzie's voice snapped Savannah back to the present, the confusion on her friend's face mirroring her own.

"Savannah, I thought you said she left town."

"I-I did," Savannah said. "Tom told us that this morning. Lizzie... who is that man she's with?"

Lizzie murmured, "What's goin' on? Aunt Natalie's not actin' normal."

Natalie hesitated as she drew closer, the weight of years of secrets and misplaced loyalty written across her face. The man leaned into her slightly, pulling her forward with him.

Lizzie studied her aunt, a hundred questions swirling in her mind. Her gaze then shifted to the man—and saw beneath the burns and disfigurement. "Uncle Earl?"

Why was Natalie behaving so oddly, and who was this "Uncle Earl?" As the tension grew thicker, Savannah tried to voice her concerns, but the words seemed to vanish before she could utter them. Suddenly the sound of hurried footsteps broke through the tense atmosphere... grit scattering, boots hitting hard. A voice, breathless and ragged, pierced the crowd.

It was Jake. "Savannah! Stop!"

Right behind him was Duke. "Natalie, don't you move."

The arrival of Jake and Duke shattered the fragile bubble surrounding Savannah, with Lizzie helplessly watching it unfold. The world seemed to close in around them as the reality of their situation crystallized. Whatever secrets lay buried in the past were now clawing their way into the open, demanding to be reckoned with.

Jake reached Savannah first, instinctively positioning himself in front of her, shielding her from the sight of a man whose face was hideously scarred. Her own face was a mixture of shock, disbelief, and dread at the approaching figure.

Jake gripped her shoulders firmly. "Savannah, talk to me. What's goin' on?"

Duke's clenched jaw and intense gaze hinted at a tumultuous mix of anger, hurt, and betrayal simmering beneath the surface. When he finally spoke, his voice was thick with unresolved emotions. "Earl Wellington— that's who he is—back from the dead, I see." His gaze shifted from Earl to Natalie, who quivered under his scrutiny.

The air crackled with tension as unanswered questions demanding to be addressed. "Let's have it, Natalie. What have you two been hiding from me and

Savannah?" Duke's eyes flicked over to Lizzie's bewildered expression. "Lizzie looks like she's in the dark too. And what's all this about warnin' Jake?" He paused briefly, then pushed harder. "You think he might know something about the accident, don't you? Earl, what's your role in all this?"

Natalie flinched, her breath catching. "Duke, please..."

Amidst the growing crowd and the hushed whispers of onlookers, Tom Maxwell surged through them, his authoritative voice cutting through the chaos, seeking to calm the tempest brewing among the group. "All right now, that's enough. Y'all step back."

Attempting to diffuse the situation, he planted himself between Duke and the slowly widening circle of onlookers. A quick assessment of the group... Earl lean-ing, Natalie shaking, Savannah frozen behind Jake... underscored the seriousness of the unfolding drama.

"This isn't the place," Tom said, knowing how quickly this could spiral. "Not here. Not in front of half the county."

Savannah looked at Tom and then at the gathered bystanders. She could sense the rising storm in Duke. The familiar surroundings of the fairgrounds suddenly felt alien and distant. "He's right. We need to take this somewhere private."

In a tortured whisper, Natalie suggested, "My... my house. We can go there."

Duke didn't respond, but he didn't walk away either.

Jake's concern for what lay ahead was evident in his eyes as he led Savannah toward Duke's truck. The sorrow and shame in Natalie, the simmering anger and unresolved pain in Duke, and the badly burned body of Earl Wellington were all pieces of a puzzle finally coming together.

Savannah quietly asked Lizzie to stay at the booth, but as they left, Lizzie's voice broke through, cracked and small. "Aunt Natalie… what have you done?"

Natalie's eyes filled, but she offered no answer.

Tom stepped back, giving them space. "Let's move," he urged quietly. "Before this turns into somethin' no one here can take back."

Savannah glanced once more at the fairgrounds… the bright tents, the cheerful families, the easy laughter. All of it suddenly felt like a different life. Because they were no longer seeking answers. They were heading straight toward the truth.

CHAPTER 23

AS Savannah entered Natalie's living room, the weight of the situation enveloped her, leaving her on edge.

Earl eased himself into the nearest chair with visible effort, the scars across his face evidence of past pain and suffering. Natalie stood rigidly beside him, her gloved hands twisting in anxiety, her nervousness apparent.

Jake hovering protectively near Savannah exuded a sense of cautious vigilance, while Duke, gripping the doorframe, seemed to brace himself for the impending revelations. The room was shrouded in a suffocating silence as Savannah finally mustered the courage to address Natalie, her voice quivering with uncertainty. "Natalie... who is this? Lizzie kept saying 'Uncle Earl.' I thought maybe he was your... ex-husband or something."

Earl looked up at Natalie, a slight curve at the corner of his mouth—just the semblance of a smile.

Natalie's reaction was immediate, shaking her head and glancing at Tom across the room. "No, Savannah," she murmured, her voice barely above a whisper. "Tom is my ex-husband. Earl is my brother."

Savannah blinked. "Your brother?" The clarification of their relationship marked a pivotal moment of revelation. Natalie Maxwell was a Wellington. Duke had said it—but it hadn't landed like this. Neither she nor Lizzie had ever mentioned it before.

Duke stepped farther into the room, confusion etched deep in his face as he studied Earl anew. Earl tried to speak, but struggled, so Duke aimed his question at Natalie.

"Earl Wellington left the winery some years ago. Folks said he'd left town... some said he was gone for good. I don't remember much from that time 'cause I was grievin' so badly." His voice roughened. "And now he's sittin' here? Burned like this? What the hell happened to him?"

Natalie didn't move. Earl didn't lift his eyes. Tom Maxwell closed the front door quietly behind them, the sound landing with a finality that made Savannah's chest tighten.

"All right," Tom said, voice low and steady. "Let's all have a seat. There's a great deal you need to hear, and none of it's simple."

Jake could feel the tension and unease that permeated the room. The question that hung heavily in his mind was why Earl was there. His disfigured appearance had left everyone with questions.

Duke tried to contain the storm rising in him. He remembered Earl as a strong and stoic figure, intent on maintaining the Wellington Winery and its rivalry with Graystone. In all the years he and Lois had been friends with Natalie and Tom, Natalie had rarely mentioned her connection to the Wellington family. But now? What was he doing here, leaning on Natalie for support, appearing fragile and worn out?

Sitting across from Earl, Savannah wondered the same. She noticed his eyes peering out from disfigured sockets, struck by the pain within them. When he lifted his eyes to hers, it was as if he was silently pleading for understanding. She looked at Natalie and saw a stranger, not Lizzie's sweet "Aunt Natalie." The Natalie in this room, hovering beside her brother, looked like a woman on the verge of shattering.

The only thing keeping Savannah grounded was Jake's steady presence by her side. He took her hand and squeezed it, trying to soothe his own nerves as well as hers.

Duke's voice cut through the tension, quiet but strained. "Natalie... why would you bring Earl here?"

Natalie's lips parted, but no words came. She looked down at her gloves as if the answers might be written there. Before she could speak, Earl lifted his hand. His voice was rough, each word a struggle as it pushed through damaged vocal cords. "She didn't want to bring me." He paused, swallowing with effort. "I asked her to."

Duke stared at him, thrown by the simplicity of the admission. "Why?" The question wasn't accusing, just bewildered.

Earl lowered his eyes again. "Because after all this time, you deserve the truth," he said quietly. Another pause. His voice was fraying at the edges when he said, "I can no longer live with the guilt."

Savannah felt a chill slide through her. There was no threat in Earl's words, just resignation. He looked like a man who had been waiting years for punishment he believed he deserved.

Natalie reached out to touch Earl's shoulder, then stopped short, curling both hands back into her lap. She looked at Duke, tears forming but not falling. "Duke... I never meant for it to be like this," she whispered. "I was tryin' to do right. Once I got caught up in it, there just seemed no way out."

Tom leaned forward, his elbows resting on his knees. "There's more to this than any of you could've guessed," he said. "Natalie didn't bring Earl here to stir up trouble. She brought him because today... all of this finally caught up."

Duke looked from Tom to Natalie to Earl, his confusion deepening. "Caught up how?"

Natalie, usually poised and confident, seemed to falter under Duke's gaze. "Because I wasn't the only one who knew Earl was alive," she said. For a brief second, her eyes shifted toward Jake... quick, tense, telling.

Jake's brow furrowed, a question forming behind his expression. He sat listening to the revelations unfolding before him, feeling like an intruder... until Natalie's glance toward him when she admitted someone else had known Earl was alive. That changed everything.

He leaned forward, eyes fixed on the man seated across from him, Earl's face marked by burns and scars.

Suddenly, the chilling details of the accident that had plagued his dreams were coming to light. As the memories flooded back, Jake felt a surge of anguish and remorse, the images of that fateful night burning vividly in his mind. His hand slipped from Savannah's. Jake's eyes never left Earl's. The name Wellington clicked.

"I remember you." He could see the pain and grief in Earl's acknowledgement that mirrored his own.

Savannah turned toward him, the revelation striking her like a physical blow. Duke stared in shock. Natalie's hand flew to her mouth.

"I remember you," he said again, this time slower. "From that night. From the accident." They were both survivors of that dreadful night, forever haunted by the memories that could never be undone.

Natalie quickly turned back to Jake. "We thought you remembered, and we didn't want Duke and Savannah to hear it from you." She took a deep breath and looked at Savannah, as if she couldn't meet Duke's eyes as she said the next part. "Someone else knew Earl survived the night. Your grandmother knew too."

Tom quietly rose to his feet, smoothing his hands over his jeans. His voice softened with respect. "I'll step outside and give you all some space. This is family business. If any of you need me, I'll be right out front." With that, he slipped out the door, closing it gently behind him.

Savannah froze, hardly noticing Tom's departure. "My grandmother?" she breathed. "Lois...?"

Natalie nodded, breaking. "She visited him. After the accident."

Duke's face went rigid. His voice thinned to a whisper. "You're sayin' my Lois went to see Earl in North Carolina after our son and daughter-in-law died...and never said a word?" His voice barely carried. *Why would she do that?* His mind raced at the implications of Lois's silence.

Duke noticed Earl's chin tremble as he forced himself to meet Duke's stare. "She shouldn't have come," Earl rasped. "But she did."

Duke's sharp gaze shifted from Natalie to Earl, his confusion slowly giving way to disbelief and a growing anger he couldn't yet name.

CHAPTER 24

FOR three long years, the memories of that dreadful night had remained fractured, full of missing pieces. Now, Jake faced the harsh reality of what truly happened. Across from him sat a man whose face was mangled and burned beyond recognition... a stark reminder of the tragedy that had unfolded. Jake looked into the eyes of the disfigured man, a rush of guilt and sorrow washing over him as he tried to come to terms with his role in the horrific event.

The sound of screeching tires, the deafening crash of metal against metal, followed by the acrid smell of smoke and gasoline, all slammed back into him with brutal clarity. He remembered the sense of helplessness and despair as he had watched the car swerve off the mountain road... the sickening realization there were people inside. Savannah's parents. The revelation struck him like a physical blow, the knowledge that he had been unable to save them a crushing weight on his chest.

The first thing he did was turn to Savannah, tears filling his eyes. Haltingly, realizing the hurt he was about to deliver, he whispered, "I... I was there. Your parents... they must have been the couple in the front seat."

He nodded toward Earl. "He was there too." Not the man in front of him now. But the man in the firelight. Earl tightened his jaw, bracing himself.

Duke, torn between anger and confusion, asked quietly, "What do you remember, Jake? Tell us."

Jake swallowed hard, the weight of guilt, grief, and remorse bearing down on him as he struggled to recount the harrowing details of that night. Savannah was weeping beside him, her shoulders trembling. Natalie looked like she was about to snap in half with grief. Earl squeezed his eyes shut, trying to shield himself from the memory.

It was Duke's face that was unreadable, his eyes focused on Jake, imploring him to continue.

When Jake continued his voice, laden with emotion, resonated through the silence. "I was on my motorcycle trailin' behind the Chevy. It all happened so fast... the blindin' headlights of another bike comin' around a blind curve, then veerin' straight into their lane. The sound of the tires when the car slammed on the brakes forced me to swerve. Without the sound, I might have run into the rear of the Chevy."

Jake winced at the brutal clarity but forced himself to continue. "The crashing sound of metal against metal was deafenin'. Then the smell of smoke and gasoline. I skidded to a stop, watchin' helplessly, as the car shot off the road and into a tree. I didn't know what to do first."

Duke moved closer to Savannah, placing an arm around her as he said quietly, "What happened next, son?"

Jake's breathing faltered. "The motorcyclist was lyin' in the road. By the time I got to him, he was already gone, so I pulled him to the side. That's when I heard screaming coming from the car."

Savannah sobbed. "Mom... Dad!" Duke's arm tightened, his own eyes stinging.

Jake lowered his head, the full impact of that night slamming into him. "I grabbed a pipe and started bangin' on the window until it cracked. I cleared the glass and was reachin' in when..." His voice cracked. "The explosion threw me back, knocked me unconscious... but not before I saw Earl climbin' out the window. I remember heat... searin', burnin' heat... then nothin' until I woke up in the hospital."

His voice splintered with the burden of knowing he couldn't save her parents. "Savannah... I tried to get them all out. I swear it. But I couldn't... I couldn't do enough." He pressed a shaking hand to his forehead. "Your parents. I couldn't save them." He turned to Duke. "I am so incredibly sorry."

Savannah could barely see through her tears.

Earl lowered his head. "It wasn't his fault," he rasped. "The fire was already taking the car. No one could've reached them in time."

Jake didn't look at Earl. He couldn't. He kept his eyes on Savannah, his chest rising unevenly, guilt spilling off him in waves. "I should've done more," he said.

Natalie finally spoke, her voice thin and breaking. "Jake... you were unconscious. You acted in the face of your own danger. You broke that window. You're the reason he had a way out." Her voice softened further. "You did everything humanly possible."

Jake's jaw clenched, but he said nothing. The truth was drowning him.

Savannah sat frozen, her mind reeling. A part of her wanted to reach for him. Another part felt the sharp sting of learning that Jake, this man she'd grown to trust, had been there on the night that changed her life forever.

But she saw the grief in his eyes. The devastation. And she knew with absolute clarity that Jake wasn't just remembering. He was breaking.

The room grew heavy with grief, each person bearing the weight of their own sorrow. Savannah curled into Duke's protective embrace, her sobs shattering the silence.

Jake hunched forward, fingers tangled in his hair, unable to meet anyone's gaze. Natalie clung to the edge of her seat as if bracing for the moment everything would unravel.

Duke's gaze drifted to Earl, the silent witness to the tragedy that had ripped their lives apart. When he finally spoke, his voice was quiet, raw, trembling. "Did my kids suffer?" The words barely made it past his lips.

They weren't a challenge. They weren't anger. They were the plea of a father who had lived three years in the dark, terrified of the answer. Savannah lifted her tear-streaked face toward Earl, desperate for truth. Even Jake looked up, breath held.

Earl finally lifted his gaze to Savannah, hollow and haunted, the nightmare of that night etched into him like scars on his soul. When he spoke, his voice cracked, remembering the moments after the crash. "Your mama didn't suffer."

Savannah inhaled sharply, heartbreak and relief colliding inside her.

Earl swallowed hard, forcing the rest out. "She died instantly. The impact took her before the fire did. She never felt the flames. Not one second of it."

Savannah pressed her hands to her mouth, sobbing. But this time, something in her grief loosened. Just a fraction.

Duke bowed his head, shoulders shaking. It wasn't relief. Not fully. But it was mercy... a single thread of peace in an ocean of pain.

Earl continued, voice barely holding together. "I saw enough to know that much. I've carried it every day since. I should've said it long ago... I just didn't know how." He looked at Savannah, then at Duke, the years of anguish etched into him, a burden he couldn't forgive himself for. "There are parts of that night that won't bring any of you peace," he whispered. "But Margaret... she didn't feel a thing. That's the truth." A long, aching silence settled over them. Margaret's mercy had been reassured.

But another truth, the one left unsaid, lingered painfully between them—one 's father and the other's son.

CHAPTER 25

EARL shifted his eyes to Natalie, a silent communication passing between them, understanding the surface had only been broken. There was more... so much more. Natalie, torn between protecting Duke from further pain and honoring the secret Lois had confided in her, felt the weight of the moment pressing down on her. Lois had been like a sister, and Natalie knew she would never have wanted to cause Duke and Savannah more anguish. But Earl's insistence on revealing the truth, whatever his motivations might be, left Natalie with a difficult choice. Her silent plea met only his grim determination.

As Duke observed the exchange between Natalie and Earl, a sense of foreboding settled over him. His protective instincts kicked in, tightening his grip on the chair and pulling Savannah closer.

He studied Earl and, for the first time, noticed something else... a challenge being passed directly to him. Accepting it with a hard, steady stare, Duke asked, "There's more, isn't there?"

Savannah shrank back at the sharp edge in Duke's voice, her mind scrambling to understand.

Jake was the first to connect the dots. He turned to Earl and softly said, "Someone's been tryin' hard to keep your presence at the accident quiet. You weren't supposed to be there, were you?"

Natalie looked as though she might faint.

Duke forced his mind to consider the truth that someone had been concealing Earl's presence at the accident. "As far as I know, David and Margaret didn't know you. You and I have had dealin's in the past but I'm fairly certain David was never part of them. So why were you in the car with them?"

He turned to Natalie with accusation, "You knew about this."

Natalie noticeably flinched, nervously wringing her gloved hands. Her glance at Earl looked like a plea for help and Duke shifted his attention to the shell of a man before him. Earl let out a sigh of resignation. He met Natalie's glance with a slight shake of his head, then turned back to Duke. "You're right. I shouldn't have been there that night."

Duke leaned forward, eyes fixed, his voice dropping to something low and unyielding. "Say it."

Savannah drew back, sensing that whatever Earl was about to reveal would change everything they believed about the night of the accident.

Jake shifted, guilt coiling through him as pieces finally aligned. He should've stayed at the hospital. He should've given a statement.

A sharp, pounding knock shattered the moment. Three hard blows—fast, urgent.

Natalie jerked upright, nearly stumbling.

Duke snapped toward the sound, tension racing through him. "Now who in the hell—"

Jake moved first. Instinct took over as he crossed the room in long strides and opened the door.

Attorney Tyler Reed stood on the porch, hat in one hand, a manilla envelope clutched in the other. "Jake," he said quietly. Then, looking past him, "I need to speak with all of you."

Jake stepped aside to let him in. "Mr. Reed... what's going on?"

The lawyer entered with a mix of solemnity and urgency, his gaze moving from Duke's guarded stare to Savannah's worry, then to Earl's dread. His eyes then lingered on Natalie.

"I apologize for coming unannounced," he began, voice steady but subdued. "I wouldn't be here unless it was necessary. Urgent, actually."

Duke's tone sharpened. "If this is about the accident, Tyler, you're about three years too late."

Reed shook his head once. "No, Duke. I'm right on time." He lifted the envelope so they could all see. A heavy pause filled the room. His presence felt like a turning point, an unavoidable reckoning closing around all of them.

"This concerns every one of you," he said quietly. "And I can't read its contents without the consent of everyone present."

Duke's voice dropped into something rough, protective. "A letter? From whom?"

Reed's answer softened with respect. "Lois. The letter was written by Lois before her death."

The mention of Lois's name landed hard, catching each of them off guard. Duke didn't move, not a muscle, as if the very ground beneath him had begun to shift.

Savannah's shock turned to a whisper of hope and fear. "Grandma?"

Natalie covered her mouth, tears instantly forming. "How is this possible. I didn't know about a letter."

Earl braced himself, his expression tightening. He could only shake his head, his eyes fixed on the envelope.

Reed clasped the letter with both hands, almost reverently. "Tom called me and said you were all here, including Earl and Jake. He mentioned you were trying to unravel what happened the night of the accident. This was the moment Lois had anticipated. I knew it was time she would want me to clear this up with her own words."

Natalie blinked, stunned. "Tyler... I didn't know anything about a letter. Lois would've told me."

Natalie's words hit Duke like a physical blow. "What do you mean by that, Natalie? That she'd tell you rather than her husband or her granddaughter?"

Earl squeezed his eyes shut in resignation.

Reed lifted a calming hand. "Easy, Duke. Lois came to me after visiting Earl. She was shaken... grief-stricken, overwhelmed by losing David and Margaret. She told me her conscience was struggling under the weight of everything she knew that happened, and everything she feared would come to light without her perspective." They were all silent, listening.

"She asked me to keep this safe," he continued, "and to bring it forward only I believed the truth would be better delivered in her own words." His eyes lifted to meet Duke's. "I believe that moment has come."

Reed's words had Duke's mind spinning with an undeniable need to rip the envelope away and read it alone, in private. The envelope wasn't just paper. It was a bridge between his wife still alive and the loneliness he'd felt since she passed. This was personal. He still felt the magnitude of his grief, the sudden heart attack taking her so soon after losing David and Margaret.

Duke's initial instinct was to protect what was left of his family. His voice, rough with emotion, demanded answers. "Before you read anything... who's it addressed to?"

The question hung in the air, heavy with implications. Despite the intensity of Duke's focus and the urgency in his voice, Reed remained composed as he looked down at the flap, hesitating, fully aware of the delicate situation at hand.

Duke pressed on, sharper now. "Is it meant for me? For Savannah? For both of us?"

Tyler Reed had always admired Duke's strength and dedication to his family. When Lois entrusted him with the letter, it was Reed who found himself caught in the middle of a brewing conflict. He was bound by his commitment to Lois. However, he couldn't help empathizing with each person in the room, recognizing their need to have clarity.

Reed steadied the envelope in both hands. "Duke, I mean no disrespect, but Lois wrote this with the intention that everyone present hear her words."

Savannah looked up, startled, her eyes wide as she looked from Natalie to Earl.

Natalie, still shocked that Lois kept something this important from her, sat frozen. Earl's instinct was to run. He couldn't imagine this would go well. But instead, he stayed still, jaw tight, guilt engulfing him.

Duke's voice hardened. "If Lois wrote somethin' for her family, then it gets read by her family. Not in front of people who have no business hearin' my wife's words."

His gaze, sharp and bewildered, cut from Earl to Natalie. Finally, his eyes settled on Jake, uncertainty and confusion flickering in their depths. Each glance carried the weight of Duke's vulnerability, the need for answers colliding with the tangled emotions that filled the room. The silent exchange spoke volumes; Duke's struggle was not just with the letter, but with the presence of those around him, each person important enough to his wife to be included.

He squared his shoulders, deciding he was not going to stand for it. "Savannah and I will take it in the back room."

Reed drew in a steady breath. "Duke... you can't do that."

Duke's brows snapped together. "Why not?"

Reed's tone stayed respectful, but firm. "Because Lois didn't write this for one person, or two. She wrote it knowing everyone here would need to hear it. I respect Lois's intentions. Her words weren't meant to divide you. They were meant to bind you."

Savannah swallowed, throat tight. "Duke, this is what she wanted. Maybe we just need to let him read it."

Reed continued, quieter but unwavering. "Duke, if I could give it to just you, I would. But that's not what she intended." Duke's confusion and grief twisted together, trying to grasp a truth he never saw coming.

Behind Savannah, Jake shifted, clearing his throat. "Maybe I should step outside. Let y'all have some privacy. I never met her." He was trying to give them space... trying to do the decent thing. He started to get up from the sofa, but Savannah reached for his arm.

"Jake..." It was her trembling voice and pleading eyes that anchored him in place. Her fingers curled around his arm. "Please don't go. Mr. Reed said she wanted you here too. So do I."

Jake met her gaze and saw everything she couldn't say... fear, grief, and the fragile trust that had grown between them. Savannah was trying to navigate the storm of emotions surrounding her, and she realized she needed the solace and strength of Jake Rollins by her side. "Jake, I need you here."

Jake sat back down beside her, taking her hand in his with a squeeze. Softly, he murmured, "There is nowhere else I would rather be. You've got this, Savannah. I'm right here."

CHAPTER 26

THE room itself remained unchanged, yet everyone inside it bore the burden of their own emotions, their faces reflecting a blend of sorrow, anticipation, and resignation. They no longer braced for impact; they were simply weary, clinging to whatever steadiness they had left.

Tyler Reed exhaled deeply, the reluctant custodian of the letter that held the key to unlocking long-buried secrets that had haunted them all. With a mix of resolve and trepidation, he stepped forward, his gentle voice a soothing balm to the frayed nerves of those around him.

"Whenever you're ready." His words were soft but firm, a gentle push toward the inevitable revelation that lay within the pages of the letter. As the words began to be read, no one spoke. There was nothing left to prepare for... only the truth they were finally about to hear.

"My dearest David,
My sweet Margaret,

I know you will never read this with your own eyes. I write these words to you with an unbearable grief, knowing you are already gone, and that what I say now will only ever be heard by those left behind. But I cannot leave this life without speaking to you both, even if it is only in the hope that some part of you can feel what my voice never managed to say.

There is no easy beginning to this. Only honesty, and the hope that you will hear it with the love I never stopped feeling for both of you.

I know that when our paths last crossed, hurt stood between us. I felt it in the way your voices raised, in the way your backs lifted with disappointment, in the way my own heart cracked as I realized I had caused a wound I didn't know how to mend. I have lived every day since with that weight.

And yet, even in my shame, even in my confusion... I loved you both. More than I could ever express.

If Tyler is reading this letter out loud, this sentiment is for Duke and Savannah as well. I never stopped loving you. I never stopped loving our family.

Before I begin, I need you all to know something that doesn't excuse anything but frames the heart I carried when all of this began.

The decisions I made were not motivated by malice. I acted out of a desperate desire to prevent a single mistake from unraveling everything else I held dear.

But mistakes don't stay contained. Nor do their consequences. Secrets fester. And guilt has a way of reshaping the truth until you hardly recognize yourself. I kept silent. And that silence became its own betrayal.

I never meant for you both to find out the way you did. You were angry with me, and you had every right to be. The last time I saw your faces, I saw disappointment I had earned, and pain I helped create.

It broke something inside me, something I never had the chance to repair before you were gone.

I am devastated by what happened. I am so deeply, helplessly sorry.

The cabin... what happened on the road that night... and what happened before and after... all of it is tied to the secret I carried.

And now, because I can't bear the lies and secrets any longer, I pray that my ailing health will take me soon. I owe the truth

to you both, but also to my husband, Duke,
and my granddaughter, Savannah.

Natalie shifted abruptly in her chair, her voice breaking the fragile stillness. "Tyler... I don't think this is necessary."

She swallowed, eyes pinned to the letter instead of the people around her. "Lois was grieving—crushed, really. She wasn't herself after the accident. Whatever she put on those pages... I'm not sure she ever meant for it to be read aloud. Not like this. Bringing it out now is only going to cause more pain."

Her gaze flicked toward Duke, desperate, almost pleading. "Maybe we should just... stop. This doesn't have to be dragged out."

Savannah took a deep breath, grateful for Jake's steady presence. Her hand tightened around Jake's forearm, fingers curling into the fabric of his sleeve. He didn't need words to communicate his support; he moved closer, his breath warm against her temple, a quiet, unspoken strength she could lean on without fear of judgement or misunderstanding.

Tyler glanced at Savannah, then Duke, then back to the letter. He took a breath... acknowledging how hard this was, but with the kind of solemn purpose that came from knowing exactly why Lois had asked him to do this.

"Natalie," he said gently, "I understand why you're frightened of what's in here. But Lois trusted me with this. She wrote this letter because she couldn't carry these truths anymore, not with what she knew was coming. She wanted her family, including you and Earl, and even Jake, to hear her words... not guesses or half-truths or whatever pieces were left behind."

He looked down at the pages, then up at Duke, steady and respectful. "If I stop now, I'm going against her final request. And I don't think any of us want that."

Duke's jaw flexed, emotion tightening his features. He didn't look at Natalie. He couldn't. Instead, he focused on the worn lines of paper in Tyler's hand, as though the answer had been sitting there all along.

Duke nodded once, firm and resolute. "Go on," he said quietly. "Let's hear it."

Tyler gave a subtle glance toward Earl, who offered a resigned nod before lowering his gaze. Then Tyler returned to the page and continued:

> *"The secret I carried began long before that night. It began the day I let my loneliness speak louder than my vows. My life here in Blue Ridge had grown into a monotonous routine—baking for events, garden club on Tuesdays, and needlepoint at the art center on Thursdays. David, you and your father were busy with the winery. Margaret was working long hours at the bed-and-breakfast in Ellijay. Savannah was still off at college.*
>
> *I was tired, lonely, and hungry for attention I should have found the courage to ask your father for. Instead, I let it come from someone who had no right to offer it.*

I met Earl accidentally on a weekend trip to North Carolina with Natalie. She introduced me to her brother who happened to be the head of the Wellington Winery. That decades-old feud always seemed foolish to me, and Earl was charming, attentive, and for a time I told myself it was harmless... just conversation, just company, just a harmless bit of feeling seen.

Duke darted a glance at Earl, whose eyes were brimming. He quickly returned his attention to Tyler and the shock of the words he was reading.

"It wasn't harmless. It was wrong.

Natalie, in her own way, thought she was giving me an escape when she helped arrange that trip. She did not intend the damage that followed, but I will not pretend she was unaware of what was happening. I agreed to meet Earl at the cabin, and in doing so, I crossed a line I can never uncross.

You were never meant to find out.

When you arrived at that cabin and found us together, the look on your faces is something I will carry with me into whatever comes next. Shock. Hurt. Disbelief. My son seeing his mother as a stranger. Margaret seeing me as a woman she could no longer respect. You had every right to turn away from me.

But you did more than turn away. You insisted on getting Earl out of that cabin, out of that situation, out of what you saw as a shameful mess. You were furious, and you were right to be. You tossed the note at me that you were never supposed to see. But I knew those roads at night, and I knew the state you were all in when you left.

God knows I should have stopped you. I should have begged you to stay the night, to wait, to cool down. I didn't.

I let you drive off with anger still scorching every word we'd just thrown at each other. I watched the car pull away with my son, my daughter-in-law, and the man I should never have let into our lives in that way. I told myself you only needed space, that you would come back when the dust settled, that we would find a way to talk when tempers had cooled.

Instead, the next thing I learned was that there had been an accident.

They told Duke and me there were only two people in the car... that no one survived. I knew, in that instant, that they were wrong about the number of passengers. I was well aware Earl had been with you, and I realized there was more to that night than anyone was saying. And later, when Natalie came to me with burns on her hands and fear in her eyes, I understood the rest, that she had found him, pulled him from the wreckage, and taken him away before anyone else arrived.

I let that truth stay buried.

I let that innocent bystander who tried to help carry questions that weren't his to bear. I let investigators build a story around a partial truth. I allowed Duke to grieve his son and daughter-in-law without ever telling him the full extent of my betrayal... that my choices not only broke his trust but set in motion the night that took them from him.

I told myself I was protecting what was left of this family. In reality, I was protecting myself from the shame of being the one who lit the fuse.

For that, there are no words strong enough. But I will say the only ones that matter:

I am guilty of it all.

And I know I do not deserve forgiveness from any of you. But I had to finally put the truth in your hands, even if it is far too late to mend what I shattered.

I cannot undo what I caused. I cannot give back what was taken. But I can leave you with this:

I loved you. Even in my failures, I loved you. All of you.

Duke... you were my partner in everything good. I let you down in the worst way, but I never stopped loving you.

Savannah, I am so sorry for the pain my choices left at your feet... to have lost both your parents because of the consequences of my actions. I pray that someday, somehow, you will find a way to forgive me.

Natalie... my friend who carried burdens you never asked for. I can't imagine the weight you've borne because of me. And your hands... so horribly painful, yet you never complain. I am deeply sorry, my friend.

And to you, Earl... I never loved you the way I loved Duke, but you did hold a place in my heart. When I saw the results of that terrible night, the horrific burns that disfigured your face, it was unbearable. I carry that guilt as well, because it never would have happened if not for me. I am so very sorry.

Finally, to the young man at the accident... if Tyler is reading this letter, it means he

*has found you. I know about your brave
actions at the scene. I came to the hospital
to thank you, but you had already left. You
were a bright spot in all of this chaos, and
I am grateful.*

*In some way, I hope that hearing this from
me will bind you, not break you.*

I love you."

As the echoes of Lois's words lingered in the air, a heavy silence settled upon the room like a heavy shroud. Tyler lowered the final page with a slow, unsteady breath. The room itself seemed to have absorbed the essence of Lois's truth, leaving behind shattered illusions and unspoken regrets. Tyler understood that revealing the secrets contained in the letter would cause pain and upheaval, but he also understood that only through facing the truth could healing truly begin.

CHAPTER 27

TYLER Reed's reading of Lois's letter unleashed deep-seated grief, leaving a trail of devastation in his wake. As he walked away with a soft click of the closing door, no one left in that room believed her words would bind them. At that moment, they all felt broken... each of them absorbing her words in their own way.

Savannah immediately reached out to offer comfort to Duke, her instinctual response to the shared grief enveloping them. Duke, reeling from his wife's confessions, found himself paralyzed in her embrace... the need to retreat gnawing at his every fiber.

"I'm suffocating in this room," he murmured, pulling back. "I need air."

He didn't wait for anyone to respond. He simply turned and walked out, swift and resolute.

Outside, Tom stepped into the driveway as Duke passed. "Are you okay?" he asked gently. Duke didn't slow down. He lifted a hand—part gesture, part warning—then continued toward the park, his need for solitude overriding any attempts at consolation. Tom let him go, recognizing the anguish etched on his friend's face.

Back inside, Savannah stared helplessly as her grandfather retreated... her own emotional shock threatening to overwhelm her. Jake came to her side, steady as ever, slipping his arm around her shoulders. "Let's get out of here," he said quietly.

She nodded, leaning into him for comfort before straightening with resolve. "I need to find Duke," she whispered. "Will you head back to the fairgrounds and help Lizzie? She's probably worried sick."

Jake brushed a strand of hair behind her ear, searching her expression. "Are you sure? That was pretty rough in there." His concern seeped into the numbness gripping her spirit. She turned to him slowly, a silent plea in her eyes. He pressed his lips against hers... gentle, comforting.

Savannah pulled back. "I'm sure," she said. Duke needed her. And she needed him right now.

"All right," he said, squeezing her hand. "Why don't you drop me at the fairgrounds, and I'll take care of things there. You can take my truck and find Duke. And Savannah... I'm here for you. You can count on it."

Savannah dropped Jake off and turned the truck toward the vineyard. She found Duke sitting on the weathered bench beneath the old oak tree, the one on the far side of the winery where he used to watch sunsets with her grandmother. His graying hair was tousled, his eyes tired... carrying a mix of sorrow and disbelief at the revelations that had shaken his world.

She felt caught in the crossfire of her family's unraveling. Throughout her childhood, she had always found solace in the quiet strength of her grandmother. But hearing the words revealing Lois might have been to blame for her parents' death had rocked the foundation of Savannah's world as it seemed to crumble before her eyes.

A deep sadness swelled in Savannah to see Duke in such despair from layers of betrayal and heartache that they never knew existed. In the face of all that had happened, she knew one thing for certain... she could not lose Duke. She had to stay strong to hold what family she had left together.

She didn't announce herself. She didn't speak. She simply lowered herself onto the bench beside him, leaving just enough space for him to breathe, offering a steady presence and a listening ear.

For a while, Duke didn't move. When he finally spoke, his voice was barely more than a rasp.

"I was blind. How could I not see it?" he said. "She was the cornerstone of our family. And I took her for granted. All those years... Lois was lonely, Savannah. She was hurting, and I never noticed."

He stared at his calloused hands, heart heavy with the realization that while he was busy providing for his family, he had failed in his commitment to his beloved wife.

"I thought our marriage was solid, built on shared dreams and commitment. But while I was busy keeping the vineyard afloat, I missed the small signs. Somewhere amidst the rows of grapevines and barrels of wine, I was too preoccupied to truly see her pain. She tried to tell me in her own way. All those nights she'd ask me to sit with her or take a drive or slow down... and I brushed her off. I told myself life was hard, that we had responsibilities." His voice cracked. "I didn't see the fractures growing between us."

Savannah's heart clenched to see him so raw and vulnerable. She had expected anger, even rage, at Earl, bitterness toward Lois, or even fury at Natalie for keeping everything from him. But this? This hollow guilt? This quiet devastation? It scared her more than anything else could have.

"Granddaddy... Duke," she began softly.

Duke shook his head. "I don't blame her. Not anymore. Not after hearing her words." He looked out toward the vineyard, eyes haunted by the weight of his mistakes and the realization of his failures. "Anger I can handle. I've lived with anger before. But guilt? Guilt settles in your bones." His voice cracked. "And remorse for things that can't be undone... that doesn't let go."

And in that moment, Savannah saw the truth with a clarity that chilled her: His self-blame was consuming him. If someone didn't pull Duke back from this edge... if she didn't... he could drift into the same emotional emptiness that swallowed her grandmother. She had lost her parents and her grandmother. She was not going to lose Duke.

She reached for his hand, not squeezing, not urging... just a lifeline. "We'll walk through it together," she said quietly. "You're not alone in this."

The hardness in Duke's eyes softened, the lines on his face easing just slightly. For the first time since Tyler read the letter, his shoulders eased by only a fraction, but enough for hope. Savannah's quiet presence and gentle reassurances offered him a path toward healing and forgiveness, not only for himself, but also for those he felt let down by.

His mistakes would never be erased, but for now, Duke could glimpse the possibility of forgiving himself and perhaps, in time, Earl and Natalie as well.

Savannah sat with Duke a while longer, letting the silence settle into something gentler. When his breathing finally steadied, she rested her hand over his for a moment, then stood. "I'll be close," she whispered.

Duke nodded, not trusting his voice, but the look he gave her held more gratitude than words could contain. As Savannah walked back toward the house, the weight of Lois's letter settled around her. She wasn't sure how they would get through the days ahead, but she knew they would. Together.

And as she crossed the gravel drive, her thoughts drifted to Jake and the way he'd steadied her when her own knees nearly buckled. The way he'd offered strength without pressing, comfort without demands. The way he'd simply sat beside her... the same way she had just done for Duke.

A quiet warmth rose in her chest. She wasn't alone either. Savannah drew in a slow breath, squared her shoulders, and pointed her truck toward the fairgrounds... completely unaware of the storm unfolding in Natalie's living room.

169

CHAPTER 28

TOM Maxwell roamed through the garden he used to tend so diligently when he was married to Natalie. He touched various flowers and shrubs planted when they first bought the house almost thirty years ago. He welcomed the distraction. Anything to keep his mind from the emotional chaos going on inside the house. When Tyler Reed finally emerged, his expression told Tom all he needed to know about what had been left behind.

Tyler approached, shaking his head. "The letter might as well have been a loaded gun. No way to soften any of it."

Tom tried to clear his head. "This is exactly what we were trying to avoid. If Jeffrey had gotten to Rollins first for a sponsorship with Wellington, he would never have ended up at Graystone and wouldn't have gotten pulled into any of this."

Tyler looked closely at Tom, the younger man he had encouraged to join his fraternity back at the University of North Georgia. Ever since, they'd had a bond akin to brotherhood. He finally admitted, coming to terms with the implications of their choices, "The letter and the money that went with it certainly backfired."

Tom answered, "Yeah, I know. I saw Rollins shovin' the letter through your office mail chute last night. I happened to be glancing out the window of the guest house at the time. I mentioned it to Natalie." He shook his head in amazement. "I don't know which shocked me more... Natalie leaving that note on Duke's door and going to North Carolina to see Earl, or Earl insisting on coming back here with her."

The lawyer nodded in agreement and headed to his car but turned to Tom for one last comment. "There's going to be fallout. I need to get back to my office and set some things in order." Tom rubbed his temple as the car sped off.

A few seconds later, Duke bolted through the door. He looked older. Not in years, but in heavy emotion. Tom's friendship with Duke was teetering on the edge of disaster. The failed gamble with the letter and the money had added fuel to the fire. If Duke discovered Tom's involvement in the events surrounding the night of the accident, their bond would be irrevocably broken.

Tom straightened. "Are you okay?" he asked softly.

Duke was in no mood to talk. His raised hand clearly signaled *I'm not talking*. Tom could only watch helplessly as Duke headed back toward his vineyard, his truck leaving a trail of dust behind him.

Tom's thoughts drifted back to his conversation with Natalie, who'd informed him that Jake Rollins, the key eyewitness to the accident, was back in town for the rodeo. Tom rubbed his temples. He didn't even know all of it, and he'd barely been able to handle it. Tom didn't even want to think about what would happen if Duke found out. He had known the letter sealed with the promise of money to ensure Rollins stayed clear of Duke and Savannah Gray was a desperate move to keep the truth from the Grays.

Seeing Rollins escort Savannah out the door, Tom realized there was an unexpected twist. That was the wildcard he would never have seen coming. Rollins had obviously fallen for Savannah. *That is why he rushed to Graystone that night.*

Savannah saw Tom in the shadows and tearfully asked where Duke had gone. Although Tom calmly pointed in the direction of the vineyard, his internal turmoil was anything but calm. The intimate farewell he witnessed between Rollins and Savannah only fueled his need to somehow regain control of the situation.

He needed to go back inside the house. It had been their home, a place where they had built a life together for nearly three decades. Tom felt a mix of nostalgia and dread. Their divorce had been one of the early casualties of that night. Now he needed to uncover exactly what Natalie and Earl remembered about that fateful night. He could only hope Earl wasn't another wildcard.

The secrets were like a tightly wound coil, ready to spring. Tom knew he had to manage the situation carefully to prevent everything from unraveling. The truth was a dangerous weapon, and he was determined to wield it wisely.

***

Inside the living room, the mood was one of shock and disbelief. Earl and Natalie each silently contemplated the significance of Lois's letter. Natalie couldn't help but feel resentment toward the woman she considered her best friend. For three long years, she had kept Lois's secrets. She had stood by her friend when she embarked on the affair with Earl, even knowing how it would devastate Duke. She had ultimately lost her own husband over it. And now, Lois just blurted it all out in a letter?

Earl shook his head with the irony of it all and the impact of his impulsive behavior. He had to admit he'd liked the idea of taking something from the arrogant Duke Gray, who thought Graystone's wine was superior to Wellington's. He had been cocky enough to think he could win Lois over. While it was platonic for a while, he had pushed for more, and Lois eventually agreed to meet him at the cabin. That decision had cost more than he could ever have imagined.

Now, he realized she'd never loved him; she was just filling an empty space. He might as well have lost his life that night too. If that cowboy hadn't been there, he would have. Instead, he lived a shadow of a life, reclusive and unable to truly function in the world.

Tom entered and closed the door behind him, not bothering with small talk. "They're all gone. That must've been some letter."

Natalie nodded without meeting Tom's stare. He took a step closer and persisted. "We need to talk."

Earl let out a slow breath. "About what?"

Tom paused to choose his words carefully. "About that night. There's something we've never addressed... something Duke is going to figure out sooner rather than later."

Natalie's gaze finally lifted. "Tom, please—"

"I'm not here to blame anyone," Tom assured them, keeping his voice steady. "But we're all circling the accident without asking the obvious question."

Earl shifted uneasily in his chair. "Which is?"

Tom looked from one to the other. "How did David and Margaret find the cabin that night?"

Natalie exchanged a glance with Earl. "Tom... we've both wondered about that," she admitted. "But every time I tried to think it through, it just—" She shook her head. "It didn't make sense. It's our sister's cabin, but since she and Paul moved to Michigan, it's hardly used... just the occasional rental." Then, as an afterthought, she added, "Of course, Lizzie would've known about it; she grew up goin' there. But she was away at school with Savannah."

Earl reached for an injured leg that was cramping from being in one position so long. "I always figured they'd found out about the family cabin and came lookin' for me," he muttered. "Maybe Lois told them about the cabin. Maybe they tracked her phone. I don't know." Then, something struck in his memory. "In Lois's letter, she mentioned David throwing a note. Things escalated from there, and I never got to see it.

There must have been something in the note that set them off."

Tom stepped farther into the room, intense and controlled. Their answers told him what he wanted to know. They knew about a note, but nothing about who it was to or David's visit to this house. A sick twist knotted in Tom's stomach. Duke would dig, and when he did, he would start uncovering things only Tom knew.

Despite his fear about his role, Tom experienced a moment of clarity. Natalie and Earl weren't hiding anything... they truly didn't know how David and Margaret had found the cabin that night. Whatever part he'd played, it wasn't the one he'd feared.

But the truth was still unfinished, and Duke would eventually seek answers. Tom owed it to himself, Natalie, Earl, and, most importantly, Duke to handle the situation delicately.

He drew a quiet breath. "I think we've done all we can for now," he said, maintaining a steady tone. "Everyone's raw. Duke needs space. We all do."

Natalie nodded, exhausted. Earl didn't disagree.

Tom softened his tone. "When things settle, we'll have to talk to Duke. All of us. He deserves the truth, all of it, but we need to approach it the right way."

Neither Natalie nor Earl objected. They didn't have it in them.

Tom moved toward the door. "Let's get through tonight," he said. "I'll figure out the right moment to talk to him and be in touch."

He didn't elaborate, and they didn't ask.

Outside, the cool air steadied him. He didn't have all the answers yet, but he knew one thing for sure... he wouldn't keep running from the truth. There needed to be conversation and honesty, however difficult it might be. Duke would hear it from him when the time was right.

Tom gripped the steering wheel, finally ready to face his past and forge a new future.

CHAPTER 29

SAVANNAH and Duke had managed to rebuild their lives, finding some semblance of normalcy and happiness. But Lois's letter changed all that... the betrayal, the heartache, the shattered illusions... it all felt like too much to bear. Leaving Duke, Savannah felt disconnected and adrift. Her once-steady life now seemed like a fragile house of cards, threatening to collapse under the weight of her grandmother's confessions.

The only thing she knew to do was the same thing she'd done when her parents were killed... throw herself into the vineyard work. Glancing at her watch, Savannah realized she could still catch the top-of-the-hour wine tasting at the fairgrounds if she hurried. She hoped that a little slice of ordinary routine might help pull her out of the chaotic world she seemed to have fallen into.

As she stepped through the fairground entry gates, the vibrant sounds and warm sunlight began to chip away at the darkness clinging to her. The glowing tents, the cheerful laughter, and the comforting scents of hay and roasted pecans felt like a balm to her troubled spirit, allowing a glimmer of hope to stir within her.

Ahead, a small group was already gathering near the Graystone tasting booth. Hay bales formed makeshift seating, wine barrels served as tables laden with bottles and glasses, and amidst it all stood Lizzie and Jake. Lizzie stood behind the table, cheeks flushed, her smile stretched thin, while Jake, with his sleeves rolled up, was talking quietly to a couple at the front.

Savannah paused, taking in the scene. Jake had been a steadfast presence throughout the ordeal at Natalie's, and now here he was, stepping in to help at their booth. Even from this distance, she could tell he was pouring samples and guiding the crowd to keep things moving until she arrived.

Of course he'd stepped in. Savannah felt a sense of gratitude and appreciation wash over her as she watched him interact with the crowd, his easy charm speaking volumes. She found herself drawn to Jake's quiet strength and unwavering support, and his presence was a warm reminder that she was not alone in her struggles.

As she approached the booth, Lizzie's smile widened with relief, signaling that Savannah had arrived just in time. "Oh, thank God," Lizzie whispered through her smile, barely moving her lips. "My place is at the cash register while you spin the tales."

Savannah's arrival at the Graystone tasting booth was noticed by several of their regular customers, including the owner of the local wine shop, Lana Peters, who greeted her warmly. Savannah lifted her chin, smoothed her hair, and stepped easily into her role at the booth, her professionalism and charm evident to everyone.

Savannah squeezed Lizzie's hand under the table in a silent *I'm here*, then addressed the waiting crowd with the ease of someone who'd done this countless times.

"Thank you all for joining us," she began, her voice warm and smooth, even if her heart wasn't. "Today we're featuring three of our wines, starting with our Mountain Harvest Rosé. It's light, floral, and refreshing... perfect for an afternoon like this." The familiar routine of pouring wine, chatting with customers, and sharing stories about various wines felt like coming home.

The crowd leaned, attentive to her instructions on how to taste each wine. Jake continued to pour samples down the line, his quiet confidence a perfect complement to Savannah's narrative. He didn't speak much—he didn't have to. Every time he handed a glass to someone, they lit up as if invited into something special.

Lizzie jumped in with her usual enthusiasm, recovering quickly with reinforcements at hand. "This one's my absolute favorite," she announced as Savannah poured the next sample. "It pairs beautifully with smoked fish, mild cheese, and pork, whatever you've got goin' on."

Laughter rippled through the group, and Savannah felt her spirits lift. She stole a glance at Jake. He caught it, and his eyes softened with a quick wink, like he was checking on her without saying a word. Throughout the tasting, their exchanges were filled with subtle gestures and stolen glances that spoke volumes.

As the last glasses were poured and the crowd began to disperse, several people stopped to compliment the "team." Lana from the wine store gave Jake an approving glance and said, "That was delightful. I do tastings at the store on Saturdays. You should join us. Oh... and I've got front-row seats for the rodeo and can't wait to see what all the buzz is about you!"

Jake chuckled and tipped his hat. "I thank you for the invitation, ma'am, but when it comes to wine, I'll leave the real magic to Savannah."

Lana looked back at Savannah with an easy smile. "Savannah knows she is always welcome." Then, with a sly grin, she added, "My dear, I think this one might be a keeper."

Savannah felt heat rise in her cheeks, thrown off guard by the insinuation. She never sought the spotlight. But Jake's knowing smile and confident swagger filled her with anticipation.

The moment the final guest walked away, Lizzie collapsed dramatically onto a hay bale. "If that had lasted thirty seconds longer," she groaned, "I'd have started weeping into the cabernet."

Savannah truly laughed, and it felt like a breath of fresh air. Jake wiped his hands on a towel, glanced toward the arena, and said, "I should check in with Graham before he sends a search party." Then, softer, to Savannah, "You okay?"

She nodded, the answer catching slightly in her throat. "Yeah. Thanks for helping Lizzie."

Before he could respond, Graham's voice erupted across the fairgrounds. "ROLLINS! Where have you been?"

Jake winced, offered Savannah an apologetic smile, and headed off at a jog. She watched him leave... the confident stride, the easy power in his shoulders... a pang of longing tugging at her heart.

***

Lizzie knew her friend well and her curious gaze fixed on the exchange between Savannah and Jake. When he'd arrived at the booth without Savannah, Lizzie had tried to question him about the meeting, but he had remained tight-lipped about what unfolded there. As soon as Jake disappeared, Lizzie shifted her focus to Savannah with a raised eyebrow, realizing something significant was brewing beneath the surface. And she hadn't missed Jake's concern about Savannah.

"Okay," Lizzie said, planting her hands on her hips, demanding an explanation. "What happened?"

Savannah turned toward her friend, visibly tense but trying to appear casual. "With what?"

Lizzie stopped placing the bottles back in the box. "Seriously? Jake was watchin' you like a hawk, lookin' as though he thought you might shatter. I'm your best friend. Whatever it is, you can tell me. Maybe I can help."

Struggling to come to terms with what had been revealed in her grandmother's letter, Savannah couldn't help asking, "What did Jake tell you?"

Lizzie leaned in slightly, lowering her voice. "He wouldn't tell me anything. Said it was 'family business.' And if he's keeping quiet? Something major must've happened."

Savannah exhaled slowly, the burden of family secrets tying their two families together. "It was a lot, Lizzie."

Lizzie's expression softened instantly, concern etched across her face. "Then tell me what you can."

Savannah knew this affected Lizzie too. "There were... things we didn't know. We were at Natalie's, just breaking the surface, when Attorney Reed arrived with a letter from my grandmother. She wrote it before her heart attack. Duke tried to get him to read it just to us, being her family, but he said the letter was meant to be read to Natalie and Earl too, and even Jake." She blew out a breath of resignation and continued. "The letter revealed things that we never would have believed."

Lizzie's eyebrows drew together, her expression tightening. "What kind of things?"

Savannah hesitated, then pressed on. "My grandmother was having an affair with your uncle."

Lizzie visibly paled, processing the implications of secrets woven into her own family. "Did anyone know?"

"Aunt Natalie knew, Lizzie," Savannah said quietly. "She promised my grandmother she wouldn't say anything." She began rolling a barrel behind the table, then paused. "There's more."

Lizzie sank onto the nearest hay bale, needing a moment. "Go on. I'm listenin."

Savannah dreaded continuing but forced herself. "The letter mentioned the night of my parents' accident. She went to your mom's cabin to meet Earl. My parents showed up. Something happened at the cabin... connected to the accident."

Puzzled, Lizzie repeated, "My mom's cabin? Why would Earl...?" She didn't finish the question. It hung between them, sharp and unfinished.

Savannah nodded faintly. "I don't know the full story yet. But the letter said my parents came there."

Lizzie stared at her, stricken. "Did my mom know too? She never said anything. Not once. And Earl..." She shook her head slightly. "Wow, I can't wrap my mind around that."

Savannah sat beside her. "I'm still trying to make sense of it too."

Lizzie swallowed hard. "So many secrets. Savannah... if something happened at that cabin and Aunt Natalie knew about it, then my family's been keeping this from yours. And from me." She paused, realization hitting her. "Oh my God... Earl's burns. Aunt Natalie's hands. Were they at the accident?"

Savannah set her hand gently over Lizzie's. "We're going to sort it out. Today was overwhelming for everyone. Duke's still processing it."

Lizzie nodded slowly, beginning to understand the impact. "Okay, yeah." She tried for a small smile. "Thanks for telling me. You and Duke must have been blindsided."

"I think Natalie was too," Savannah said. "She's carried this knowledge for three years."

Lizzie pondered aloud, "Hey... how did your parents even know about the cabin?"

Savannah considered. "I obviously knew about it from you. Maybe I mentioned it to my parents. But I couldn't have told them where it was. I only knew it was about an hour from Blue Ridge." She shrugged. "Just another question in a sea of them."

Lightening the mood, Lizzie angled her head toward the direction Jake had gone, a sly smile emerging. "And your cowboy actin' all protective makes a whole lot more sense now."

Savannah tried to hide her reaction. "He's not my cowboy... but he has been very thoughtful."

"Girlfriend..." Lizzie pointed at her. "That man looked like he was ready to build you a storm shelter with his bare hands."

Savannah let out a quiet laugh and pushed herself to her feet. "Let's finish breaking down the booth. I need something simple to focus on."

"Good plan," Lizzie agreed, gathering a stack of tasting cards and the afternoon's order forms. "My brain's still spinning."

They worked in companionable silence, finding solace in the simple task of tidying up. Neither spoke, but their silent solidarity spoke volumes of the unwavering friendship. They both understood that something had changed, and whatever lay ahead was just the beginning.

As they loaded the last crate into the truck, Lizzie brushed off her hands. "Well," she said, "we survived the day. Want to grab an early dinner? Or a drink? I could use something that doesn't involve wine or hay."

Savannah hesitated, some loose ends tugging at her. "I really should go check on Duke. He didn't say much when I left."

Lizzie nodded, instantly understanding her concern. "I can stop by the ranch on my way home if you want. Make sure he's okay. I don't mind at all."

Savannah's felt her shoulders relax. "Would you? That would really help."

"Of course." Lizzie replied with a small smile. "You can take a rain check on dinner. We'll try again when the world feels a little less upside down."

Savannah returned the smile, feeling grateful. Her gaze drifted toward the arena, where the sounds of distant work... hammering, voices, a low thud of boots on dirt... still echoed across the fairgrounds.

"In that case..." she said softly, "I think I'm going to stop by the arena. Jake did a lot to help Duke and me. I'd like to thank him."

Lizzie smiled, genuinely hopeful for her friend. "It's time you met a man who recognizes how special you are, just like we all do. Go... I'll check on Duke."

They parted with that quiet, easy understanding that only old friends share. As Lizzie secured the tailgate of the truck, Savannah turned toward the arena, where the evening light cast a soft, golden haze over the dusty ground. She looked around her, admiring the stunning array of colors in the fall foliage.

And she knew exactly where she needed to be.

CHAPTER 30

AS Savannah approached the arena, the day's weight pressed heavily on her shoulders... betrayal, confusion, and a faint thread of determination pulling her forward. Her thoughts drifted to Jake, who was busy tending to his chores at the arena. His steady presence during those dark hours offered her understanding she hadn't felt in a long time. The gratitude she felt toward him settled somewhere deep within her... a quiet flutter, elusive and unnamed, yet undeniably real.

Her gaze lingered on his shirt, casually tossed over the fence. Watching him, his back turned, she saw the muscles in his shoulders tense and relax with each motion. There was undeniable strength in him, but it was the kindness in his eyes and the warmth of his smile that truly captivated her.

As she neared the fence, it was the sight of Jake's quarter horse that brought her back to the present. Seeking a distraction from the day's chaos and her musings about Jake, Savannah reached for an apple from a nearby basket. The horse's ears perked up, his eyes steady and curious. His presence was calming... solid, aware, patient in a way only animals could be.

She exhaled slowly, extending the apple. "Hey there... good boy," she murmured. "Looks like you've had a long day too." The horse took the apple gently, crunching it with an unhurried confidence that coaxed a small, grateful smile from her. The simple rhythm of feeding and interacting with him gave her a chance to collect her thoughts, easing the day's numbness. She rested her fingers on the fence rail, letting the quiet settle between them.

"You're lucky," she said to the horse. "You don't have to explain what you're feeling. You just... carry what you can." She didn't know why the words slipped out, or why a tightness pressed against her ribs. Maybe because it felt safe here... safe to admit something she wasn't ready to share with Jake. The horse nuzzled her sleeve, and she let her hand rest on his shoulder. "It's been a really long day."

The sound of boot steps broke the moment. Savannah turned to see Jake standing in the corral, paused in the middle of a chore he'd clearly forgotten upon seeing her. He didn't seem surprised... just watchful.

Their eyes locked, and a silent understanding passed between them. Jake's presence was reassuring, a force she couldn't quite explain. He didn't speak directly to Savannah, instead ambling over to the horse and beginning to stroke its neck and shoulder.

"There, now, Charro. Looks like you've found yourself a pretty lady... What's that, boy?" He lifted his brows with a teasing nod. "You think she's somethin' special? Yeah... I'd say you're right."

He turned to Savannah, a hint of seriousness layered beneath the playfulness. "Ma'am, this here's Charro... a fine quarter horse ready to take us straight across that finish line day after tomorrow."

Savannah eased right into it, "Why, Charro, it's wonderful to meet you." She scratched his nose, earning a pleased nicker. "I hear you've paired up with quite a cowboy for the rodeo. I'm looking forward to seeing you two show off your skills."

Jake suddenly shifted tactics, speaking conspiratorially to the horse. "You're stealin' my thunder, boy. Time for you to head to the stable." With a quick tilt of his head toward the barn, he added, "I've got it from here." A stable hand whistled, and Charro trotted off, leaving Savannah with a wistful smile.

Jake vaulted over the fence with ease, landing beside her with a solid thud. "Evenin', ma'am," he said, tipping his hat.

Savannah shook her head, amused by his effortless rapport with his horse. "You really talk to Charro like he understands you."

Jake stepped closer, his warmth radiating toward her, impossible to ignore. "Oh, he understands plenty. Especially when a beautiful woman wanders into his corral."

She blushed, a mix of surprise and intrigue prompting her to play along. "Is that right?"

Jake's grin deepened, slow and deliberate, full of confidence. "He was tryin' to impress you, darlin'.

Thought if he looked good, maybe you'd stick around long enough for me to get a word in."

A soft laugh escaped before she could stop it. "Well... he did a fine job."

Jake studied her intently, seeing past the strain of the day and the raw emotions he knew were there. "You look worn down," he said gently, unable to resist rubbing his thumb along her cheek. "Today was tough. Yet you came to work the booth, and no one would've ever known."

She sighed deeply, her exhaustion evident. "The longest day I can remember. I just... came to say thank you and go home."

Jake shook his head, decision firm. "No, ma'am. Not like this."

Savannah blinked, confused. "Like what?"

"Like someone carryin' too much alone." His voice filled with sincerity. "Come on. You need to eat. Let me get you somethin' simple. Nothin' fancy. Just some fresh air and a bite of food, so your body remembers you're still here."

Savannah hesitated, uncertainty nagging at her. "Jake. I..."

"Listen, there's a band playin' over in Blue Ridge tonight. The town square should be all lit up." He could see his coaxing was getting through, so he continued, "Food truck'll be open. Good hotdogs. Good people. Good noise to drown out a bad day." He gestured toward the parking lot. "Ride with me. Ten minutes, tops."

She opened her mouth to protest again, but the thought of going home alone with nothing to do but think about what happened sounded much worse. Something inside her that was tired of being strong relented. "Hotdogs and banjos?"

"Savannah..." He gave her that smile that made his eye twinkle and her heart melt. "This is exactly the kind of night you don't realize you need." With a gentle tug on her hand, Jake led her toward his truck. The fairgrounds were thinning out... lights dimming, voices fading into the evening.

As she climbed into the truck, the familiar scents of hay and dust filled her senses. But once beside Jake, it was his scent, warm leather and clean spice, that drew her in.

Jake started the engine, glancing at her as the dashboard glow touched her face. "You good?"

She nodded, feeling a little of her normal steadiness return. "I think so."

"Good." He drove onto the gravel, then the road. "We'll fix the rest."

The ride was peaceful. Cool fall air slipped through the cracked windows as Blue Ridge came into view, its storefront lights twinkling along the sidewalk.

The town square was alive with energy, not crowded but comfortably bustling. Strings of lights arched between lampposts, casting a subtle glow over families, couples, and locals lingering in town. A line gathered at the food truck by the curb, and a small band played upbeat tunes... fiddle, banjo, and guitar weaving into the night.

Jake parked and came around to her side, leaning an elbow on the open door. "C'mon," he encouraged. "Let's start by gettin' you somethin' to eat."

Savannah stepped down, feeling a small part of the day's heaviness lift, guided by Jake toward the music and the promise of a lighter evening.

They found an open bench near the edge of the square, close enough to hear the music drifting from the pavilion but far enough for a small pocket of quiet. Jake handed her a hot dog loaded the way he liked his own... mustard, onions, a little relish... nothing fancy.

"Careful," he said. "These things tend to have a mind of their own."

Savannah chuckled, taking a bite anyway, determined to set aside the day's events for a moment. When Jake mimicked the rodeo announcer's dry voice, it was so unexpected she couldn't help laughing.

Caught up in the lighthearted moment, she noticed the smear of mustard at the corner of his mouth and couldn't resist. "Oh, hold still," she said, lifting her napkin.

Jake caught her wrist gently, a flash of amusement in his eyes. "What are you doing?"

She tilted her head, unfazed. "Saving you from yourself. You've got a situation here." She leaned in and dabbed lightly at the corner of his mouth. Showing him the napkin, she added, "The evidence, sir."

The sound of Savannah's laughter was like music to Jake, and all he wanted was to keep the easy banter going with a lighthearted sense of humor.

They sat on that bench, indulging in hotdogs and laughter, until Savannah felt a sense of contentment wash over her. In Jake, she had found not just a friend, but a kindred spirit... someone she could rely on when things were hard, someone who could coax her back to the good times. She looked at him as if truly seeing him for the first time.

Jake smiled when her shoulders noticeably relaxed. Impulsively, he stood to offer his hand with a sudden spark of mischief that made her pulse quicken. "Come on," he said. "Now that we've had something to eat, we might as well go work it off with some music." She let out a soft laugh and took his hand.

They walked together toward the pavilion, a few locals turning their heads to see the Graystone granddaughter about to dance with the star rodeo cowboy. Savannah exchanged a smile with Eddie, who was strumming out a fast tune... all energy and noise. But when Jake lifted his arms to lead her into a square dance, Eddie signaled the band, and they brought the pace down to a slow medley, a warm, steady rhythm that invited closeness without asking.

"Really?" Savannah mouthed over at Eddie.

Jake winked at Eddie in appreciation. "You up for it, Miss Gray?"

Before she could think of a teasing response, Jake slipped a hand to her waist, guiding her in with a natural two-step that surprised them both. Savannah's arm rested on his shoulder, leaving a hint of space between them at first.

But as they moved, the space disappeared. Savannah eased closer without thinking, her arm tightening around Jake's neck. Jake's hold shifted too... a quiet pull that drew her fully into him. Their steps fell into rhythm, slow and natural, as if they'd done this a hundred times before. The connection was there, in each other's arms. They both knew it... there was no going back.

CHAPTER 31

DANCING with Jake, with the music swirling around them, Savannah couldn't ignore the growing attraction she felt for him. With his arms securely around her, she experienced a unique sense of safety and understanding in a world of uncertainty. His easy smile and kind eyes revealed a cowboy with a heart of gold and a gentle touch that seemed to soothe the ache in Savannah's heart.

As Jake reached for her other hand, pulling it around his neck, he drew her closer. It was as if he was silently telling her that she didn't need to pretend to be strong around him.

When the band finished their final song and began packing up, Eddie waved goodbye. A rush of melancholy swept over Savannah as the evening came to an end.

Jake watched her intently. "You doin' okay?"

Savannah nodded, though exhaustion tugged at the edges of her smile. "Better than I was a few hours ago."

"Good," he replied softly. "Why don't I take you home?"

Savannah hesitated, unsure how to voice her feelings of loneliness and vulnerability. The word *home* stirred up thoughts of Duke's silence, the letter, the cabin, and Natalie's shaken voice... all waiting for her the moment she walked into the ranch.

They were walking hand in hand toward the truck when Savannah, in a moment of quiet courage, searched his eyes and confessed, "I don't..." She swallowed, attempting again. "I don't really want to be alone tonight."

That one simple statement allowed Jake to see a raw and honest part of a woman used to putting on a strong face... for the public, for her friends, and for Duke.

"Savannah, talk to me. What do you need?"

Her voice was quiet, stripped down to the truth. "Just somewhere I can breathe."

Jake nodded, realizing she was exhausted and not ready to dive back into the drama of the day. "My place isn't far," he said. "Just a small rental cabin I'm using during the rodeo. But it's quiet. And you don't have to be alone there. You're welcome to come with me."

Her response was gentle yet certain. "I'd like that, Jake. Thank you." Then, with a tired sigh, she added, "I should call Duke. On top of everything else, he doesn't need to worry about me."

"That sounds good. You can call from the porch to have some privacy, and I'll stoke up the fire and fix us some of my famous hot buttered rum with cinnamon."

Savannah smiled at the thought of Jake preparing hot buttered rum. "I can't wait. The call shouldn't take long. I just want him to know where I am. We will have to deal with things tomorrow, but tonight we can delay the inevitable a little longer."

He parked the truck in the driveway and opened the door for Savannah. After he unlocked the front door to let himself inside, he turned and said, "Take whatever time you need. I'll start the fire, then I'm going to hop in the shower to get some of this dust and mud off from the chores. I'm surprised you could tolerate me tonight."

That made Savannah laugh, thinking "tolerate" was not exactly the word she'd use. "Jake, do what you need to do. I'm just happy to be here."

"Okay, I'll be quick. Maybe you can help me with those buttered rums?"

Savannah stood on the porch of the small cabin, gazing at the faint outline of the foothills in the distance. The nearly full moon cast a shimmering glow over the scene, and the stars twinkled overhead. For a moment, she could pretend she hadn't heard everything she did in Natalie's living room.

Here she was at a cabin with Jake... unlike the cabin that now haunted her thoughts, where her grandmother had last seen her parents before the accident. She shook her head in sadness, trying to picture them in the heat of an argument. She recalled her mother telling her to never go to bed angry with a loved one because you never knew what the morning would bring... a lesson learned young but never forgotten.

Why hadn't her mom taken her own advice? Savannah rubbed her eyes in frustration, then reached for her phone. Duke answered on the first ring. "Savannah? Are you okay? I've been worried."

Savannah tried to push down the guilt for not being there for her grandfather. "I'm sorry, Duke. Lizzie was supposed to come check on you. I went into town with Jake for a hotdog. Eddie's band was playing, so we danced a bit."

Duke shared that Lizzie had visited the ranch and brought soup, unaware of Savannah's plans. Savannah braced herself and got to the point. "Duke, I know we have a lot to soak in and deal with. If it's okay, I'd like to wait until tomorrow. I'm going to stay at Jake's tonight." After hearing Duke's shock, she clarified, "It's not like that... really. With everything that we learned today, I just need the company right now."

As soon as she said the words, she winced at her oversight. Of course, Duke might need company too. Holding the phone a little closer, she softened her voice. "Duke, I think I might be falling for Jake, and the rodeo is day after tomorrow. Then he'll be gone. I want this time to get to know him better."

"Okay, thanks, Duke. I love you too. See you in the morning."

Savannah stepped inside the cabin, which was already warming from the fire blazing in the fireplace. The living room smelled faintly of cedar and burning hickory. A soft lamp glowed in the corner. A folded blanket rested over the sofa, and a pair of boots waited neatly by the door.

She was about to take off her jacket when Jake emerged from the bedroom, his wet hair combed back. He wore a flannel shirt over jeans, sleeves rolled up with a single button fastened near his waist, leaving an unguarded view of his muscular chest.

He stepped behind her. "Here, let me help you with that jacket." When his hand brushed across her shoulders, he could feel the tightness. "How did the call go?"

"As well as could be expected. I think he was pretty shocked I was here."

Jake nodded, "I suppose so. You can trust me, Savannah." Then, with a playful tilt of his head and a smile, he added, "Now, come help me with the drinks... but you have to swear to keep the recipe secret!"

Savannah caught the connection Jake missed. "I think we've had enough secrets for one day, don't you?"

Jake rolled his eyes, annoyed with himself. "Leave it to a cowboy to stick his foot in his mouth. I'm sorry. You're right. Full disclosure on how to make the hot buttered rum drinks." She followed him to the kitchen, sitting on a bar stool as he gathered the ingredients.

Savannah watched, trying not to focus on his bare chest. "I really don't know that much about you. With all your fan following, is there one special someone in your life?"

"I travel around too much to settle down. Whenever I need a dose of home, I head back to Arkansas. My parents are there, and my sister and her kids usually visit whenever I'm around." As if thinking aloud, "Love those three kids... two boys and a girl. Uncle Jake loves spoilin' them, that's for sure. It makes me look forward to havin' a family someday whenever I decide to stay put."

Jake handed her the hot drinks and laid the blanket from the sofa by the fire. They sat quietly, sipping their drinks. He looked at her tentatively and asked, "Are you relaxing a little?"

Savannah nodded, rubbing her neck. Jake set down his drink. "I have an idea. Why don't I rub some of those knots out of your shoulders? If Charro were here, I bet he'd give me a good reference."

The idea sounded great to Savannah, who was ready for anything that would relieve the lingering tension. "A massage sounds wonderful. Where do you want me... sitting or lying down?" He started to rub her shoulders seated, but her long hair got in the way and he couldn't get the right angle.

Frustrated, he looked at his hands. "My hands are calloused, but I have a balm I use on my muscles after a rough ride. If I use that, it might help. Why don't I get you a sheet to use so I can rub the balm into your shoulders and back?"

"Honestly, the balm might be just what I need, and don't worry about your hands. But Jake, if I take off my blouse, it is for the massage, right?"

"Savannah, you can always trust me not to cross a line with you that you don't want crossed. For now, let's get you comfortable." He gave her the sheet, dimming the lights to just the firelight, then turned his back while she removed her top and lay face down on the blanket. She had pulled a clip out of her bag to put her hair up.

Jake turned around to see Savannah's bare back in the glimmering firelight. Reminding himself of his promise, he knelt beside her. He placed a hand lightly on her back, gauging his touch. Savannah gave a quick involuntary jump at the unfamiliar sensation, then relaxed. It was hard for her to sort through her feelings. Part of her longed to roll over onto her back and rip off his shirt, desperate to feel skin on skin. But practicality won. "Your hands are fine. Will you try it with the balm?"

Jake scooped balm onto his hands. Rubbing them quickly together, he created a warmth that he then transferred to Savannah's shoulders. He made it a challenge. Each knot along her neck, shoulders, and back, was a door. He couldn't get inside the door until the knot was released. One by one, the doors opened and he would smile. A few times, her tiny sighs and moans pushed him to forget his promise. But he didn't and vowed to himself he never would.

Savannah was lulled by the warmth of the drink, the fire, and Jake's healing touch, drifting into a place of peace and calm.

"Savannah?" Jake whispered. No response, just the soft rhythm of sleep.

He closed his eyes for a moment, feeling something warm and unexpected open inside him. A tenderness he hadn't planned on... a protectiveness he didn't know he had room for. Carefully he lifted his hands away.

He retrieved a pillow and blanket, gently moving her to the sofa. Removing the clip from her hair and placing a pillow under her head, he felt her hair spill over his arm like silk. Then he draped the blanket over her shoulders, tucking it around her with tender care.

Savannah sighed in her sleep, peaceful for the first time all day.

Jake lingered only a second, observing her in the soft lamplight... the curve of her cheek, the way she relaxed fully only now, here, in his home.

"Goodnight, Savannah," he whispered softly, then dimmed the lamp, leaving only the faint glow from the kitchen light. He moved quietly, his footsteps almost silent as he walked down the hall to his room, deliberately choosing not to glance back at Savannah.

It wasn't that he lacked the desire to look back... it was that he knew if he did, he wasn't sure he could find the courage to leave her.

CHAPTER 32

SAVANNAH awoke to an unusual silence that left her feeling disoriented. Groggy and bewildered, she took in her surroundings... the dying embers in the fireplace, the cool air brushing against her skin, and the soft sofa beneath her. As she pieced together the events of the previous night, memories flooded back. She remembered the warmth of the fire and Jake's reassuring presence beside her. His gentle touch, his comforting words, and the promise he'd made... all came back in fragmented pieces, slowly forming a coherent picture.

Relief washed over her once she realized she was safe and unharmed, yet a wave of embarrassment followed when she noticed her missing blouse, leaving her feeling exposed and vulnerable in the dimly lit room. Yet, when she glanced around, it became apparent that Jake had meticulously arranged everything with care. Her blouse was neatly folded, her jacket placed beside it, and a blanket and sheet were arranged around her like a protective shield.

She'd fallen asleep, and Jake had merely ensured her comfort and safety. Standing up, she felt a sense of gratitude mixed with lingering unease. Dressing quickly, she found solace in the familiar routine. With each button fastened, she felt more like herself, more in control of the situation. Despite the strange circumstances, she knew she wasn't alone, and as she made her way to the restroom, a faint smile tugged at the corner of her lips.

When she came out, face washed and her hair tucked back into a low bun, Savannah was met with the savory smell of cooking bacon and the sounds of Jake bustling in the kitchen. She hesitated for only a second before stepping toward the kitchen.

Jake stood at the stove, barefoot, wearing only jeans, his back to her as he cracked eggs into a pan. The morning light filtered in through the window, catching on his shoulders while he moved around the kitchen with ease. His hair was still damp, darker than the night before by the firelight. For a brief, disconcerting moment, it felt almost too intimate to witness. Not because of what he wasn't wearing, but because of how natural the scene seemed, as if this were simply how mornings began.

Sensing her presence, he turned, pausing just a fraction longer than necessary before slinging a kitchen towel over his shoulder. "Mornin'," he said, his voice still rough with sleep. "Hope you're hungry. I'm rustlin' up some breakfast. Those hotdogs are long gone."

She nodded, suddenly famished. "I'm starving."

He slid a mug across the counter toward her with a grin. "Coffee's fresh."

Grateful for something to do, she wrapped her hands around the mug and took a sip, finding a glimpse of normalcy in a world recently turned upside down. She watched him, marveling at how comfortable he was in his own skin.

Jake gave her that casual smile that reached his eyes. "Did you sleep okay? You were out like a light. I hope you don't mind that I moved you from the floor to the sofa. Thought it would be a tad more comfortable."

It then dawned on Savannah that he had carried her, shirtless, and she couldn't deny that the thought was tantalizing. She was looking down at her coffee, but when she met his gaze, she suspected he was thinking the same thing. "You were very gallant, and I appreciate all you've done for a casual acquaintance."

"Anytime. And Savannah, in case you haven't noticed, we've moved far beyond casual acquaintances."

They stood there for a moment, the quiet between them carrying the weight of everything they weren't saying. Not awkward, just aware.

"I heard from Duke this morning," Savannah said, keeping her voice steady as she changed the subject.

Jake glanced at her. "Everything okay?"

"He wants a meeting today." She took another sip of coffee. "Just the four of us... him, Natalie, Earl, and me. He said he's having breakfast with Tom. Sounds important since there are still so many questions."

Jake agreed, understanding the challenge ahead. "I'll head back to the fairgrounds after breakfast. Still plenty to do before the rodeo."

"I need to go home, too. Shower and change. Get ready for whatever's coming." Savannah hesitated, then added, "Lizzie will be back at the Graystone booth alone again."

He set a plate in front of her. "She's tough and better at it than she gives herself credit for."

"I totally agree," Savannah said. "But I hate that she keeps getting left holding things together while everyone else falls apart."

Jake didn't disagree. "Will you call me when you're done?" he asked, reaching his hand across the kitchen island.

She took it, amazed at how close they'd become in such a short time. "I will."

They ate their hearty breakfast quickly, not expecting to linger. The eggs were good, the toast warm, and the coffee strong. That would have to do for now.

As they prepared to leave, Jake pulled on a sweatshirt, grabbed his boots, and opened the door for her. The morning air was crisp and bright. "Savannah," he said, stopping her just outside the door. She turned to him. "I meant what I said last night."

Touched, she understood exactly which words he meant. "I know." Their eyes filled with hope, and Savannah reached for him this time, confident he shared her feelings. The kiss was intense and empowering, encouraging them to face the uncertainties of the future together. After one more parting kiss, they separated, each returning to their own responsibilities.

Savannah drove home with the window cracked, feeling a mix of trepidation and resolve. She showered quickly, washing away the scent of cedar and smoke, choosing her clothes with care. Nothing dramatic. Just herself determined to face whatever was coming her way.

CHAPTER 33

DUKE sat at the corner table in the café next to the art center, brooding over what questions he intended to ask at the meeting. Although he knew Mabel, he barely noticed when the waitress approached with a pot of coffee. Seeing the expression on Duke's face, she decided it was best to let him be, so she poured his coffee the way he liked it and discreetly slipped away.

He had arranged to meet Tom for breakfast and arrived early, hoping to clear his mind. His steel-blue eyes scanned the menu without truly seeing it, his thoughts tangled with the revelations of the previous day. The sleepless hours had left lines etched around his eyes and mouth... lines that told a story of both joy and sorrow.

Despite his best efforts, he couldn't shake the knowledge that his wife had carried hidden truths that he had been blind to. He had turned to Tom, a loyal friend and trusted confidante, seeking strength to face the truth, all of it, no matter how difficult it might be.

Mabel showed Tom to the table, handing him a menu. After he set his jacket over the back of the chair and sat, she filled his coffee mug and refilled Duke's.

"Mornin', Duke," Tom said.

"Mornin'," Duke replied. His hands held the coffee mug with a sense of purpose, finally noticing the waitress, mumbling, "Mornin', Mabel."

The friendship formed between Duke and Tom was a direct result of the closeness between Lois and Natalie. Their wives were constantly planning events for them to attend or dinners out together. Duke looked across the table at Tom, realizing he had been so consumed with grief over losing David and Margaret, then Lois, that he hadn't been there for his friend when Tom and Natalie divorced. Now he started to wonder if the divorce had anything to do with what Natalie was hiding. Once Tom moved to Murphy, it just compounded Duke's grief with the loss of yet another person he was close to.

Tom knew Duke well enough to see his pain. Words were hard to come by at a time like this, so he let Duke lead the conversation and allowed periods of silent understanding when he thought it was needed. All he wanted was to reassure Duke that he wasn't alone.

"I'm touched that you asked me, Duke. Natalie and Earl want me involved too," Tom said, keeping his voice even. "I've arranged for a room upstairs in the art center. We won't be disturbed."

Duke nodded in appreciation. "That's good."

"It's quiet up there," Tom added. "Plenty of privacy. We won't be rushed."

Duke took a sip of his coffee before setting the mug down next to his untouched biscuit. "I'm not looking for blame or explanations, Tom," he said, his voice sounding weary. "I just need to understand what happened. The order of it. What was known and when."

Tom met his eyes. "That's exactly how I'll keep it."

Duke exhaled slowly. "Savannah doesn't need to hear everything."

"I understand," Tom replied. "I'll do my best, but Savannah is an adult. This involves her parents and grandmother. She deserves to know as much as she can handle."

Though his instinct was to shield her from pain, Duke knew Tom was right. Duke's shoulders relaxed just a fraction. He stared past the window for a second, at nothing in particular, then back to the table.

"I keep kickin' myself," Duke said quietly, "about why Lois carried things without me noticin'. Why didn't you say somethin'?"

Tom didn't answer right away, reflecting on the past. How many things could have been done differently. "I don't have an excuse. I was going through a lot in my own house with Natalie." He paused, thinking of his divorce, then gently added, "Duke, Lois knew you loved her."

Duke's mouth tightened, but he didn't argue or agree. He simply accepted the words, knowing he would consider them later when he could face the true depth of her feelings.

They finished their coffee, and Tom checked his watch. "We should head over soon."

"All right."

They stood, and Duke slipped on his jacket slowly, straightening it with deliberate care. Whatever awaited him next door, he would face it standing tall.

Making their way toward the door, Tom walked beside him. Just before they reached the sidewalk, he paused and rested a reassuring hand on Duke's back. "You're not alone," Tom said quietly. "I'm right here."

Ready to face the truth with integrity, Duke looked at his friend with gratitude. "I know," he said. Together, they walked out into the morning light.

Duke glanced around, checking his watch. "Savannah said she'd meet us there... ah, there she is."

Savannah stood near the low stone planter at the top of the stairs. Her nerves were taut as she waited, hoping to avoid Natalie and Earl until Duke arrived. When she saw him, she straightened.

"Hey," she greeted, pushing away from the planter. Her eyes went first to Duke, then to Tom. "Did you have a good breakfast?"

"We did," Duke said. "Didn't want to keep you waitin'."

"I just got here," she replied, though it was clear she'd given herself extra time. She glanced toward the front doors. "They've opened the meeting room for us. I think Natalie and Earl might already be inside."

Duke took in the building's architecture... the sculptures flanking the stairs, a place meant for reflection rather than confrontation. "All right," he said. "Let's do this."

Savannah reached for the door but paused, turning back to them. "Before we go in, I need to say something."

"What is it, Savannah?" Duke asked.

"I don't know what this meeting will uncover," she began carefully, "but whatever comes out, I want it all on the table. No more circling around pieces and hoping they'll line up on their own. We need the truth."

Duke exchanged an affirmative look with Tom, both silently agreeing that Savannah should get full disclosure. He looked back at his granddaughter, his expression thoughtful. "I agree. It's time for honesty and transparency, no matter how difficult."

Tom held the door open. "Then let's start unraveling the truth."

Savannah pushed through the door with determination and stepped inside.

CHAPTER 34

NATALIE and Earl were already seated in the meeting room. Upon seeing the others enter, Earl struggled to rise to his feet, extending his hand, hoping to avoid any confrontation.

Tom noticed Duke's hesitation and stepped forward to shake Earl's hand. "Morning, Earl." He then turned to Natalie, offering the same courtesy. "Natalie."

Duke acknowledged them both with a brief nod and took his seat without a word. The absence of a handshake hung in the air longer than the gesture itself might have.

Savannah, taking her cue from Duke, chose the chair beside him, her posture straight and her hands folded neatly in her lap.

Once everyone was settled, Tom leaned forward, addressing Natalie and Earl directly. "I had breakfast with Duke this morning," he explained. "I asked for this meeting because he and Savannah deserve clarity about what happened the night of the accident and

Lois's subsequent death. The letter Tyler read yesterday left many unanswered questions."

His gaze moved deliberately between Natalie and Earl. "We're not here to assign blame. We're here to understand the truth—all of it."

Natalie, caught up in a whirlwind of emotions and loyalties, didn't hesitate. She turned toward Duke, her posture tense, her voice resigned. "I suppose there's no point saying I'm surprised we're having this meeting."

With eyes filled with sorrow and shoulders slumped, Natalie briefly glanced at Savannah before returning her gaze to Duke. "I spent years trying to keep things contained. Not out of disrespect for you and Savannah, but because I believed reopenin' old wounds would only cause more harm than good."

She paused, her jaw tightening. "Lois made choices I was aware of. I won't deny that I kept some of that information to myself," Natalie admitted, her honesty cutting through the tension in the room. "I did it believing I was protecting people already carrying enough loss. I didn't expect it all to surface this way... or now."

Filled with regret, Natalie's voice softened as she addressed Duke, her emotions evident in the tremor of her words. "What disappoints me most is that the decision to reveal everything was taken out of my hands once Tyler read the letter. It wasn't easy to hold it inside all this time, seeing you almost every day." The weight of her confession pressed upon her in this moment of reckoning as she faced Duke and the consequences of withholding the past.

"Natalie," Duke began, "I know you're a good woman, and I believe you meant well. But that time has passed. Now I need to understand what my wife was hiding. Not pieces of it... all of it. Can you do that?"

Savannah listened in silence beside Duke, her mind turning over the memories of Natalie. Natalie had been present throughout Savannah's life... someone she trusted and leaned on in times of need. She was "Aunt Natalie" to her as much as she was to Lizzie. Yet as the conversation unfolded, her sense of closeness and familiarity was suddenly at odds with what she was hearing, and Savannah began to question how many choices she'd considered her own had been quietly guided by Natalie's influence.

Natalie cleared her throat and focused on Duke. "About a year before the accident, you were in Memphis at a wholesalers' meetin'. David and Margaret had taken Savannah up to Knoxville to settle her in at the university. Lois was facin' the weekend alone, and I was already plannin' a long weekend at the family ranch in Asheville with Tom. When he couldn't go at the last minute, I asked Lois if she wanted to join me." Natalie gave an ironic chuckle. "We actually laughed at the feud between the wineries that had gone on for so many years, no one could even remember why." She looked at Duke to gauge his reaction to the feud.

"Go on," Duke said quietly.

Earl sat up straighter. "If you'll allow me, I think I can fill in this part."

Duke took a deep breath in, uncertain of what to expect. "All right."

Earl's scarred face twisted slightly, an attempted smile at the memory. "Natalie showed up at the Wellington ranch with Lois, the prim and proper wife of the untouchable Duke Gray."

Duke half rose from his seat but Tom gently asked him to sit down. "Let him go on."

"I was newly single after a nasty divorce and up in years... the last thing I wanted was a tryst with a married woman. Natalie and Lois got settled in and changed into casual clothes. I was on the porch reading the paper when Natalie said they were going down to the river. What caught my attention wasn't their carefree laughter; it was Lois. Her hair was down, chestnut brown with streaks of gray that glistened like sunlight. She wore simple khaki pants and a button-down white shirt. Simple, no jewelry. It was as if she could feel me watching. Half-way down the hill, she turned mid-laugh, and our eyes met." He sighed, "I didn't know it at the time, but with Lois, it was the pursuit she wanted... not to be unfaithful."

Savannah tried to picture her grandmother on that riverbank, her hair flowing freely, lonely and yearning to be truly seen.

Duke squeezed his eyes shut, letting Earl's words sink in. *She wanted the pursuit, not to be unfaithful.* The flush of guilt he felt was overwhelming. "I get the picture. How about getting to the time of the accident." Trying to restrain the anger from his voice, he asked, "Was the cabin somewhere you met often?"

Earl was about to answer when Natalie placed her gloved hand on his to continue. Natalie said, "I know the answer to that and no, the family cabin was used as a rental and was mostly occupied. Earl can confirm this but, Duke, up until that night it had mostly been phone calls, texts, and the flowers or notes that were sent to Lois at my house."

Earl nodded. "That's the way she wanted it. At least, until that Friday night. She called me and said there was an argument, then you left for your weekly poker game with Tom. She was upset and said she needed some space to breathe and relax. I mentioned the cabin and that Natalie had the calendar of the rentals. I offered to meet her there and, for the first time, she said yes."

Duke was confused. "I don't remember an argument. But after learning about the accident, everything else seemed to melt away."

Natalie continued, "Lois must have called me after Earl. She asked about the cabin and said she needed a place to get away for a couple of days. The cabin wasn't rented and was only an hour away, so of course I said she could use it. That's when she mentioned Earl was coming. Lois begged me to keep it to herself, that she needed time with Earl to see if there was any future with him."

Earl looked at Natalie, astonished, but she continued. "Early Saturday morning, after you went to work in the vineyard, Lois picked me up. She said she left you a note telling you she wasn't going far, but she needed to clear her head and would be back in a few days. I was to ride with her to Morganton and meet Earl at the old post office. He was there when we arrived. Earl went with Lois in her car, and I drove Earl's car back to my house."

Duke shook his head. "Something doesn't make sense. I never got a note. I thought she was with you for a day of shopping in town. She was back by the time the police came to tell us about the accident."

Tom suddenly spoke up. "This is where I might have a piece of the puzzle. David came to our house Saturday looking for Natalie. When she wasn't there, he asked me about the cabin and where it was. I thought it was odd and hesitated. He seemed worried about Lois... said he found a note that she'd written."

Duke looked at his friend. "Why didn't you say anything?"

Tom shook his head in regret. "At the time, I didn't think anything of it. Then Natalie showed up with Earl's car, and we argued about her involvement in getting Earl and Lois together. She begged me to keep quiet. That this would blow over and no one would get hurt. Then she got a hysterical call from Lois and she stormed out." Tom took a long breath. "After all that happened, our marriage couldn't survive it. That's when I moved to Murphy."

Duke was mentally trying to sort out the pieces. To Tom, he asked, "So David took the note. He obviously didn't want me to see it. You said he mentioned the cabin. If the note didn't say where she was going, how did he know about the cabin?"

Savannah had been listening intently when it suddenly became clear; he knew about the cabin because of her. "Lizzie grew up going to the cabin every summer. She talked about it a lot. I'm sure I mentioned it to Mom and Dad." Her eyes welled up. "He... he knew about it because of me."

CHAPTER 35

EARL sat in his chair, the weight of the past bearing down on him. The memory of that fateful day swirled in his head like a storm threatening to consume him. With a heavy sigh of resignation, he began to unravel the tangled web of emotions that still haunted him.

"During the drive to the cabin, an awkward silence hung in the air between us. We hadn't been alone together since her visit to North Carolina, and this was meant to be our first overnight. I attempted to put Lois at ease, placing my bag in the upstairs bedroom to give her the space she seemed to need. I had no idea about a note to Duke or what excuse she'd made to come to the cabin, but Lois's call on Friday night suggested we both had something we needed to find out."

Although Duke's hands were clenched, he remained silent.

"To provide a distraction," Earl continued, "I suggested we hike up to a nearby waterfall. It was a long way up, giving us a chance for earnest conversation, and Lois began to noticeably relax. She spoke a great deal about Blue Ridge and its people and atmosphere. There were so many things she seemed to love about the small town; it made me curious about what was wrong. I remember her saying she wasn't quite sure there was any particular thing that had caused her discontent. She expressed a restlessness inside her. I told her I understood, but, in truth, I'm not sure I did. Coming back down the mountain path, I could tell she was having second thoughts about the two of us. By the end of the hike, we had agreed there would be no pressure between us and we would let things unfold naturally. Never in a million years did we see what was coming.

"Back at the cabin, we decided to shower, change, and go into town for dinner. I heard the knock on the door from upstairs. Lois was still in her shower, so I came to the door in my robe, and it was David. I had never met him, so at first, I wasn't sure who it was. With me in my robe, he came to all the wrong conclusions. He demanded to see his mother. There was no stopping him. He banged on the bathroom door, calling for Lois. She came out, startled to see both David and Margaret, then quickly realized how it must look with both of us freshly showered."

Earl's voice trembled with emotion as he recalled the heartbreaking moments that changed everything.

"Lois tried to calm him and explain. In truth, we were there together. Was there desire? Yes. Was there expectation? Probably. Would anything have happened? We will never know. When I told David my own car was back in Blue Ridge, he insisted on driving me back. When Lois said she would drive me back, David refused, telling her he no longer trusted her. I could see the hurt in her eyes. She pleaded with him, but he was obstinate. I saw no other alternative but to dress and go with them. All I know, looking back, is that the misunderstandings and hurtful accusations unfolded like a tragedy in slow motion leading to a devastating conclusion none of us could have foreseen."

Duke tried to grasp what he was hearing. "So you and Lois were never intimate?"

Earl sighed in defeat. "Nope. We won't ever know how things might have unfolded with us. What I do know is that if David and Margaret hadn't come to the cabin, they'd still be alive, and I wouldn't look like this. If we'd understood each other sooner—if any of us had—that night would have ended very differently."

***

Savannah was sitting perfectly still, absorbing Earl's words, when her phone vibrated in her pocket. She ignored it. His words had affected them all, their heaviness still lingering in the air. No one had moved. Duke's gaze remained fixed somewhere beyond the table, his hands resting flat against the wood as if anchoring himself there. The idea that David and Margaret, and even Lois, might still be with them seemed impossible to bear.

The phone vibrated again. Sharper this time. Insistent. Aware of the disruption, Savannah glanced down to see who was calling. Lizzie's name glowed on the screen. Savannah frowned. Lizzie knew where she was. She knew better than to interrupt unless it mattered. Despite her initial reluctance, when she heard the phone a third time, she knew the situation must be urgent.

Savannah inhaled slowly and stood, the chair legs scraping softly against the floor. "I'm sorry," she said, excusing herself from the somber gathering and already moving toward the door. "I need to take this."

As she excused herself from the room, Tom quietly indicated his approval. Natalie hardly noticed, her gaze faced downward. Duke, however, looked up and met Savannah's eyes. He understood her well enough to recognize and admire her unwavering sense of duty and natural role as a problem solver. Savannah responded to Duke's silent inquiry with a reassuring nod. Her gesture conveyed confidence that she was prepared to manage any unexpected challenge that had come up.

She stepped outside, the cool air a welcome contrast to the stifling tension inside. She swiped to answer, bringing the phone to her ear with a mix of anticipation and apprehension. "Lizzie?" Savannah's voice was barely audible above the construction going on across the square.

"Savannah, thank goodness," Lizzie's voice came through, a mixture of relief and urgency. "I know you're in the middle of something. I wouldn't call if I didn't have to."

Savannah leaned back against the cool wall, pressing the phone closer to her ear. "What's going on?"

As Lizzie began to speak, Savannah felt a sense of duty pulling her in two directions. Inside, the room held secrets and revelations that needed tending. Outside, Lizzie's voice pulled her toward another matter, one that demanded her attention and care.

Lizzie's voice was tense as she explained the situation to Savannah. "There's a man here," she said, her words hurried. "At the fairgrounds. He says he has an appointment with Duke, but Duke isn't answerin' his phone. He flew in this mornin'. He's waitin' for me to reach one of you. Savannah, he's from Italy."

Italy? Savannah closed her eyes briefly. It wasn't the first time Duke had arranged a meeting without mentioning it. He'd done it before. More than once. "From Italy? This must be important. What could he possibly want?" she asked, the responsibility of covering winery business in Duke's absence ingrained in her.

Lizzie hesitated. "He says he's here about a collaboration, I think. He keeps askin' for you. Said if Duke wasn't available, he was to meet with Duke's granddaughter."

"Me?"

"Yes," Lizzie said. "He said your grandfather spoke highly of you. I didn't know what else to do. I didn't want to interrupt Duke, but I can't just leave him standin' here."

Savannah listened, the weight of Earl's words colliding with the urgency in Lizzie's voice regarding the unexpected visitor from Italy seeking a collaboration with the winery. Savannah's instincts kicked in, ready to represent her family's legacy. "You did the right thing. I'll come."

"You're sure?" Lizzie asked. "I know today's—"

"I'll handle it," Savannah said gently. "Just let him know I'm on my way." She ended the call before Lizzie could apologize again.

Savannah stepped back inside the meeting room. Tom had been speaking and paused. She apologized for leaving, explaining there was urgent business at the fairgrounds.

Duke started to stand, but Savannah quickly assured him she had it under control, suggesting he stop by the booth after they finished. She was determined to handle the situation with grace and professionalism, already in motion toward the fairgrounds.

Savannah shifted into problem-solving mode: a visitor from Italy, here for a potential collaboration with the winery, and her grandfather unavailable. She could so clearly envision Duke in her mind... calm, deliberate, never outwardly rushed or flustered. It was just like him to assume that things would be handled smoothly, even in his absence. For a fleeting moment, Savannah wondered if this was what her grandmother had experienced all those years... Duke simply trusting that she would manage anything that came their way, confident that his family could carry on without him stepping in.

She shrugged off the reflection, ready to handle any situation concerning the winery. Driving the familiar road winding toward the fairgrounds, the meeting with Earl and Natalie faded slightly with each mile, its weight present but no longer crushing. What was being said in that room would still be there when she finished with business.

Savannah parked near the main gate and walked through the gate, the distant voice of the announcer echoing across the fairgrounds as he spoke of tomorrow's rodeo. She noticed people's attention drawn toward the practice arena, where Graham stood smiling and waving a flag in acknowledgment of the crowd's cheers.

Not far from Graham, she spotted him. Jake sat astride his horse near the far rail, relaxed, one hand resting easily against the saddle horn. Sensing Savannah's gaze, Jake turned with an easy smile and tipped his hat in silent greeting before returning his attention to the crowd. His acknowledgement assured her he had been watching for her arrival.

Just knowing he was close by, a calm settled over her, helping prepare her for the unexpected conversation ahead. Her resolve toughened... she was ready.

CHAPTER 36

SAVANNAH stepped onto the fairgrounds in her element. Years of honing her craft—learning the art of winemaking and the science behind it—settled into place as she pushed aside the weight of the meeting and focused on the task at hand.

The Graystone canopy came into view, with a small group of guests drifting away with tasting bags in hand. Savannah saw Lizzie behind the table, methodically clearing glasses, but when she scanned the nearby area, she didn't see a man waiting. Lizzie's face lit up with relief as soon as Savannah stepped beneath the canopy. She knew Savannah's no-nonsense attitude was what was needed when meeting with an esteemed guest, unlike the bundle of nerves she became. Lizzie had tried to hold her own with the Italian man, but she could tell he quickly sized her up and dismissed her, deciding to wait for Savannah.

"Okay," Savannah said, skipping pleasantries. "What did I miss?"

Lizzie leaned in, speaking in a low volume. "He's a big shot, Savannah. He could tell real quick I wasn't the one he should talk to, so he stepped away for a minute. Said he'd watch for you and be back."

Savannah's brow lifted. "The Italian? Who is he?"

"He said his name was Tiziano Piaggi," Lizzie said. "He's here from Siena... his family winery is Tenuta Piaggi. Sounded like it was important."

Savannah's father had instilled in her the importance of hard work and dedication, and she had taken those lessons to heart as she let the Tenuta Piaggi settle in her mind. He had also taught her the importance of the vine's lineage. That was it. She remembered reading a recent article regarding Tenuta Piaggi. The son had taken over after his elderly father's death and was actively expanding the business. She thought she remembered he was looking especially for innovation.

The fact that he was here to meet with Duke piqued her curiosity because one thing was certain... Savannah's passion for winemaking was matched only by her fierce determination to succeed. Savannah asked, "When did he arrive in Blue Ridge?"

"While you were in the meeting. I didn't know how long you'd be, and I didn't want him to leave." Lizzie hesitated. "I'm sorry I called you out of there."

"You did exactly what you should've done. That was quick thinking on your part," Savannah said. "Did he taste anything yet? We need to present Graystone in the best light."

Lizzie smiled. "I led with the new vintage, the cabernet-franc. I figured that's where you'd want to start."

"Good decision. You led with strength." Savannah folded her arms loosely. "And?"

A slight smile played on Lizzie's lips. "He took his time. Really analyzed it—the aroma, the palate, the finish. He asked about the vines, the soil, how the grapes were handled. Closed his eyes like he was somewhere else entirely."

Savannah studied Lizzie's face. "Did he say anything?"

"Not really." Lizzie lowered her voice. "Some guests came up to the booth, and I needed to speak with them."

Savannah looked around. "Where is he now?"

Lizzie glanced across the aisle. "He noticed the Wellington booth."

Savannah followed her gaze. "Maybe he came to meet with both wineries. Considering everything going on right now between our families, it's probably not the best time if he has an interest in us both."

"I don't think he had a scheduled meeting with them. When he saw the booth, he asked who they were. I told him and he walked over to Jeffrey."

Savannah watched Tiziano interact with Jeffrey Maxwell, their heads angled toward each other, gestures precise and deliberate. Duke had always regarded the Wellington cabernet as respectable. Seeing it evaluated by a palate like Piaggi's made Savannah wish she'd been there herself. Nevertheless, she trusted Graystone's wines to speak for themselves. They always had.

Lizzie chewed on her bottom lip with concern. "He's been there a while."

"I'm sure Jeffrey's enjoying the attention," Savannah said, trying to push aside the irritation of having to leave such an important meeting. "Let's be ready when he comes back."

She reached beneath the table. "Pull the family reserve. Open one bottle and let it breathe." She knew their family reserve was truly special, and she was determined to convey that to him.

Lizzie agreed. "Great idea. I'm on it."

Savannah turned as movement caught her attention. Tiziano Piaggi was already walking back toward their booth.

Savannah studied the man approaching, gauging her strategy. He was undeniably handsome, confident in his stride toward her. What was it about Italian men? It must be in the genes. From the article, she knew he was in his fifties, about the age that her father would be. Just the fleeting reminder of her father standing behind her with pride in his eyes gave her the strength to communicate the unique qualities of Graystone wines with poise and expertise to such a sophisticated and discerning Italian visitor.

"Mr. Piaggi," she said, offering her hand. "I'm Savannah Gray. I apologize for missing you earlier."

He took her hand lightly and kissed both cheeks without hesitation. "Ciao, Savannah," he said, smiling. "A pleasure to meet you. Call me Tiziano. Duke spoke very highly of you. He said you were a 'passionate winemaker who respects tradition but is open to new opportunities... someone who honors the past while embracing the future.' These are things I came here to discuss."

Engrossed in the conversation, Savannah never noticed a certain cowboy staring at the exchange from his horse in the practice arena.

Savannah gestured toward the small table behind the booth. "Please... it would be an honor to stand in for Duke. I never saw the meeting on his calendar, or we would certainly have been here to meet you."

Tiziano said easily, "It was my mistake. I arrived early. My visit in California finished sooner than expected." He smiled. "After I arrived, I took the liberty of stopping at Graystone first. Walked the rows a little. Took a few soil samples."

Savannah, surprised by his brazen admission, replied, "You did?"

"Duke mentioned most of the vines were planted by his grandfather, who was Italian. That would have been your great-great-grandfather. I could see the challenge he faced with the red clay. The thoughtful cultivation has produced very good soil," he said. "I recognized some of the older vines. Those are of great interest to me."

Lizzie returned with the opened bottle. "This is the family reserve."

Turning to Savannah, Tiziano coaxed, "Tell me about it."

Savannah spoke simply. "You are correct about the red clay soil that posed a unique challenge to my great-grandfather and the other early settlers arriving in this region. With meticulous care, my family managed to coax the vines to thrive, yielding wines that are as complex and robust as the terrain where they originated." She offered him a glass, adding, "The family reserve is processed exclusively with the original Italian vines."

Tiziano savored the complex notes and subtle nuances of the family reserve, his wealth of knowledge and skilled palate shining through. Savannah smiled at his reaction. With each sip, he seemed to uncover the true essence of the Gray family's heritage and the dedication that goes into each bottle of their wine.

"Your family has achieved something remarkable," he said. "That is not always the case when I visit a winery outside of Italy. It seems we share a passion for preserving tradition in a rapidly changing world."

Savannah met his gaze without hesitation. "That is true. However, we use some of the latest innovations in our other vintages. We would love to extend an invitation for you to come to the vineyard for further tastings and a tour of the facility."

He stood and handed her his card. "That is most kind. When Duke becomes available, I would like to accept your invitation."

"Of course," Savannah said. She passed him a bottle of the reserve. "Please—accept this bottle with our compliments."

He inclined his head. "Grazie. Until next time."

As he walked away, Savannah noticed he didn't head for the exit. He returned to the Wellington booth. Savannah watched Tiziano rejoin Jeffrey, with the sinking realization that they were not the only winery competing for a collaboration with Tenuta Piaggi.

CHAPTER 37

SAVANNAH'S departure had not disrupted the meeting; if anything, it had brought a newfound clarity to the unfolding situation. What had already been said in the room could not be taken back, and Duke had no interest in revisiting intentions or explanations. His piercing gaze took in every word and gesture. He wasn't seeking reassurance or comfort; he was searching for the truth, for the threads that held the intricate web of deceit together, and those that threatened to unravel it.

Tom seemed to recognize the gravity of the change. He remained seated, his questions measured now, his tone deliberate. He no longer pressed for confessions or defenses. Instead, he sought answers to the sequence of events that led to the night at the cabin... a consistent series of truths. It was not easily forthcoming.

Earl answered carefully, offering only what was required. Efficient. Contained. Exhausting. Natalie spoke little, giving no additional help. She avoided Duke's gaze, not out of defiance, but awareness.

Tom leaned back slightly, folding his hands, trying to restrain his frustration. "Whatever happened back at the cabin," he said quietly, "it can't be undone. We all know that. And pretending otherwise hasn't helped anyone." He paused to let his words sink in. "What we know is that there was a note to Duke and that David found it and took it. We don't know how he knew to look for Lois at the cabin. He came looking for Natalie to get an address for the cabin. Since Natalie wasn't at the cabin, she didn't know about the note until I questioned it later, after the accident." Natalie silently agreed, her eyes down.

He looked directly at Earl. "You're the only one alive who was at the cabin. You mentioned David threw the note. Did anyone say what it said?"

Earl rubbed his temples trying to remember. "It all happened so fast. Harsh words were spoken. I don't think anyone mentioned the cabin."

Duke, ever perceptive, suddenly grasped the implication of something. "Tom, you said you mentioned the note to Natalie after the accident." Barely containing himself, he turned to face Natalie. "That's why you were so quick to offer to help pack up Lois's things after her death. I thought you were doing it out of friendship. But that wasn't all of it, was it? You were looking for the note, weren't you?"

The shock on Natalie's face showed the impact of the accusation. It was Tom who gently asked her, "Did you find the note, Natalie?"

The door opened quietly, but the timing made it impossible to ignore. Jeffrey paused just inside the room, one hand still on the doorframe, as if he sensed the tension he had stepped into. No one spoke, waiting on Natalie's answer. Jeffrey absorbed the scene in a single sweep: Tom leaning back, Earl rigid in his chair, Natalie staring down at her hands, Duke standing, alert and unnervingly still.

"I'm sorry," Jeffrey said, breaking the silence. "I didn't realize you were still meeting." No one told him to leave.

Tom finally addressed his son as he explained, "We're trying to understand what happened." Then, as an afterthought, "I thought you were tied up at the fairgrounds. Who's covering the booth?"

"I've got someone handling it," Jeffrey replied easily. "They're fine for now." He shifted his weight. "Something came up that seemed worth mentioning."

Duke didn't look at him, his voice like a deep rumble. "We're not finished."

"It won't take long," Jeffrey said. He hesitated just long enough to get Duke's attention. "It involves Graystone as well."

Duke finally lifted his eyes, shifting his attention to Jeffrey. "Then say it here."

Jeffrey nodded. "An Italian winemaker stopped by the fairgrounds. He went to the Graystone booth, but Savannah wasn't there yet. While he waited, he came over to our booth and tasted Wellington's wine. Asked questions. Took his time." He paused. "He mentioned expansion. Said there was potential."

Duke's mind sizzled in calculation. Titiano Piaggi was not supposed to be here until tomorrow... that must be why Lizzie called her away. He looked down at his phone to see the missed calls. He realized that with everything going on he hadn't mentioned the meeting to Savannah. Wellington was not supposed to be involved.

A glance at Earl's calm demeanor didn't fool Duke. He knew Earl well enough to know he was thinking strategically about the implications of Jeffrey's information and what it might mean to Wellington.

"I'm not saying anything was offered," Jeffrey added. "Only that the interest seemed genuine." Earl remained still, hands folded, saying nothing. His intuition told him, especially from Duke's reaction, that something significant was unfolding, and he wanted Wellington to be part of it.

Duke had set the wheels in motion by arranging this meeting. His plan to elevate Graystone to new heights of success and prominence on the world stage had nothing to do with Wellington. "That conversation about expansion," Duke said evenly, "belongs to Graystone."

Earl's gaze lifted briefly, then lowered again. "No one forced the Italian to walk over to the Wellington booth. I think you would agree with all that has happened over the last two days, we've learned timing is everything." No one corrected him. No one agreed as this added yet another complication between them.

The vibration against the table was faint, but Duke felt it. He glanced down at his phone to see a text from Savannah:

He arrived early. Went to the fairgrounds.
Met with Jeffrey while we weren't here.

Duke typed a brief reply:

Jeffrey's here now.

Savannah's response came quickly.

I have his card. I extended an invitation to
come to the vineyard once you're available.
But Duke, after that, he went back to the
Wellington booth.

Duke stared at the screen for a moment longer than necessary. Wellington's involvement hinted at a larger game at play, one that involved calculated moves and strategic decisions. He needed to leave now.

Duke set the phone down. "This isn't finished," Duke said directly to Natalie, standing. Not as a warning... as a fact. "But there's nothing more to say right now."

No one stopped his leaving. As he reached the door, he heard the subtle exchange between Earl and Jeffrey that hinted at further behind-the-scenes scheming. The unresolved tension combined with the recent power dynamics in play left an air of uncertainty. The meeting was not just about what was said but what was left unsaid... where words held weight and silence spoke volumes.

Duke left and never turned around, leaving behind a flurry of whispered questions and uncertain glances.

CHAPTER 38

DUKE walked with purpose, not patience. Returning to the fairgrounds with a sense of urgency, he was not there to idly pass the time but to make significant moves.

Savannah was anticipating Duke's arrival, but when she looked up and saw him, she knew something had happened. Even under normal circumstances, Duke's presence commanded attention, but the intensity in his expression left no room for doubt.

"Duke, what is it? Did something happen at the meeting other than Jeffrey showing up?"

Savannah's concern was evident, so Duke forced some calm into his voice. "Let's just say Jeffrey arrived at an inopportune time. We'll have to deal with that later. For now, by Tiziano showing up early and meeting with Jeffrey, Earl sees an opportunity for Wellington. This meeting was for Graystone."

Savannah's back stiffened. "So, let me understand, Duke. A meeting important enough to be worried about

Wellington interference and affect the long-term legacy of *our* family winery, was not important enough to tell me about? This family is down to two, and I'm the other half, Duke. I am not all right with your making major decisions without me."

Duke ran his hand through his hair. She was right. Savannah was not only capable and efficient, but she also possessed a calm strength that complemented his more forceful approach. "I intended to tell you. Honestly. The meeting was set right before Earl's arrival in town, and I honestly forgot about it until this afternoon. I saw an article about Tenuta Piaggi's expansion plans and reached out to him to invite him here. When I told him of our original Italian vines, he said he would try to fit us into his schedule."

Savannah quickly assessed the situation. "Now I know where I saw the article. It was in your study. Thankfully I read it before meeting with Tiziano. So your concern is that Tiziano might also want to involve Wellington Winery? They aren't even located in this state. Why would that be a problem, Duke? Is it the old feud? Is it Earl?"

Duke looked at Savannah with admiration. She had a keen intuition, which made her a forceful partner in the winery, and he relied on her insights without question.

Duke, calmer now, said, "We won't know if there is a problem until we meet with him, will we? You said you extended an invitation. Let's move on that quickly. Where's his card? I'll call him."

Savannah reached into her pocket and handed him the card. "There might still be time to meet with him this afternoon."

Duke nodded and stepped just far enough away from the booth to hear clearly. Savannah kept working, close enough to watch his face.

"Tiziano. This is Duke Gray. I understand you met with Savannah."

A pause.

"Yes, she certainly is. My schedule changed as well. Let me make it up to you this afternoon." Duke's jaw tightened almost imperceptibly. "I understand you've had the opportunity to taste other wines while you're here."

Another pause.

"I see. You're referring to a winery from Asheville."

He covered the receiver and glanced at Savannah, mouthing, "Wellington."

Savannah nodded.

Duke uncovered the phone and spoke evenly, "Our vineyard is especially lovely at sunset. Please allow Savannah and me to give you a Southern welcome and a tour of the winery to see if Graystone might be a fit with your plans."

He listened, then pressed once more. "Yes, at the ranch. Five o'clock."

When he ended the call, Savannah searched his expression.

"He says he's intrigued," Duke said. "But no commitment. He already has a meeting scheduled with Wellington first thing tomorrow."

"We don't have time to waste. We need to get home and prepare for his arrival," Savannah said.

"Absolutely," Duke agreed. "Let's get this booth broken down." Even as he said it, he looked around and noticed Lizzie had done most of the work while giving them privacy to talk. He and Savannah pitched in, efficiently working together... not as grandfather and granddaughter, but as partners guarding their legacy.

Lizzie subtly gestured toward the Wellington booth just as Savannah's sharp eyes noticed the movement at the far end of the row. "They're back," Lizzie murmured.

Earl Wellington had returned, moving with Jeffrey's careful assistance, his cane tapping against the pavement as he lowered himself into a chair at the Wellington booth.

Duke handed Savannah the final box. "Finish this. I'll be right back." Crossing the aisle without hesitation, Duke approached Earl with a calm resolve that spoke of unshakable determination.

"Duke," Earl greeted, surprise thinly veiled. "Didn't expect you over here."

"I imagine you didn't," Duke replied evenly.

Jeffrey stepped aside, giving them space. Earl's injuries were a reminder of unresolved tensions, his guarded posture a shield against his physical vulnerability. But his eyes shone with an alertness that betrayed a mind as sharp as ever.

Duke's composure never wavered, his voice steady and unwavering as he laid down the terms of their interaction. "I heard you've scheduled a meetin' with Tiziano Piaggi tomorrow mornin'," Duke said.

Earl's mouth curved slightly, ready for a clash of wills. "I've never been one to let an opportunity slip through my hands."

The double meaning wasn't lost on Duke, but he refused to rise to the bait.

"Tiziano was scheduled to meet with Graystone, and I will find out this afternoon if a collaboration with Tenuta Piaggi is a fit for us," Duke said calmly.

Earl's grip tightened on the handle of his cane, delivering his veiled threat, "Yes, and we will find out if Wellington is a fit tomorrow morning. It makes sense for him to explore options."

Then, without raising his voice, Duke said, "Earl, whatever happens with Tiziano doesn't change any-thing between us." The message was clear, reinforcing the long-standing animosity between their two families.

"I guess we'll see how it plays out," Earl said.

"Indeed, we will," Duke replied, already turning away.

Savannah observed it all with a keen eye, her in-tuition finely tuned to the human dynamics between Duke and Earl. When he returned, Savannah was wait-ing, ready to give her full support. "They're in play," she said, already knowing the answer.

Duke nodded once. "But not ahead of us."

The task complete and cart loaded, Savannah straightened. "Then we don't need to waste another minute."

"Let's do this," he said.

Savannah nodded. "Exactly."

They stepped away from the booth together, already mentally preparing for the meeting ahead.

***

Savannah and Duke moved steadily toward the parking area, their cart laden with the remnants of the booth. On the top was the banner with the dining photo of Jake and Savannah. As they walked, Savannah paused to look at it, a thoughtful expression crossing her face. "Give me just a minute," she said to Duke. "I need to say something to Jake. I won't be long."

Duke acknowledged her with a nod. "I'll be by the truck," he replied, giving her the space she needed.

She watched him move on before turning back toward the arena, her steps slightly hesitant yet determined. Jake was standing by the fence, engaged in conversation with one of the cowhands when he noticed Savannah coming his way. He turned his attention to her, searching her expression.

"Hey," Jake greeted, his tone gentle but sensing the gravity in her stance.

"Hi," Savannah responded, the simplicity of the word a contrast to the complexity of their situation. The surrounding world seemed to fade away, leaving behind only the unspoken emotions that lingered in the air between them. It seemed ages since they'd parted that morning.

"I'm heading out," Savannah finally said, breaking the silence. "I've got a meeting."

For a brief moment, Jake wondered if she was avoiding him, then casually asked, "Late one?"

"Late enough," she replied.

Their conversation was sparse, yet heavy with meaning. It was not a typical farewell, but rather an acknowledgment of the paths their lives were taking.

"I'll be around tonight," Jake offered. "After things wrap up... if you want to talk."

Savannah hesitated, considering the uncertainty of her evening. "I don't know how long it's going to run."

Jake's response was calm, accepting the unpredictability of their future. "I figured. Lots goin' on. I'm not going anywhere before the rodeo."

She held his gaze, searching for something she didn't quite have words for. "I know you'll be leaving soon."

His jaw tightened slightly, a silent admission of the truth. "Yeah."

The moment stretched between them, filled with a sense of acceptance, of understanding that some things were beyond their control. Savannah finally broke the silence. "I didn't want to just drive off."

"I'm glad you didn't," Jake replied, a faint smile softening his expression.

She nodded, the smallest smile touching her lips. "I'll find you later—if I can."

"That works," he said. "And if not... we'll talk."

It wasn't a promise. It wasn't a goodbye. It was simply the truth of where they were.

Savannah stepped back. "If I don't see you tonight, good luck tomorrow at the rodeo. We'll be there rooting for you."

"Hope your meetin' goes okay," Jake answered, his sincere words carrying a lingering warmth.

She turned before he could see the emotions threatening her... questioning what possibilities could be waiting for them if they were just brave enough to reach for them.

CHAPTER 39

DUKE was preoccupied on the drive back to Graystone, his mind already working... his thoughts focused on the impending meeting with Tiziano Piaggi. A collaboration with Tenuta Piaggi had the potential to be a pivotal moment that could shape the future of Graystone.

Savannah barely noticed, lost in her own jumble of thoughts tugging at her. On the one hand, there was Jake, a cowboy who'd shown up out of nowhere and turned out to have been at the accident when she lost her parents. Then there were the secrets Natalie kept about her grandmother, and the letter that revealed the far-reaching impact of that night at the cabin. And, in the midst of it all, this opportunity presented itself to build the future of Graystone.

Duke reached across the seat and gave a comforting pat to Savannah's hand. "Sweetie, we can't unhear the truths that have been said over the last few days. There's no reset button we can push to make it all go away. We'll have to deal with it all the best we can. But

Savannah, we're in it together. For now, we need to put that aside to give our full attention to a possible future with Tenuta Piaggi. We need to present a united front."

Savannah squeezed his hand back. "You're right. Let's see what he has to say, but I'm with you a hundred percent."

They had barely unloaded the truck when Tiziano's taxi could be seen in the distance. A smile of encouragement passed between them... a silent acknowledgment of their shared mission. Savannah looked at Duke with confidence. "Let's do this."

Despite all the uncertainties that loomed around them, Duke remained steady and composed. He knew he'd done his homework in preparation for the meeting, and his knowledge of Tiziano and the winery was comprehensive. Earl would only have this evening to learn about Tenuta Piaggi.

While they quickly prepared the library for the meeting, Duke briefed Savannah on Tiziano's background. "Tiziano comes from a long line of Italian winemakers and recently inherited the family estate, Tenuta Piaggi, located in the countryside near Siena in Tuscany. He is supposedly a master of his craft, having studied enology in renowned wine schools in Italy. What intrigues me most is his signature approach... blending traditional methods with modern techniques to create wines that are rated nothing short of exquisite. I'd love to bring a taste of Italy to Blue Ridge, but also to expose Graystone to those same techniques."

Tiziano lingered at the door before knocking, taking in the sprawling rows of vines set against the misty foothills landscape. During his earlier visit, he had immediately identified the original Italian vines, and his soil samples had reflected thoughtful cultivation and meticulous care that had coaxed the vines to thrive. Impressive. The door opened and Duke graciously introduced himself before ushering him to the library, where some of Graystone's finest wines were waiting.

Once Tiziano was seated at the long mahogany table, he started with, "I must apologize to you both for my early arrival. I did not intend to disrupt your day. But, as it turned out, I discovered another winery from North Carolina that also looked promising would be here in Blue Ridge for the fair. I will meet with them tomorrow morning. My dealings with you separately should not have any effect on the other, as you are in two different states."

Duke stated clearly, "Yes, you mentioned your meeting with Wellington Winery on the phone. If you are considering an arrangement with both wineries, you should be aware of a long-standing animosity between the Gray and Wellington families. It was never our intention to be involved with Wellington, given the history."

Tiziano considered the unexpected turn of events. "Do you mind telling me what happened?"

Savannah watched Duke for his reaction, but he simply stated, "The feud goes back generations. It started over land, and never really got resolved."

"I see." Tiziano reflected, wondering if there might be a potential bridge between these rivalries. "And is this land still owned by one of the families?"

"No, it has long since been lost so neither family was able to take advantage of it. I think it might be a subdivision now."

Tiziano was determined to remain open-minded. "There is one important factor you and Wellington, as well as the California wineries I visited, have in common. You each have thriving vines that originated in Tuscany. Those original Italian settlers brought precious vines with them, braving unfamiliar terrain and climate. That intrigues me. I am eager to explore all opportunities that would expand and showcase the excellence of the Tenuta Piaggi wines while bringing innovative new blends into the world of American winemaking. After my initial tasting of both of your wines, I see potential in each of you. Would you mind presenting a new tasting with your comments so I might take notes?"

Savannah lined up a row of glasses to present a showcase of their finest wines, from the lightest of whites to the deepest of reds, concluding with their unique ice wine, produced from late-harvest grapes not picked until the first heavy frost. While she poured, Savannah spoke of their heritage. "As a young girl, my grandmother would tell me of the massive migration into the United States in the late 1800s. The hardships abroad were real, and the United States was considered the 'land of opportunity.' My great-great-grandfather, Lorenzo Grigio, was a young immigrant from Italy, determined to create a legacy that would transcend time. When he came here to Blue Ridge, he had already Americanized his name to Gray. There is a massive granite boulder at the edge of the land that has probably been there for thousands of years. It impressed Lorenzo enough to name his winery Graystone."

After the tasting, they toured the land, and Tiziano saw more of the Italian vines and took a picture next to the granite stone. Tiziano said to Savannah, "Thank you for sharing the story. I never knew how the name Graystone originated. Nunzio Rossi and Lorenzo were from neighboring vineyards close to Tenuta Piaggi. They came to the United States together to make their fortune. Did your grandmother mention how Nunzio decided on the name Wellington?"

Savannah chuckled. "She said they traveled by sea with a French chef. After they cleared Ellis Island, the three men got a flat together in Brooklyn trying to share their earnings. When the chef landed a big job in Manhattan, he brought home a beef filet to make the newest rage in France... *Beef Wellington*. It supposedly made quite an impression on Nunzio, and he eventually changed his last name to Wellington."

As the sun fell behind the foothills, Duke said pointedly to Tiziano, "Their story went well for a while. They could never agree on how the soil should be cultivated on the plot of land they purchased together. Their disagreements got worse. By the time they dug up their vines and parted, they weren't even speaking. They built their respective wineries to compete against each other. That sentiment was instilled in generation after generation."

Tiziano raised his hand to his chest, more thoughtful than decisive. "Thank you for your honesty, Duke," he remarked. "Understanding history is important. Sometimes doors must be reopened to see opportunities right in front of us." His eyes moved briefly between Duke and Savannah. "Still," he added, "there are instances where opposing strengths lead to surprising outcomes." He gave a courteous nod. "I look forward to continuing our discussion after I meet with Wellington."

As Duke watched Tiziano leave, a sense of anticipation and excitement stirred within him. Would he agree to work with Wellington if it was the only way to take advantage of the opportunity? He realized no decisions had been made, but also that nothing had been ruled out. Graystone was still in the running.

CHAPTER 40

JAKE stood on the dock at the marina, wrestling with a mix of emotions. He had been waiting for Savannah's call, and now that she was on her way, he felt conflicted. What was he doing here? Deep down, he was a wanderer, his life a series of adventures driven by a passion for the rodeo and a love for the open road. He picked up a rock and skimmed it across the water, watching the ripples widen and fade.

Looking out across the lake, Jake tried to put his finger on what made Savannah different. There was something about her that intrigued him, a feeling of connection that he couldn't quite explain... strong and fragile at the same time. The reality of the situation hit him hard. If the accident hadn't haunted his dreams the last three years, he would not have returned to Blue Ridge. If fate had shifted just slightly, he and Savannah might never have met.

He saw her car pull up, and when she got out and began walking toward him, he realized what it was. Meeting Savannah was like stumbling upon a rare anchor in a storm of constant change. Being around her, he felt a sense of calm and purpose in a way he hadn't realized he'd been missing.

Savannah stepped out of her car, pulling her jacket a little tighter, though the chill that moved through her wasn't from the night air. Despite her initial reservations, there was a magnetic pull drawing her toward the cowboy waiting across the parking lot. And the turmoil of the last few days surrounding Lois, her parents, and now Jake, had left her unprepared to think clearly. She might have grown up in a small town, but she had big dreams of making a name for herself in the world. Meeting Jake had played havoc with her carefully laid-out goals for the future, challenging her to question the path she had always envisioned.

Yet under the glow of the streetlamp, with Jake's gaze locked onto hers, a sense of belonging enveloped her. With each step, her heart whispered that this was where she needed to be. Without a second thought, she closed the distance and melted into Jake Rollins's embrace, finding in him a silent promise of safety amidst the chaos.

The crisp night air carried the scent of the fishermen's recent catch, mingled with the faint aroma of coffee wafting from a nearby shop. Jake paused, glancing around at the closed restaurant fronts, their signs swaying gently in the evening breeze. He pulled Savannah closer, his voice barely above a whisper. "Looks like most of the restaurants are closed." He held her a moment longer before pulling her into a tender kiss.

Savannah, with a gentle smile, gestured to the warmly lit coffee shop. "That's okay. I'm not that hungry. Maybe just a cup of coffee?"

With a nod, Jake took her hand, leading her inside. Moments later, they emerged, each cradling a steaming cup of warmth. "Let's sit out on the dock if it's not too cold," Jake suggested, his eyes searching hers for agreement.

The dock stretched out into the lake, wooden planks creaking softly underfoot. They settled on the bench at the end of the dock, the lapping of water against the boats providing a soothing soundtrack. Savannah wrapped her hands around her coffee cup, seeking more than just physical warmth. "I wasn't sure I'd see you tonight," she confessed, her voice a blend of relief and vulnerability. Her fingers trembled slightly, betraying the emotions she struggled to contain.

Jake shrugged lightly, pulling another stone from his pocket to skim across the water. "Wouldn't feel right just leavin' after the rodeo without talkin'. There's a lot we haven't talked about."

A silence settled between them... profound but not uncomfortable. A couple passed by, their easy laughter reminiscent of simpler times.

"There's so much going on," Savannah admitted. "More than I could have imagined... definitely more than I planned for."

Jake nodded, understanding without pressing. "I know that." He inhaled deeply, gathering his thoughts. "We can't just keep circlin' what's painful. The guilt was bad enough thinking about the accident when I didn't know who the victims were. But now, when you're in my arms, knowing it was your mom and dad, it crushes me. There had to be a way I could have done more."

Beside him, Savannah's eyes were cast downward, listening to the whispered echoes of the past. The truth had unraveled the web of deceit that had cloaked that fateful night, leaving her heart raw with grief. She reached for Jake's hand, seeking strength to voice her own turmoil. "I can't bear the thought of my grandmother's role in the chain of events that led to the confrontation at the cabin and then the accident. It is like a knife to my heart, cutting deep into my soul."

They sat, hand in hand, enveloped in a cocoon of shared pain. The weight of their words hung heavy in the air, yet there was a sense of release, of finally confronting the shadows. Jake struggled to come up with the right words. His voice, tinged with sorrow and acceptance, broke through the turmoil. "As much as we'd like to, there is no turning back the clock. No amount of guilt or blame can undo the tragedy. But Savannah, my gut feeling is that the more we dwell on it, the more it will deepen the wounds. Maybe the first step toward healing is to let go of the blame and anger that consume us."

Savannah turned to him, her eyes searching for solace in his words. In that quiet moment, they both understood the need to let go of the past, to release the grip that consumed them.

As they rose to leave, Jake extended his hand to Savannah, offering a glimmer of hope. She wrapped her arms around his neck, wishing the night would never end, that this moment of connection would last forever. Their kiss lingered, filled with both longing and uncertainty.

Savannah shook her head and began, "With Duke in talks with the Italian winery, I don't know what the next few weeks look like. Or where I'm supposed to land after all this."

Jake's response was unexpected, his honesty a balm for her uncertainty. "Same with me. After this rodeo, Graham and the team travel to Birmingham." He paused, his gaze drifting over the water. "I've spent a long time movin' from one thing to the next. Never really stoppin' long enough to ask if it still fit." He looked at her, his vulnerability laid bare. "Lately, I've been askin'."

Savannah offered a faint smile, finding contentment in their shared exploration of the unknown. "And?"

Jake met her gaze, his sincerity unwavering. "And... I don't have the answers yet."

She found comfort in his uncertainty, in the shared exploration of unknown possibilities. As their cups emptied, they began to walk along the boardwalk, unhurried. Savannah paused by the railing, resting there as she gathered her thoughts. "This might sound strange," she began, "but I don't need things tied up. I just didn't want them to be left unsaid. And what you said tonight about letting go of the guilt and blame gave me a lot to think about."

Jake turned, his eyes meeting hers with understanding. "I'm glad. I'm going to try too."

"You have been amazing this week. I honestly care about you, Jake," she said simply, her words unguarded.

Jake's expression softened, a new openness in his gaze. "I care about you too, Savannah."

They stood side by side looking out at the water, Jake's arm around her shoulder, comfortable being together. Savannah reflected on the other night by the fire. "And, Jake, that line you talked about... you've never crossed it."

After a moment, Jake's smile returned, easy and familiar. "Not yet."

CHAPTER 41

THE ranch was quiet at this time of the morning. Duke got up before the sun, hoping for some quiet time to sort things through. He shrugged on his weathered jacket, feeling its familiar weight on his shoulders, and stepped out onto the porch with a steaming cup of coffee. The warmth seeped into his hands, a comforting contrast to the crisp air.

Looking out over the rows of vines, a wry smile crept across his lips. The first light frost of the season dusted the leaves, a delicate lacework of ice crystals that caught the early light. By the time the rodeo kicked off, the sun would have chased away the chill, but he knew the weekend promised a deeper freeze.

Duke's thoughts wandered to Tiziano. If he was still in Blue Ridge, perhaps Duke could introduce him to his latest wine. He wandered over to the late-harvest grapes and checked the lightly frosted edges. The plan was to wait for the deep freeze, to capture the essence of the frozen grapes in a bold, innovative ice wine... a rarity in North Georgia. Success in the past few years had bolstered his confidence, and he felt he was on the brink of perfecting something remarkable.

The thought of Tiziano inevitably raised the question of whether he would consider a collaboration with Tenuta Piaggi if Wellington was involved. Hearing the story of Nunzio and Lorenzo again, from Savannah's perspective, made the rivalry that ended a friendship seem even more tragic. His conversation on the phone with Tom gave his tangled web of thoughts a sounding board. Patience was not one of Duke's strong points... it gnawed at him that Tiziano would meet with Earl this morning.

One thing Tom said during the conversation kept hovering just outside Duke's memory, stubbornly elusive yet significant. Since Natalie's involvement in the accident was just revealed, Duke never quite understood its impact on Tom and his wife. Grief had consumed him when Lois passed, and Tom's move to Murphy was behind him, leaving questions unasked.

Now that Duke was aware, he had asked Tom if Natalie's role in the accident had led to their split. Tom's answer was the part Duke couldn't quite reconcile. "It was more than the accident," Tom had said. "Our paths were moving in different directions, and the secrets just kept coming. I finally couldn't take any more." It was the "secrets just kept coming" that refused to settle in Duke's mind, a mystery that tugged at his curiosity. Was there even more about Lois? How could he have been so blind?

At that moment, the screen door swung open, and Savannah came out to the porch with coffee in one hand and a plate of biscuits in the other. "Morning, Duke. I brought you a fresh biscuit." One glance at Duke as he took the biscuit told her he was deep in thought. His brow was furrowed, eyes distant, as if he hardly registered the warm, flaky bread in his hand. Savannah watched him quietly, recognizing the familiar signs that Duke was processing something important, lost in the tangle of memories and worries that had been piling up since the revelations of the past few days.

How could he not be? So many things had been thrown at them. She wished she could ease Duke's pain.

Duke remained quiet, so Savannah softly said, "I saw Jake last night."

That got a nod, and Duke asked, "Is he ready for the rodeo? Between his sponsor duties and getting tied up in our family business, he hasn't had much time to practice."

"He came to Blue Ridge because of the accident. He's been carrying a lot of guilt. He said something last night that goes for you and me too. We can't undo any of it. It's time to start healing. Look what happened to Lorenzo and Nunzio. They were too stubborn to forgive or forget, and their rivalry has gone on for generations. Duke, don't you think it's time for that to stop?"

Duke was about to answer when he thought to check his watch. There was just enough time to take a shower and get to the early morning meeting at city hall. The planning committee was gathering to confirm last-minute details about the rodeo and the final ceremony.

He hugged his granddaughter tightly, his pride in her swelling. "We can try."

***

Duke entered the council chambers and walked directly up to the mayor, who was greeting members with authority, ready to preside over the gathering. His stride was purposeful, but it faltered ever so slightly when he saw Natalie. She stood off to the side, her notebook clutched tightly, a diligent keeper of every detail. The same Natalie, yet different from the one he'd come to know over the last few days.

Her presence threw him off. The transformation in how he perceived her had left him unsure how to navigate the sudden rift between them. As he observed her, something peculiar caught his attention... *her gloves.*

Then something registered. Why was she always wearing gloves? It made some sense now with the chill in the air, but thinking back, she wore them in the summer too.

A flicker of uncertainty crossed her face—how he might treat her now, after everything. She instinctively moved toward the back door, seeking escape, but Duke blocked her path, clearly intending to speak with her.

"Duke, not here. Not now."

"There's somethin' I've been meanin' to ask you," he said quietly, his tone gentle but insistent. "All this time, I never thought to ask why you always wear gloves. I just assumed it was something you liked. But I don't recall them before the accident." He hesitated, searching her face. "They are from that night, aren't they? Do you want to tell me?"

Natalie squeezed her eyes shut, her composure wavering, the images rising unbidden. She had kept that night locked away, shared only with Earl and Tom, but not by choice. No one else... not even Lizzie, nor her closest confidant, Lois.

Duke stepped closer. Gently, he took her hands, easing the gloves off to reveal the scars beneath... raw and uneven, the kind of marks that time could not erase.

His eyes met hers with the question that pierced her defenses. "From saving Earl?"

Tears welled up, spilling over as she shook her head. "No," she whispered, her voice trembling. "From reaching for David."

CHAPTER 42

HAVING grown up in the Wellington vineyards and winery, Earl possessed an extensive knowledge of winemaking techniques and a discerning palate that guided him in creating the distinctive flavors of Wellington wines. Before the accident, his attention to detail was evident in every aspect of his winemaking process, from selecting the finest grapes harvested from the old Italian vines to meticulously monitoring the fermentation and aging stages.

Earl's sharp gaze missed nothing as he assessed the dynamics in the parlor at Tiziano's hotel. Although Jeffrey had brought several bottles for tasting, Earl knew he lacked the hometown advantage. Duke was able to entertain Tiziano at his ranch with a tour of the winery. Whatever it was that Tenuta Piaggi was offering Duke, he wanted in on it.

He had always taken great pride in personally pouring tastings for visitors and sharing the stories behind each wine, fostering a sense of connection and authenticity that set Wellington Winery apart. With his physical limitations, Earl had asked Jeffrey to do the honors.

Sitting across the table, as Jeffrey began to pour, Earl felt the scrutiny of Tiziano's gaze, a man who seemed to hold the key to a potential partnership between their wineries. It wasn't in the words so much as the pauses... the way Tiziano's gaze lingered over him, not with the respect or challenge Earl was accustomed to, but with a kind of gentle pity.

Earl hadn't sat across a negotiating table like this for three years. That night had not only taken away Earl's ability to move freely but also fractured his confidence in running his family winery in the hands-on manner he was accustomed to.

As the discussion proceeded toward the prospect of a partnership between Tenuta Piaggi and Wellington, Earl tried to assert his role. "Tenuta Piaggi's expansion interest aligns with the new directions Wellington is considering. Our location and distribution capabilities enable our wines derived from Old World vines to get out into the market quickly." He let that information sink in since it was the edge he had over Graystone's more remote location.

Tiziano inclined his head but did not immediately respond. Instead, he glanced toward Jeffrey, who finished pouring and passed the glasses for the tasting.

"So Jeffrey, you have been running Wellington lately. What are your thoughts on expansion?"

Jeffrey shot a sideways glance at Earl, not eager to overstep his boss. "I worked under Earl as an apprentice until he was injured. When he asked me to take over the day-to-day management, I never envisioned expansion."

Annoyed, Earl spoke up to regain Tiziano's attention. "If you don't mind me asking, what is it you are looking for in a collaboration here in the United States?"

Tiziano tried to look past Earl's disfigured face as he spoke directly. "I have a strong interest in the vines from our region in Tuscany that were brought here to the States and cultivated to thrive. I have met with several wineries in California. When Duke approached me, I found out about the two neighbors, Nunzio and Lorenzo, who came over with their vines. I did my research and discovered Nunzio established Wellington Winery in Asheville. I called the winery to arrange a visit and was told Wellington was being represented here in Blue Ridge at the fair. So I changed my flight to arrive early."

Tiziano added, "What struck me was not how similar your wineries are... but how different."

Earl's posture straightened, his curiosity piqued. "Different how?"

With a thoughtful gesture, Tiziano intertwined his fingers, contemplating his response. "Wellington offers scale, and you are right about its strategic location in Asheville. Graystone thrives on innovation, a blend of experimentation and tradition. Each complements the other in a business capacity. However, it is how these vines have adapted to the different terrains that fascinates me. I believe we can capitalize on that."

Jeffrey sat back at the table, intrigued.

"In Italy," Tiziano continued, "we often look for contrast when we create something lasting. It is not about dominance. It is about balance." He paused. "What interests me is not choosing between you but understanding whether a mutual collaboration can exist without conflict. It would also require full-time oversight."

Earl absorbed the words slowly. This was not the outcome he had anticipated. Tiziano was not offering reassurance, nor was he closing doors. He was describing something that required full-time stability... something Earl was no longer certain he could provide on his own.

"A partnership requires continuity," Tiziano added gently. "Not only in leadership, but in presence."

Jeffrey finally spoke up, carefully weighing how truthful he should be. "That's been a challenge recently." He looked directly at Earl and added, "I honestly don't think this is a fit for us right now. Without you at the winery, the momentum hasn't been there, and it's affecting growth."

Tiziano folded his hands on the table, his voice calm but resolute. "That is an issue I have to consider."

Earl leaned forward, a last attempt to grasp the slipping reins. "Meaning?"

Tiziano closed his notebook with a decisive snap. "Meaning there is potential here, but not without a strong, present leader."

Earl's carefully laid plans had unraveled before him, leaving him exposed. He remained seated for a moment longer than necessary before using his cane to assist with standing. Neither Tiziano nor Jeffrey pressed him.

CHAPTER 43

THE discovery of Natalie's burned hands, and the revelation that they were burned trying to save David, shook Duke to the core. There was a war of emotions going on inside him. Duke found himself torn between his feelings of betrayal caused by Natalie's unraveling secrets and a growing sense of compassion for the woman who had kept so much hidden for years.

Still gently holding Natalie's hands, his heart softened as he realized the extent of her suffering, her guilt, and her attempts to make amends for the past. He then remembered the unanswered question from the meeting. Looking into her distraught eyes, he asked the question again. "Natalie, when you went through Lois's things, did you find the note that was meant for me?"

Natalie had wanted to keep the existence of the note to herself, but at the meeting, Earl had mentioned that David brought the note to the cabin. Even Tom had confirmed that David mentioned a note.

"I tried to find it, Duke. I looked all through her things. But I never did. Maybe, after the accident, she threw it away."

The idea of a note meant for him leading to such a tragic outcome fueled Duke's determination to find it. He wanted to see with his own eyes the truth it held and the part it played in the events at the cabin. Duke reached for his jacket, then turned to Natalie. "I have to go back to the ranch. I'll meet you at the rodeo venue." He tried to muster a small smile. "And Natalie, take that notepad with you. It has everything that needs to be complete before the opening ceremony. I'll be there soon."

***

Duke moved through the ranch house with a quiet urgency, opening drawers he hadn't touched in years, lifting lids, checking the backs of shelves where things slid and were forgotten. Papers lay in uneven stacks across the desk. A box from the closet sat open on the floor beside the bed. The note seemed to have vanished into thin air, adding to Duke's irritation and sense of loss.

Lois's jewelry box rested in his hands longer than the others. He opened it, not because he expected to find the note there, but because it had been hers. Memories flooded his mind, with the weight of her absence pressing heavily upon him. He set the box down carefully and lowered himself to the edge of the bed, elbows on his knees, his gaze fixed on the scattered papers across the room.

A sharp sound from downstairs broke the still-ness... the front door closing.

"Duke?" Savannah's voice carried up the stair-case, edged with concern. Her footsteps came quickly down the hall before she appeared in the doorway. She took in the room... the open drawers, the boxes, the look on his face, and asked, "Duke, what is it? What happened?"

His voice was broken. "There was a note. I didn't find out until after you left the art center. Lois wrote it to me before she left for the cabin, but I never saw it. David found it instead, and it led him and your mother to the cabin. Earl saw David challenge Lois with it. I need to find it... to find out what it said that mattered enough for them to go after her."

Savannah looked around the room at the open drawers and boxes. "Maybe she discarded the note after she realized how much pain it caused." She hes-itated before adding, "For now, though, time isn't on our side. The opening of the rodeo is just a few hours from now. I promise I'll help search more later. Why don't we drive together?"

Duke knew she was right. The search would have to wait. But even as they left for the rodeo venue, Duke couldn't shake the feeling that the note was still out there, waiting to be found.

On the drive to the venue, Duke was still preoccu-pied. Savannah knew there was more from the way he avoided looking at her. "There's something else, isn't there? There can be no secrets between us, Duke. We agreed to learn the truth together."

Duke drew in a large breath, dreading telling her, but knowing he had no other choice. "I saw Natalie at city hall this morning. I asked her about her gloves… she let me see the burns."

Savannah said, with relief, "Right, Lizzie said she burned her hands a while back." When Duke remained silent, it came to her. "Oh no. Natalie got the burns at the accident." Duke nodded, still not looking at her. "So, she and Earl were both burned. Did she burn them moving Earl?"

Duke's heart was pounding. "No, Natalie went back to the car and reached for David."

"He was still alive?" A gut-wrenching sob overtook Savannah with an intensity she had never experienced before.

Duke pulled over to the side of the road and pulled Savannah into a sheltering embrace. "I didn't want to tell you." As soon as he said the words, he began to understand why Natalie had kept the hurtful secrets to herself. He held her for a few more minutes, cringing at the pain they shared. He then muttered, almost to himself. "Damn, sometimes the truth is harder to take than the secret."

CHAPTER 44

AS Duke comforted Savannah, a sense of clarity washed over him, urging him to confront the shadows of the past and embrace the light of honesty, no matter how difficult. However, the sudden vibration of Duke's phone shattered the poignant moment. The unexpected sound was a reminder that time was moving outside the truck.

Duke shifted back to the driver's seat to reach for his phone. "It's from Tiziano. He says he has a promisin' offer for Graystone and an intriguin' opportunity for you."

Savannah sat up and wiped her eyes with Duke's handkerchief. "Me? He has an opportunity for me? And an offer for Graystone?" Savannah let a glimmer of hope and excitement seep into the part of her where darkness had taken hold.

Duke read the rest, then shared with a spark of anticipation in his eyes, "Tiziano says he will be at the rodeo today to discuss further. Savvy, this could be a new path for us and the legacy of Graystone." Duke started the engine and pulled back onto the road.

Savannah looked at Duke with renewed hope. "Maybe this is fate stepping in to get us through all the hard truths of the past to pave the way for a new beginning. Let's hurry."

When they arrived at the rodeo venue, it was alive in its final preparations. Temporary seating framed the arena, and extra truckloads of dirt were being spread by workers eager to get the rodeo underway. Savannah left Duke to go deliver Jake's shirts with the Graystone sponsor emblem. Before they parted, she said, "I'll meet you at the sponsor tent before the opening ceremony so we can go in together."

Duke nodded and went to look for Natalie to finalize last-minute details for the city council VIP suite. He scanned the grounds the way he always did... methodical, attentive, trusting what he could verify with his own eyes. This part of the rodeo had always mattered to him, the foundation everyone else took for granted.

He joined Natalie, her clipboard tucked under her arm, calling out observations as they walked the grounds. She sensed his spirit had lifted so she tucked away her curiosity about his earlier reaction to Lois's note.

"The south entrance still needs one more directional sign," she said. "And they haven't finished stringing lights near the sponsor tents."

Duke replied, "I'll take care of the tents."

Natalie flipped a page on her clipboard. "I'll take these last-minute announcements over to the MC." Duke agreed, each slipping easily into their roles.

Jake was by the stables, brushing Charro's coat until it gleamed in preparation for the opening parade. Savannah had just dropped off the sponsor shirts, and he was still grinning from the gleam in her eyes and her words of support. She hadn't stayed, moving on to finish the sponsor tent.

When Jake looked up and saw Duke and Natalie working together, he raised an eyebrow in brief surprise before setting the thought aside as Duke headed his way.

Duke had been hoping to have a few words with Jake. The last few days had shown him Jake Rollins brought much more to the table than simply his skills as a rodeo competitor. There was a quiet confidence about him... one that fit Duke's own straightforward, no-nonsense attitude.

"That's a fine-lookin' horse," Duke said. "Are you two ready for today's events?"

Jake responded with an easy smile, setting the brush down. "As ready as we can be. Just anxious to get started."

Duke glanced toward the line of freshly installed sponsor tents bordering the far side of the arena. The Graystone banner hadn't been raised yet. Then he smiled as he saw Savannah and Lizzie hanging it. "I'd like to go over a few last-minute changes to your role at the reception afterward," Duke said. "Nothin' complicated. Just wanna make sure everythin' runs smoothly."

Jake nodded immediately. "I've got time now if you do."

They walked toward the tents together, talking easily with the kind of quiet familiarity that comes from mutual respect.

A short distance away, Natalie paused near the volunteer table, confirming names and assignments. She'd always had a soft spot for the rough-and-tumble atmosphere of the rodeo, and today was no exception. When her gaze drifted back to Duke, her hand slipped into her pocket, brushing against her gloves. A quiet sense of relief washed over her. At last, the one secret she had never revealed to anyone had been shared with the one who mattered most.

Her hands busily organized the stacks of flyers, and her voice carried with confidence as she directed volunteers, her mind momentarily free from the weight of recent days. The simplicity of the tasks was a welcome distraction. They grounded her, each completed chore a small triumph.

Natalie glanced at the nearby post clock, a subtle gesture betraying her anticipation. Earl and Jeffrey's meeting with the representative from Tenuta Piaggi Winery had been scheduled for that morning, and by now, the outcome should be known. Earl's determination to secure a deal that could strategically position Wellington ahead of Graystone was evident, and she knew Duke would be waiting just as anxiously for news.

Jeffrey had never intended to return to the fair-grounds. Before Earl arrived in Blue Ridge, his plan had been simple... pack up the Wellington booth after the final day of the fair and head back to Asheville. Clean. Set. Back to work. That plan dissolved the moment Natalie brought Earl into town.

The meeting with Tiziano had been a bold move. Jeffrey would have liked more time to prepare. They hadn't brought up the rivalry between Wellington and Graystone, but Tiziano was fully aware of it. Duke must have brought it up. Earl did not like to be challenged. He would remember this. And he would not forget Jeffrey's comment about his absence.

Jeffrey moved through the fairgrounds with purpose, scanning faces as he went. He needed to find Natalie before Earl did. Not to interfere. Just to make sure she wasn't blindsided.

But as he walked, his attention turned toward the center of the grounds, where the sounds of hammers and shouted instructions filled the air. In the distance, he spotted Duke Gray with the cowboy. Jeffrey slowed.

Approaching Duke hadn't been part of his plan. But after the morning's meeting, the idea no longer seemed out of place. If anyone understood what it meant to stand opposite Earl Wellington and refuse to bend, it was Duke.

Jeffrey exhaled, bracing himself as he adjusted his direction. He hadn't come to Blue Ridge looking for a confrontation. But he suspected one was coming. And this time, he wasn't sure he intended to step out of its way.

CHAPTER 45

JEFFREY crossed the fairgrounds toward Duke, questioning his own motives for seeking out Wellington's rival. The meeting with Earl and Tiziano had unsettled him more than he cared to admit. As Earl's nephew and heir to the winery, he had stepped in to keep the family business running when Earl couldn't. He'd told himself he was maintaining things... that Earl was still deciding the future. But the meeting made one thing impossible to ignore. A partnership with Tenuta Piaggi was possible, but Tiziano questioned whether Earl could lead Wellington into that future. Knowing that Graystone was also being considered, Jeffrey had to act fast.

The question pressing on him wasn't about business. It was about loyalty. Did he stand behind Earl and watch the winery falter... or step into a role Earl could no longer fill?

Duke saw Jeffrey approaching and muttered to Jake, "This should be interesting."

Jake saw the shift in Duke's stance and said with an easy smile, "I'd better get back. We've finished here, and I have to put on some fancy duds to lead the parade. Your granddaughter brought me one with fringe on the sleeves and the Graystone emblem on the back."

"We're proud to have you wear it, son. Do your best out there... we'll be rootin' for you. We'll see you after at the tent."

Jake tipped his hat and left as Jeffrey got close. Duke spoke first. "Jeffrey, is everything all right? I didn't expect to see you here."

Jeffrey tugged at his collar. "I didn't expect to be here. Do you mind if we talk privately?"

Duke could see the worry on Jeffrey's face. "Sure, Jeff. Does this have to do with Wellington's meeting with Tiziano this morning?"

Jeffrey replied, "Yes... well, indirectly. The meeting didn't go as Earl hoped."

"Is Tiziano no longer interested in a partnership with Wellington?"

"No, he's very interested in both Wellington and Graystone. He's just not interested in Earl remaining involved. That was not received well."

"I can imagine... but why come to me? You know Earl and I don't harbor any affection for each other. As Tom and Natalie's son, you have a stake in what the future looks like for Wellington. Why not speak with them?"

"I will. But Duke, it's you I need to talk to. If Wellington and Graystone both go into a partnership with Tiziano, it means we would be working together. I need to know that if Earl is out of the picture, could you put the old feud aside and be willing to work with me?"

Duke absorbed the implication behind Jeffrey's words. "Does Earl know you're talking to me?"

Jeffrey was about to answer when his phone rang. Looking at his phone, he said, "It's Earl. I need to take this."

Duke knew Tiziano planned to see him at the rodeo. He gave a quick thought to tipping his hand but decided against it, keeping options open. "You take it. I have to get to the tent to head into the rodeo for the opening ceremony."

Jeffrey answered the phone, nodding to Duke as he turned, already walking toward the entrance.

The sound of the loudspeaker thundered through the air as the announcer began the fifteen-minute countdown to the opening ceremony parade. Duke hurried toward the Graystone tent to meet Savannah and head into the rodeo together.

Lizzie had already gone inside, and Savannah rushed out when she saw Duke. "You're late. We need to hurry. I don't want to miss Jake and Charro leading the parade."

Duke and Savannah were swept into the lively crowd pouring through the gates. Duke smiled to see Savannah's eyes darting eagerly among the faces of the cowboys lined up for the parade outside the arena, searching for one in particular. He could see the excitement on her face when she spotted Jake at the parade's starting line... a stark contrast with her demeanor just a short while ago on the side of the road. Duke felt a gentle pang, knowing Jake would soon be just a memory, leaving behind a girl who deserved all the happiness in the world.

They made their way to the city council suite, where they found their seats as Savannah searched the entry gate where the parade would kick off the opening ceremony. Her growing feelings for Jake had been a blessing the last few days, and she refused to dwell on what she would do once the rodeo was over and Jake was long gone. She spotted Natalie tending to the refreshment table in the suite. Part of her wanted to hate Natalie for all the secrets, but another part wanted to hug her for trying to save her father.

Her thoughts were broken when Duke patted her knee with a gesture toward the stands. "Tiziano. He could be a turning point for us." Savannah nodded with a mixture of excitement and apprehension. As the opening ceremony began and the parade kicked off, Savannah couldn't shake the sense of impending change.

The parade music swelled. The riders entered with Jake, confident and smiling, as the center of attention. Jake's hat was in the air welcoming the crowd, and Charro trotted proudly, his head high. Duke and Savannah were focused on Jake—but Tiziano was focused on them.

CHAPTER 46

THIS year, the annual Blue Ridge rodeo was not just a showcase of cowboy skills and fierce competition. Natalie had volunteered for the refreshment table at the city hall suite, just inside the glass partition, where she spotted Duke and Savannah. Although Graystone Winery, as a rodeo sponsor, had provided wines for the suite, Natalie had smuggled in a few bottles of Wellington cabernet. She was pouring a glass of it for one of the city commissioners when she accidentally spilled some on her glove.

The commissioner, Harold Wiley, saw the spill, and taking his glass, said, "Natalie, white gloves might not be the best idea."

Natalie looked down at the pesky stain. She hadn't brought a spare pair, and she realized any attempt to wash it would only make it worse. The sound of the announcer and the music signaling the start of the parade caught her attention, bringing her closer to the open bleachers for a better view. She looked out at the arena to see Jake leading the parade. The roar of the crowd spoke to his larger-than-life persona that was clearly captivating the crowd. One look at Savannah's focus on Jake's winning smile told Natalie the cowboy had won Savannah's heart.

When she looked over at the stoic man beside Savannah, she knew the one secret that had led to her persistent silence on the others. Natalie had worked with Duke on city matters since before Savannah was born. She understood his work ethic and dedication to the legacy of Graystone. When Lois faltered and felt left out, Natalie tried to point out to her friend how much Duke truly loved her, but Lois always seemed to doubt it. Natalie had watched from afar, helpless to rectify their relationship while her own with Tom was slowly falling apart. After her divorce and Lois's death, she had tried to console Duke, hoping that someday he would see her as his biggest fan.

But now... because she had kept her promise to Lois and helped Earl, Duke saw in her only betrayal. That morning, for just a second when she allowed Duke to remove her gloves, she not only bared her hands, but she also laid herself bare. Natalie forced her eyes away from Duke and scanned the crowd in the VIP section. She spotted Jeffrey, sitting between Earl and the Italian vintner. Impaired by his injuries, Earl looked stiff and uncomfortable. But before Natalie turned back to the refreshment area, she saw Mr. Piaggi turn around and look directly at Duke with a nod of acknowledgment.

***

Tiziano Piaggi had been born into a family with a long legacy of land stewardship in the rolling hills of Tuscany, raised to honor tradition while recognizing authenticity. Here at the Blue Ridge rodeo, his instincts quickly recognized the difference between performance and something more genuine. The enthusiastic roar of the crowd prompted him to find the focus of their attention.

The rider at the head of the parade, with the words "Graystone Winery" proudly displayed on his shirt, exuded a confidence that resonated with fans in the audience as well as Tiziano. It was not just sponsorship that adorned the fabric, but a heritage and pride of the community that could not be manufactured. He remembered the cowboy, Jake Rollins, from the banner at the Graystone booth. As he observed the crowd's reaction and the aura surrounding the Graystone family, Tiziano found himself drawn to the people behind the names.

His gaze then shifted to the bleachers where Duke and Savannah were seated. His meetings with the young woman had revealed a quiet strength about her and familiarity with her heritage that resonated with him. Recognizing her as the woman from the banner photo with the cowboy, he saw that her unwavering focus on the rider revealed layers far deeper than a smiling pose. He hoped it would not be a complication, because Tiziano understood clearly that Savannah was not just a bystander, but an integral part of a legacy that would influence the future of Graystone.

Turning his attention to Duke Gray, Tiziano recognized a man familiar with being at the center of attention without seeking it, a self-assurance that spoke of history and responsibility. Tiziano hoped Duke Gray would demonstrate that he understood preserving heritage was more than just maintaining traditions... that it required connection to the land, a respect for history, and a willingness to listen and learn from those who came before.

In contrast, seated nearby, he was aware of the strained presence of Earl Wellington, and the uncertain demeanor of Jeffrey Maxwell, the Wellington nephew. In truth, Tiziano was weighing the value of both wineries, but even more, the people behind them.

Duke spotted him, and he and Tiziano exchanged a knowing glance that they would connect soon. As he turned his attention back to the last of the parade and the entrance of the rodeo clowns, Tiziano's mind was already working to juggle the personalities before him, each with their own expectations and their ability—or inability—to move past a decades-old feud.

CHAPTER 47

SAVANNAH leaned forward in her seat, eyes bright, as the annual Blue Ridge rodeo thundered to life below. Maybe it was the sense of community... laughter erupting as the crowds watched the antics of the clowns. Or was it the thrill of watching the fearless cowboys compete in dangerous events? Maybe it was just a chance to escape the emotional rollercoaster she'd been on for a few hours.

As the announcer's voice boomed through the loudspeaker, reeling off the order of events of the day, then introducing the arena director and the stock contractor. Finally, he introduced the star of the show:

> "Ladies and gentlemen, riding out from Fort Smith, Arkansas, this man has dominated the circuit from Houston to Kissimmee! With over thirty-five wins this season and a heart as big as this arena, he's not just chasing a buckle—he's chasing history! Put

your hands together for the reigning PRCA Eastern Division Champion... Jake Rollins!"

The audience stood up cheering as Jake walked into the arena leading Charro and waving his hat. Tall and ruggedly handsome, with a confident swagger, Jake was clearly the star of the rodeo. He was the one everyone came to see, the one everyone cheered for. Savannah found herself unable to look away. She couldn't deny the flutter of excitement in her chest as she watched him mount Charro with practiced ease, his eyes focused and determined... that is, until he looked up and locked eyes with Savannah. He tipped his hat with that easy smile meant just for her.

Savannah turned to Duke. "Jake's first event is the saddle bronc riding. This group of bucking horses are supposedly some of the fiercest. I want to go down to the arena to see which horse he picked and wish him luck. I won't be long."

Tiziano's nod across the stands made Duke certain the Italian would come up to the suite soon. But there was no way he was going to dampen the happy enthusiasm in his granddaughter. "Wish him luck for me, too, but get back soon. I'm expectin' Tiziano to come talk to us."

From the far side of the suite, Natalie set down an empty glass she hadn't realized she'd been holding. She had observed Savannah leave without casting her even a glance. Had all the years watching Savannah grow up—and having both her and Lizzie underfoot all the time—blown up in smoke? The truth about her grandmother and the night of her parents' accident was too much. Should it all have been kept hidden? Natalie looked over at the seat Savannah had left and paused her focus on the back of Duke's head. She'd never wanted to cause him pain. Just the opposite... she wanted to see his smile again and be happy.

When he shifted in his seat, Natalie snapped her attention back to the refreshment table.

***

As Savannah reached the edge of the arena, she caught a glimpse of Jake preparing for his first event. She told herself she had come to wish him luck. In truth, it felt more like fate bringing them together. Savannah hesitated for a second, unsure of how to approach him, but then she remembered her grandfather's words about seizing opportunities when they presented themselves.

She was still holding her program and quickly came up with an idea. "I saw the list of bucking horses. The article said you draw numbers to find out which horse you ride."

Part of Jake wanted to jump over the fence to take Savannah in his arms, but right now he needed to focus. "Yeah, that way no one gets too familiar with a certain ride. Makes it fair, I suppose."

"Which one did you get?" Savannah asked.

Jake dug the slip of paper from his pocket and passed it over the fence to her. She read the name next to the list in the program and looked up at him with worry. "Maximus? You chose Maximus? Oh Jake, it says he's really dangerous"

Jake adjusted his shirttail. "Hey, he's just a horse. I've got this. I have to go get in the lineup now." Jake looked closer at the worry on Savannah's face. No one other than his mom and sister had ever worried about him getting on a fifteen-hundred-pound horse bucking out of control. He added, "I'll be fine. And Savannah... we're not finished yet." With the tip of his hat and an easy smile, he winked. "Now let me go win this rodeo."

***

Tiziano's Mediterranean features, a reflection of his Tuscan roots, stood out to the crowd of North Georgia revelers. In a small town, rumors can form quickly about a stranger sitting with Natalie's nephew and a badly burned man. One whisper to the next passed between them that Tiziano Piaggi had built a successful winery in Italy and had set his sights on expanding his legacy to the United States, seeking partners who shared his vision. Someone finally realized the burned man was Earl Wellington.

Oblivious to the small talk, Tiziano found himself at the Blue Ridge rodeo as a guest of Earl Wellington and his nephew, Jeffrey. Earl's winery in Asheville was a key possibility in his U.S. expansion plans, but he couldn't shake his concerns about Jeffrey's ability to handle such a significant endeavor.

Meanwhile, Duke Gray of Graystone Winery embodied a different kind of energy—one that embraced the future with a willingness to adapt and evolve.

Tiziano saw potential in Duke, recognizing his drive and passion.

But it was Savannah Gray who truly captured his attention. Her grace and intelligence hinted at a talent waiting to be nurtured, and the idea of offering her an apprenticeship in Tuscany lingered in his mind as a path to greatness. However, after seeing her reaction to the rodeo cowboy, he wondered about her openness to such an idea.

Determined to get discussions started with the Gray family, Tiziano rose from his seat.

Jeffrey glanced at him. "Everything all right?"

Tiziano gave a small nod. "I have some business to attend to, signaling his intention to seek out Duke."

As Tiziano made his way through the bustling crowd, Earl and Jeffrey's puzzled expressions followed him. Their eagerness to secure Wellington's future was palpable in the tension left hanging in the air between them. Finally, Jeffrey said with a conviction that was new to him, "Earl, if we allow past grievances and this long-standing rivalry between Wellington and Graystone to let us miss this huge opportunity, I don't know that I can move forward simply being the *staged* manager of Wellington with you pulling all the strings."

Jeffrey could hear the raspiness of Earl's breathing. When he gave no answer, Jeffrey added, "You have to somehow bridge the gap between you."

Earl sat there, hating every word that he heard. But he took a hard look at himself for the first time since before the accident. He had made mistakes... and he was paying for them every day. Was there a way to move forward? Could he make this right and extend an olive branch of reconciliation? Would Duke accept it? He looked at Jeffrey and nodded. "Let's do it."

CHAPTER 48

L EAVING Earl and Jeffrey, Tiziano found himself caught between Wellington and Graystone. Aware of the delicate balance of power at play, he set out to bridge the divide between the families.

Savannah was returning from the arena when she saw Tiziano approaching the elevator to the upper-level suites. She ran to the nearest stairwell, taking the stairs three at a time to get to the suite before Tiziano.

She got to the door of the suite just as the elevator doors were opening and scooted inside. Duke was just inside the door. Savannah said hurriedly, "Tiziano is almost here. Let me catch my breath—Duke, Jake chose Maximus as his horse for the saddle bronc ride. He's the most aggressive. We have to watch, okay?"

Duke craned his neck to see Jake on the sideline waiting for his number to be called. He told Savannah to go ahead and get seated as he answered the door to welcome Tiziano. Despite the distraction, Duke remained focused on supporting Jake, knowing that a win for the cowboy would not only be a personal victo-ry but also a win for Graystone.

"Tiziano, welcome! Our sponsored cowboy, Jake Rollins, is about to compete so you will have to excuse me. Please... help yourself to a plate of refreshments. I will be with you as soon as he finishes." Duke glanced at Natalie, who overheard his suggestion.

Natalie came up to Tiziano with her widest smile of hospitality. "Here, let me help you. May I offer you a glass of wine?"

Duke joined Savannah. Tiziano could feel the rise of tension in the suite. He looked inquisitively at Natalie, and she explained. "Jake has become like fam-ily to Duke and Savannah. For the saddle bronc event, the cowboys draw numbers to see which horse they will ride in the event. Jake's draw was Maximus, the most feared horse in the competition."

When she saw the question in Tiziano, she contin-ued, "It means with Maximus, Jake's chance for injury increases, but if he can last through the buzzer, he has the highest odds for best score."

Tiziano walked over and leaned against the door-frame to the bleachers, eager to watch the cowboy test his skills. Duke and Savannah were on their feet as the audience cheered and called out their support while Jake mounted the powerful horse with steely resolve in his eyes.

Jake knew the next few moments would test his ability and courage like never before, but he was ready to take on the challenge and make Duke, and especially

Savannah, proud. Eight seconds... that was all he needed.

Maximus broke hard out of the chute, and the clock started when his front feet hit the dirt. Tiziano was mesmerized, his eyes rapidly moving from rider to the clock.

Midway through the ride, a crossfire kick caused Jake's body to momentarily pitch forward. His free arm dipped slightly, and a collective gasp rose up in the crowd. Savannah's stomach dropped, and she clutched Duke's arm. But Jake righted himself and reclaimed his rhythm to make it to the buzzer. The pick-up men brought their horses alongside, and Jake swung cleanly onto one of them as Maximus was guided away from the arena.

Jake stood in the ring waiting for his score. Savannah didn't realize she was holding her breath. The scoreboard came to life as the announcer called out, "Ladies and gentlemen, we have our highest score of the event! Jake Rollins' score of 90.2 is the score to beat with three more riders yet to ride."

The roar of applause was deafening and Tiziano found himself swept into the adrenalin-pumping frenzy. After seeing Jake ride, it was clear he was more than just a sponsored cowboy... he was a symbol of resilience, determination, and the spirit of Blue Ridge.

Once the competition continued with the other riders, Duke and Savannah walked back up to the suite beaming with pride over Jake's success. Different council members were patting Duke on the back. "Nice ride." "That's one fine cowboy." Everyone was full of praise and anticipation for his next event.

Savannah checked her program. To Duke, she said, "They should start bringing the calves down in about forty-five minutes. Then Jake's order is seventh in the tie-down roping."

Reaching Tiziano, Duke shook his hand again. "I apologize for leavin' so abruptly. Our boy knocked it out of the park, don't you think?"

Tiziano's excitement was evident. "I have never been to a rodeo before, and I admit it was easy to get caught up in all the enthusiasm. Will he compete again?"

Savannah's excitement mirrored Duke's, and she explained. "Jake has three events. His next one involves roping and tying a calf's legs. Where the last event was judged, this next event will be timed to see how quickly each cowboy can complete the task. We should have a little over an hour. Tiziano, Duke received your text this morning. There is a quiet area in the lounge."

The attention of the others in the suite was already focused on the next rider. Tiziano nodded. "I am eager to share my ambitious vision for a partnership that will aim for a new legacy in the world of winemaking."

The group retreated to the lounge to have a more in-depth conversation. Tiziano wasted no time outlining the potential benefits of partnering with Tenuta Piaggi. "It is my belief that the ideal alliance is between Graystone, Wellington, and Tenuta Piaggi. However, with Wellington's lack of upper management involvement, I have concerns about Wellington, and that casts a shadow over my plan."

Just as Duke and Savannah began to see their hope of a future with Tenuta Piaggi fade, there was a resounding knock at the door of the suite. No one except Natalie was close by, so she answered the door and was shocked to see Earl and Jeffrey. Natalie scrutinized her brother, whose demeanor looked both resigned and defeated. He had even allowed Jeffrey to push him in a wheelchair, as though he had given up on the effort to walk.

"Is Tiziano here? We would like to speak with him." Earl's voice seemed even raspier than usual to Natalie.

"Yes, he's here. What's goin' on? He's over in the lounge speaking with Duke and Savannah." Natalie closed the door to the suite behind them. The muscle twitched in Jeffrey's jaw, but he remained quiet. Natalie looked at Jeffrey to get a straight answer, "You're not going to ruin this for Duke and Savannah, are you?"

Instead of Jeffrey, Earl hesitantly replied, "Just the opposite. If I had a white flag, I'd be holding it."

CHAPTER 49

WHEN Tiziano outlined his vision for a partnership with both Graystone and Wellington Winery, Duke and Savannah were intrigued. But their focus was on Jake's upcoming tie-down cattle roping event, and Tiziano agreed to wait until the competition was over.

Savannah spoke up. "We are the ones sponsoring him. The least we can do is to be out there watching his competition. Tiziano, you seemed to enjoy the rodeo. We have an extra seat if you'd care to join us."

They were about to get up to return to the bleachers when Natalie ushered in Jeffrey, who was pushing Earl in a wheelchair. A stunned silence fell over Duke, Savannah, and Tiziano.

Natalie tried to explain. "I am sorry to interrupt, but Earl said it was important."

Duke raised his eyebrows with sudden curiosity, staring intently at Earl. "Well, Earl, what is it that you want? We were just takin' a break to watch the tie-ropin'."

Earl mustered what strength he could and cleared his throat. "Tiziano has made it clear his vision for expansion includes both Graystone and Wellington wineries. My current health makes my role at Wellington questionable. I am here to explore the possibility of a future where our wineries could work together... to bury the hatchet of our past grievances." Earl's words echoed in the air like a tantalizing dream.

Duke assessed Tiziano's reaction, then glanced at Savannah. "An intriguin' idea. For now, though, we need to table this discussion so we can support our cowboy."

Tiziano opened his mouth to speak but Duke was already standing, with Savannah quickly following his lead. Duke added, "We'll continue after we get the scores for the tie-ropin'. The barrel racing should give us some time before Jake's last event."

As the group made their way back to the bleachers to watch Jake's performance, Savannah led the way with a sense of excitement and determination. But there was something more. Although she graciously showed Tiziano to an empty seat, she barely glanced in the direction of Natalie, Earl, and Jeffrey. Tiziano had been intrigued by Savannah's knowledge and passion about the wine industry, but, observing her now, he wondered if she would be able to fulfill the role he had in mind that would require working closely with Wellington.

The sounds of the rodeo surrounded him... the music and cheers blending into the background.

Tiziano watched quietly, taking in every detail. If Earl was willing to let go of the old animosities in the spirit of progress, a gesture that hinted at a new chapter in the relationship between Graystone and Wellington, would Duke be able to do the same?

Before Duke could sit, Mayor Winfield stopped him with a congratulatory pat on the back, praising Jake's previous high-score saddle bronc ride and expressing optimism for his next performance. "The stakes are high this year. With a record number of sponsors like yourself, the take-home purse for the winner is at an all-time high. If Rollins wins, he'll be sittin' pretty. I hear the time to beat for the tie-down ropin' is 7.5 seconds."

As Duke settled in the seat next to Savannah, the announcer's enthusiastic voice came over the loudspeaker, introducing the first competitor. Duke casually looked back toward the glassed-in area of the suite to see Natalie maneuvering Earl's wheelchair and getting a chair for Jeffrey. Natalie glanced up and caught his eyes. Duke could see the question in her expression. Earl's unexpected appearance had shifted the dynamic in his discussions with Tiziano, sparking a potentially different conversation that lingered unspoken between them. Would he be willing to meet Earl halfway? Could he get past the idea of Earl and Lois together? As hard as it was to accept, Lois would never have reached out to Earl if he had not failed her in their marriage. That had nothing to do with Earl.

Savannah grabbed Duke's arm with nervous excitement. "Jake's next." She kept her eyes trained on the dirt below, but Duke saw the way her fingers worked together in her lap... the way her shoulders held tight, as if she could will the next few minutes to go Jake's way. There was pride there, and worry, and something else Duke had only recently begun to recognize in her... how much she'd let herself care. Only then did he turn toward the arena.

Jake and Charro moved along the fence line at a steady walk, lining up near the chutes. Even from a distance, Duke could see the calm in Jake's posture... focused, deliberate, like a man who'd done this a thousand times and still treated every run like it mattered.

The announcer's voice rolled over the crowd. "Next up... Jake Rollins!" The moment of truth arrived as Jake entered the arena, and the collective anticipation reached its peak.

Savannah leaned forward, her gaze fixed as the calf was guided into position. Across the aisle, Tiziano sat eagerly, taking in this new event with the cowboy who meant so much to the Gray family. But Duke could feel the question sitting between them... the earlier mention of a future that included both wineries, the shock of Earl appearing in the suite, the surprising words that had followed. Unspoken tensions and unfinished conversations hung in the air just as the chute gate snapped open.

Jake was off in a burst of motion—horse surging, rope swinging, the loop flying true. The calf broke hard to the right and Charro matched it with a clean pivot that drew another surge from the crowd. Jake's skill and determination captivated them, drawing out a sense of pride and awe among the revelers.

Savannah's breath caught, her eyes never leaving Jake.

Jake dropped the slack, stepped off in one smooth motion, and the world narrowed to boots pounding dirt, hands moving fast, the practiced rhythm of a man who didn't waste time. For a second, Duke thought he saw a hitch... something small in Jake's shoulder when he went down... but Jake didn't falter. He finished the tie and snapped his hand up, marking the time. The flag went up. The crowd erupted. The leader-board lit up with the record time: 6.9 seconds.

Savannah finally exhaled, her whole posture loosening as if her body had been braced against impact and was only now realizing it had been spared. She turned her head just enough to find Duke, eyes bright.

Then, as Jake jogged back toward Charro and swung up into the saddle, Duke's pride shone through in that moment, a shared triumph for the group in the suite and throughout the audience. Even Earl and Jeffrey were clapping, and Tiziano was shaking his head in amazement. Duke raised a glass with a toast. "That's our boy!"

The day might be far from over, filled with promise and possibility that extended beyond the confines of the rodeo arena, but Duke wanted to savor the victory. Jake was still out there, and there was one more event to determine the victor.

CHAPTER 50

DUKE'S investment in the Blue Ridge annual rodeo ran deep. He took pride in supporting community events like the rodeo. Watching Jake's performance in the tie-down roping event filled Duke with satisfaction, realizing his growing respect for Jake went far beyond mere sponsorship. His remarkable skill had put him in a strong position to claim the grand prize.

The plan was to reconvene with the Italian vintner, Tiziano, to discuss business matters during the interim before the final event of bull riding, where Jake had a chance to secure the overall victory. Duke's mind, however, was preoccupied with thoughts of Jake's well-being.

Just as Duke was contemplating how to address his concerns with Jake, a discreet staffer slipped into the suite and handed him a note that demanded his immediate attention. Without a second thought, Duke excused himself from the festivities, slipping away unnoticed, not even by Savannah, who was engrossed in a discussion with Tiziano about his hometown of Siena.

When Savannah turned to her grandfather to continue discussions with Tiziano, she was puzzled to find an empty chair where Duke had been seated just moments ago. Confusion creased her brow as she scanned the crowded suite, searching for any sign of Duke's whereabouts.

She leaned in toward Tiziano to ask, "Did you see Duke leave?"

Tiziano was eager to pursue a plausible collaboration, and suggested, "Perhaps he just stepped out for a moment. Shall we begin without him?"

Savannah stood up and noticed Natalie standing behind Earl. She couldn't avoid Natalie forever, and Savannah had to admit that if anyone had noticed Duke leave, it would have been Natalie. Taking in a breath of resolve, Savannah walked up to Natalie. "Duke seems to be missing. Did you happen to see him leave?"

Natalie was about to answer when Earl's raspy voice intervened. "I saw him leave. Someone handed him a note, and he lit out of here like there was a fire that needed putting out."

Savannah hesitated for a moment, realizing she was being assessed by Tiziano, Earl, Jeffrey, and even Natalie. Savannah raised her chin and stiffened her spine. "If Duke left like that, it must have been important. But there is no reason we can't continue the discussion where we left it before Jake's event. Shall we return to the lounge?"

Not wanting anyone to question her moving forward, Savannah turned on her heels and walked toward the lounge. To her relief, they all followed.

***

Summoned by the rodeo medic with news of a shoulder injury, Duke struggled to balance his role as a sponsor with his concern for Jake's safety. Before he reached the medical support tent, he could hear Jake's defiant voice. "I am fine and I can push through the pain. I WILL be riding that bull!"

Duke raised the flap of the tent and entered, coming face-to-face with a determined Jake Rollins. Seeing Duke, Jake was immediately contrite but rolled his eyes toward the medic. "You sent for him, didn't you?"

The medic looked helplessly at Duke and said, "We think he has either a dislocated shoulder or a torn rotator cuff. We need imaging to determine which it is. Please talk some sense into him. It would be a huge mistake for him to get on a raging bull with this shoulder."

Duke tried to reason with Jake. "Son, your well-being is more important than winning a rodeo. You need to get the imaging to rule out any serious injury."

Jake tried to restrain the stubborn pride that flared up within him by tightening his voice. "I will not be scared off by some medic's overzealous need to yank me from the competition. I know my own body, and it's not as though I haven't pushed through pain before." Jake looked at the medic, then at Duke for support. "Just give me whatever paper I need to sign to release all liability, then tape me up good. I'm not letting anyone down today... not the fans, not Graystone, and not Savannah."

Hearing him refer to Savannah, Duke expressed, "But Jake, Savannah would never want you to ride if you're injured."

"Perhaps... and that is why you're not goin' to tell her. I'll be fine. I just need enough points to get an overall winnin' score."

Duke saw Jake's commitment to not disappointing anyone drive him to make a risky decision to compete in the bull riding event despite the potential consequences. Torn between a desire to protect Jake and his respect for the cowboy's fierce independence, Duke felt compelled to accept Jake's unwavering belief in his own abilities.

To the medic, Duke said, "Have him sign the release. Then, when you think you have him fully taped up, tape some more."

Duke's acceptance touched Jake... there were no words. Jake simply looked at Duke and nodded.

Duke left the tent wondering whether Jake's determination and grit would be enough to overcome his injury and secure victory—or whether his stubbornness would prove to be his downfall.

***

"Damn fool!" Graham came charging into the medical tent. "What the hell are you thinking, Rollins? Obviously, you aren't thinking." He muttered, "Tryin' to get yourself killed... well, not on my watch."

Jake was trying to button his shirt over his taped shoulder when Graham suddenly came over and tugged

Jake's right arm. Jake yelled in surprise as much as in pain. "What was that for?"

"To prove a point. If a simple tug has you yelling, what do you think is going to happen with a bucking bull? The bull you picked… he can smell fear. He'll find your weakness and dig in. You should know that."

Jake stood his ground. "I'm not givin' in, Graham. I've done this before. I just have to stay on that bull for eight seconds."

Graham shook his head. "And after the eight seconds, when you slide off the bull and land on that shoulder, how the hell are you goin' to get up and get out of its way?"

Jake was already grabbing his glove. "I'm ridin' and that's it. The cowhands will get me up if need be."

Graham could see Jake was not backing down. "Well, if you're going to be stubborn enough to do this, then I'm going to be your rope man in the chute. And I will be out in the ring pickin' up your pigheaded ass, so you don't get tromped on."

Jake understood the affection behind Graham's grumbling. He gave Graham a smile and said, "Thanks, Graham. Couldn't ask for any better."

"Hurry up, then. The chute boss has called the fifteen-minute warning."

***

Meanwhile, in the suite, Savannah was preoccupied with the high-stakes discussion with Tiziano and Earl regarding how Tiziano planned to handle the expansion, unaware of the danger Jake was about to face in the bull riding ring.

Duke came in out of breath, as if he'd been running. "They just gave the fifteen-minute warning to Jake. The announcer is introducing the first rider now."

By now, they all knew nothing would get in the way of watching Jake Rollins compete. They shuffled papers and began to move toward their seats. But Duke held Savannah's shoulder back. "I need to tell you why I was called away. Jake was injured in the last event. His shoulder. I tried to talk him out of riding the bull, but he insisted."

Alarm set in. "Duke, we need to stop him."

"It's too late. He's probably already in the chute. Savannah, he didn't want me to tell you." Duke glanced up at Natalie, who was gaping at the news, jaw dropped.

Savannah looked up at Duke, curious. "Then why did you tell me?"

"Secrets haven't worked out so well for us in the past. Thought it was time for a change."

Savannah's gaze inadvertently shifted to Natalie, whose wry smile and small nod prompted Savannah to look back at Duke. "Then let's not start now."

The announcer's voice rose above the crowd. "All right, folks... next up, riding for the overall title... Jake Rollins."

Savannah didn't wait for another word.

CHAPTER 51

J AKE knew he could trust Graham. With the deafening roar of the crowd, his signals needed to be
understood immediately. His approach to the chute
had to be calculated with precision. Jake needed to
clearly position himself as unafraid. The chute was narrow; every move was significant. He climbed the railing
and placed one foot on the bull, warning him he was
there. Graham helped brace him for the inevitable buck
inside the chute. Jake eased down onto the bull, his feet
on the side rails, pointed forward. He had considered
removing his spurs to not set the bull into motion too
early but, in the end, he preferred to have them.

Once seated, Jake tightened his legs around the
bull, pushing from side to side to signal the bull who
was in charge. Graham held the bull rope loosely so
Jake could adjust it to a position that felt the least likely to further harm his shoulder. He adjusted his grip so
that his pinkie finger lined up against the bull's spine.
He then rubbed the part of the exposed rope up and
down until it warmed and turned tacky in his glove.

When he was satisfied the rope would stay in his gloved hand, he hit it as a signal for Graham to pull the rope.

Checking the tension, Jake realized it needed to be tighter. He signaled Graham, who responded by pulling the rope more. Jake took the rope from Graham and wrapped it securely through and around his hand and flipped the excess rope behind him. With his good arm, he lowered the brim of his hat and straightened his posture. The injection the medic had given him was kicking in, and Jake read the bull, adjusting forward and back, determining which way the bull would turn out of the gate. He cocked his hips, putting his right leg forward. Jake was betting the bull would go left.

Jake took a deep breath. Eight seconds. That's all he needed. He tipped his hat in a nod that signaled the gate to be opened. For a millisecond, the bull shifted like he was switching to a bolt to the right, but Jake added tension to the squeeze of his knees, warning the bull. *You're not the one in control. I am, and I'm not goin' anywhere.* The bull bolted to the left, bringing Jake back upright from his cocked position. Man against animal in an age-old test of wills. The bull twisted sharply and kicked hard, as if to rid himself of the venomous snake on his back.

Maybe his free arm wasn't high enough or his posture straight enough, but Jake dug in and refused to be jolted off. When the buzzer signaled the eight seconds and it was time to dismount, Jake was so focused he didn't hear it. Graham rushed into the ring with two clowns wearing protective barrels to distract the bull so Jake could fall off. Graham was on the left and the barrel men on the right. When the bull swung right, Jake made his move and fell onto his left side, protecting his injured shoulder as much as possible.

A shot of pain rushed through him, greeted by the collective gasp of the crowd. But Graham was right there, shielding Jake to help him out of the arena. Outside the gates, the medics were waiting.

***

Savannah didn't realize she'd been holding her breath until her gasp overshadowed the shock that echoed through the stands. She'd stood in front of her seat, binoculars in hand, ever since Duke had told her of Jake's injury. She had watched as he cautiously climbed into the chute, and she could see the bulge under his shirt where the taping was. Her fingers tightening on the binoculars, Savannah lived through every one of those eight seconds with Jake, willing him to make it through unharmed. It wasn't until he landed hard in the dirt with Graham quickly at his side that she knew where she needed to be.

Turning to Duke, she said, "I have to go. I need to be there."

Duke gave her a quick hug. "I know you do. Jake is stubborn, but he's strong. He's gonna be okay. Before you go, is there anything I should know about the talks with Tiziano while I was gone?"

Savannah adjusted her position so Tiziano couldn't read her expression. "He has some ambitious ideas, and there's one concerning me that we need to discuss. There is another one I'm not so sure you're going to like. Earl seems to be on board, but you and I need to have some further discussion. But Duke, right now I have to be by Jake's side."

"Did you even see his score? Even with his injury, he got an 81. That puts Jake in line for the grand prize. Now get down there. I'll take the business side of things from here. Sounds like you did good work keepin' things movin'."

***

Savannah was rushing toward the medical tent when she ran into Lizzie heading in the same direction. "Lizzie, do you know how badly Jake is hurt? You probably had a better angle watching from the judges' box."

Lizzie was helping the judges tally the scores. "That's what the judges want to know. There are still two riders left, but so far Jake's score is the highest on the leaderboard. They want to be sure he can make it to the awards ceremony."

Savannah and Lizzie arrived at the tent Graham greeted them at the entrance. "Hello, ladies. Jake is undergoing imaging at the moment. Before his ride, I ordered a portable machine so it would be here by the end of his ride. As soon as the doctor reads the scan, we'll know more."

The medic came up to Graham. "The images are complete. I've given him something for the pain. He's resting, but you can see him now."

When Jake saw Savannah, he tried to get up, giving her a lopsided smile.

"Easy there, cowboy. You may have bested an eighteen-hundred-pound bull, but you don't want to go up against me if I'm trying to help you. Now lie back and relax until we get the results of the scans." Savannah spoke in a voice that would not take no for an answer.

Jake settled back into his pillow and couldn't help his smile. "That's why I didn't want you to know before I rode. It was enough to contend with Duke and Graham."

"Well, Duke told me. But not until it was too late to do anything about it. And while we're on the subject of secrets, I'm done with hiding the truth, Jake. Whatever it is—we might not like what the truth costs us, or someone we care about. However, over the last several days, we've learned the hard way that secrets come with consequences."

Graham and Lizzie watched in awe as the injured cowboy who could duel with a dangerous bull was speechless when it came to standing up to Savannah.

Lizzie asked the medic, "The judges want me to ask if Jake can make it to the awards ceremony?"

When Jake overheard her, he responded, "You let them know that if they have a trophy waiting for me, I'll be there."

There was a twinkle in Lizzie's eye when she answered, "Oh, I think it will be a little more than a trophy."

Lizzie turned to leave, and Savannah squeezed Jake's hand. "I'll be right back. I need to speak with Lizzie for a minute."

Lizzie walked outside with Savannah. "What is it?"

"Remember Tiziano, the Italian vintner? He made me an offer. He wants me to go to Italy. I'd be in Siena at the same time you're in Florence."

Lizzie started jumping up and down. "What? That's incredible! When do we start packing?"

"I haven't spoken to Duke about it, and I have no idea how Jake is going to react. We feel good together, Lizzie... but there's been no commitment."

CHAPTER 52

JAKE tolerated the chastisement being so eloquently verbalized by the doctor. He could hardly blame the man. He knew he had been foolhardy. Jake wasn't normally the reckless type. Savannah had even picked up on that. Winning the rodeo had become important to him... more than he'd realized.

He'd signed up for the Blue Ridge rodeo because of a puzzling letter from a local attorney about an accident that continued to give him nightmares. Never had he imagined how the week here would evolve.

Savannah walked back into the tent as the doctor was telling Jake to report at the hospital first thing Monday morning to schedule surgery. Once the doctor left, Savannah sheepishly said, "He didn't look very happy. I guess you don't need another person telling you that you were crazy to pull such a stunt."

Jake gave a resigned sigh. "Yeah, the doc said that after surgery it would take four to six months to recover. Guess I won't be ridin' any more bulls for a while."

Savannah let his words sink in but only said, "The awards ceremony is about to begin. Are you up for it? Duke wants you to be down here for it but said you don't have to go to the Greystone post party."

Jake got into the wheelchair the doctor had ordered. "He says I can walk out to the podium if I will ride in the chair behind the scenes. And Savannah, I'm up for all of it if you're by my side."

It seemed the most natural thing for Savannah to lean down and kiss Jake, gingerly avoiding his injured shoulder. He was beginning to feel like home to her, filling a loving hole in her heart left vacant by the loss of her parents.

Savannah pushed his chair toward the arena. Graham had gone ahead to gather the other cowboys winning various prizes and awards. But when the crowd got a glimpse of Jake, the roar that erupted proved he had won their hearts with his impressive performances and fearless attitude. He had become a local hero.

With a torn rotator cuff and his arm in a sling, Jake stood tall as the announcer declared him the grand winner of the rodeo. The mayor came up to the podium and asked Jake to join him. Duke came up and stood next to Savannah, both of them beaming with pride for the cowboy who just a short week ago was a stranger to them.

The mayor spoke. "There are times when, as your mayor, I have the privilege of honoring who had come into our community and left a mark on it. I have seen that in the way you've stood behind this young man."

Turning to Jake, the mayor lifted a large symbolic key from the table. "Jake Rollins, would you accept a key to our fair city of Blue Ridge, Georgia? It would be our honor to call you neighbor." Jake took the key, tears welling in his eyes as the entire audience, including Tiziano, Earl, Natalie, and Jeffrey, came to life with cheers and applause.

Jake had expected a trophy cup and a check, but the check that was walked out to the stage by Graham and Lizzie was a huge 30" x 72". But it wasn't the physical size of the check that astonished Jake. It was when he saw the number of zeros! "$10,000" came flashing on the leaderboard in neon lights. Jake had won ten thousand dollars! Everyone was losing their minds with excitement over the good fortune of the man who stood injured before them. Savannah screamed until she no longer had a voice. Duke beamed with pride.

Jake tried to compose himself and raised his hat with his good arm to quiet the audience in order to speak. When there was finally enough order, he began, "Mr. Mayor, citizens of Blue Ridge, you have no idea what this means to me. A week ago, I was a stranger in this town. But I can tell you with certainly, today Blue Ridge feels like home. I'm not exactly sure what I would do without a homemade biscuit and a cup of Mountain Mama coffee in the mornin' and a glass of Graystone cabernet to come home to every night."

The crowd roared, and Savannah jumped up and down.

Jake continued, "I know riding that bull seems like a heroic move. It wasn't. I have been trained well, but I can tell you... my rodeo boss and dear friend, Graham

Ross, was by my side. He had my back. Graham... thank you. And, if you haven't noticed the restaurant photo at the Graystone tent of me with a beautiful young lady, she is your friend and neighbor, Savannah Gray. Both she and Duke have made a huge impression on me over the last week, and I consider them family. And to all of you in Blue Ridge, thank you for coming out and supporting the rodeo. It's fans like you who encourage cowboys like us to do what we do!"

With that, the entire team of rodeo athletes came out, along with the clowns, to take a bow... then Graham, then the stock contractor, and finally the judges.

***

Well-wishers surrounded Duke and Savannah, buzzing with excitement about Jake's big win and the chance to meet him at the Graystone post party. Graham had taken Jake to help him clean up a little before meeting them at the Graystone tent. Lizzie had gone there directly after the awards ceremony to open it up and turn on the lights.

Duke took Savannah's arm to hold her back. "Let's take a few minutes to talk." They found a bench behind the stands where it wasn't too loud with the workmen already breaking down the venue.

Duke began, "After you left, Tiziano told me about Italy. Did he tell you it would be for six months?"

"No. Just that he was interested in my going there to learn the traditional wine-making process and share more about the innovations we use at Graystone. But six months? Granted, after we harvest the grapes for the ice wine, the vines will be dormant for the winter. In exchange, he mentioned sending over a supervisor to move between Graystone and Wellington. I didn't think you'd take kindly to someone interfering in our business."

Duke looked down at the ground in thought, then back at Savannah. "I discovered something important this week. The woman I loved dearly was lonely and unhappy because I was so caught up in the winery that she felt left out. Savannah, you have been a saving grace at Graystone since the accident, but I'm not a fool. I know how much you've wanted to go to Italy to learn the traditional ways. The timing couldn't be more perfect. Lizzie will be close by in Florence for winter semester, and you'll be back in time for growing season. Sweetheart, I don't want you to lose this opportunity. And who knows? The supervisor might be able to teach this old dog a few tricks."

Savannah gave herself a moment to absorb Duke's words. Dare she believe such a dream would come true? Her throat had that involuntary catch she got whenever she thought of her mother. She knew her mom would tell her to follow her heart. Even in the cool night breeze, it was clearer than day. The was one thing she wanted more than Italy. To Duke, she asked, "What about Jake?"

Duke sighed. There it was. His granddaughter had fallen in love with the cowboy. "This is too big of an opportunity for you to pass up. If you and Jake are meant to be together, you'll find a way. And six months isn't forever."

Duke chuckled to himself at the irony. Just moments ago, eight seconds seemed like an eternity.

CHAPTER 53

THE party was in full swing, filled with celebratory laughter and clinking glasses. Savannah could tell Jake was exhausted, although he smiled and chatted relentlessly with his fans. She eased her way through the group with a chair and a comforting smile. "Thought you might need this, cowboy."

"Thank you, ma'am, but I can't be sittin' if everyone around me's standin'."

Savannah saw Tiziano across the room, so she said to Jake, "All right, but I'll be back in ten minutes to give you a break." Jake tipped his hat and gave her a look that said he was counting on it.

Tiziano was speaking with Jeffrey. Savannah hesitated for a moment, somewhat surprised to see Jeffrey here at the Graystone event. However, when she followed Jeffrey's eyes, she saw Natalie and Earl in a far corner. Realizing more must have happened in the suite while she was with Jake, Savannah couldn't help but wonder if this might mean a new beginning for Graystone and Wellington, working together rather than being at odds. Her gaze found Duke, in his element among his guests. He caught her glance and winked.

Jeffrey saw Savannah approach and excused himself. Tiziano stepped to the side for a little privacy. "I imagine you have questions."

"Yes, I do. Duke mentioned you were offering me a six-month apprenticeship. Why me?"

"That's a fair question. It was Duke. He told me the history of your original vines... and of you. He said if I decided to do business with Graystone, I should get to know his granddaughter. I admit I was curious about such a girl, yet that first day at the tent when you introduced me to your family reserve, I could see the potential. It would be my honor to host you in my home and be treated as one of our own."

Savannah stared at Tiziano in wonder. "What a generous offer... one that I gladly accept. However, I must stay for the ice wine harvest and Jake's surgery. My friend, Lizzie, is leaving for art school in Florence in two weeks. Would that timing work for you and your family?"

"That would be perfect. I will make the arrangements. Duke asked me if I would stay to see the grapes harvested for your new ice wine, and I agreed if the predicted frost arrives this week. Then I will spend a few days in Asheville to fully understand the capabilities Wellington brings to the table."

"Thank you, Tiziano. I won't let you down."

Savannah turned to go rescue Jake when she saw Lizzie across the room, looking at her with bright eyes filled with anticipation. Savannah nodded, and she could hear Lizzie squeal in delight. Tiziano heard her too and smiled.

A feeling of relief came over Savannah. She had made the decision to move forward with her life. She hoped for a future with Jake, but she had decided on Italy for herself. Now she just needed to tell him, although she didn't want to do anything to ruin his huge day.

Winning the rodeo and receiving the key to the city felt like a dream come true for Jake. The $10,000 prize money was an amazing bonus, giving him the much-needed time to heal his shoulder and explore his growing feelings for Savannah. He looked up and saw her walking toward him, wondering what a new chapter would look like with Savannah by his side.

Jake gladly took Savannah's hand and thanked the few lingering fans. Whispering to Savannah, Jake said, "I thought you'd never get back. Why don't we get out of here? I just need to thank Graham and Duke."

By the time Savannah realized Graham was talking to Lizzie, everything dropped to slow motion. Savannah tried to shake her head in warning, but it was too late. Lizzie had told Graham, and it just slipped right out of his mouth. "How about your girl, Jake? Lizzie just told me the news. Six months in Italy… that should be incredible."

It took just one beat of Jake's heart for his dream to crash and for him to cover his shock. "Savannah has always longed to see Italy. This should be a grand opportunity for her. Now, if you'll excuse me, I must say good night to Duke."

Savannah started to follow Jake, but he held up his good arm and attempted a smile. "I'll be back soon."

As soon as he left, Graham shook his head. "He didn't know, did he? And I opened my mouth and stuck a foot in it."

Lizzie looked distraught. "I'm sorry, Sav. I was so excited."

Savannah sighed in resignation. "I was about to tell him. A wise man recently told me there's no going back... no do-overs. All we can do is move forward."

Duke recognized the look on Jake's face, and it was not the look of a major winner of the Blue Ridge rodeo. After the past week, Jake was like family to Duke and Jake felt the same way. Duke placed a hand on Jake's back and led him out of the public eye. "Do you want to tell me what happened?"

"Savannah's goin' to Italy." Jake's heart sank as he realized the weight of those words, but he couldn't bear to hold her back from pursuing her dreams, even if it meant letting her go.

Duke took pity on the young man before him who had obviously fallen for his granddaughter. Wasn't it only a couple of hours ago that Savannah had told him the only thing that meant more to her than Italy was Jake.

Forcing Jake to look at him, Duke said, "Let me ask you a question, son. That recklessness out there in the arena today is going to cost you getting surgery on that shoulder, right?"

Jake didn't know if he could handle another lecture, but he answered with a sigh, "Yeah."

"Seems to me I heard the recovery was about four to six months before you could consider gettin' back to the rodeo." Duke had Jake's attention, so he continued, "You've got all that time to heal and ten thousand dollars in your pocket. You don't think they have rehab facilities in Italy? I'm bettin' that if you could hold on to the reins of Maximus for eight seconds and ride a hard-twistin' bull with a torn-up shoulder, you can find a way to hold on to my granddaughter."

"Yes, sir." The smile that lit up Jake's face was worth its weight in gold to Duke. It was time they all found some happiness.

CHAPTER 54

SAVANNAH wasn't sure what to expect when Jake returned. The shock of seeing him bolt over to her with excitement gave her pause.

"Let's get out of here." Jake reached out his good arm, and without a second thought Savannah took it and left with him.

As they reached the parking lot, Jake tossed her the keys. "You should drive."

Savannah tried to make sense of his urgency, "Jake, we need to talk. I was going to tell you about Italy, but you were surrounded."

"None of that matters." Jake took her in his arms, with an awkward adjustment for his shoulder. He then let all caution dissolve into the air and spoke from his heart. "I love you, Savannah Gray... more than I could ever have imagined."

A flush of happiness swept over Savannah. "I love you, too, Jake. I'll be here through your surgery. It's only six months. I'll be back before you know it. Are you planning to stay here in Blue Ridge or back home in Arkansas while you recover?"

This was the moment he'd been waiting for. "Well, I was thinking of recoverin' somewhere a little more exotic… maybe a foreign country?"

Savannah couldn't dare hope. "Italy?" Jake simply smiled as he nodded. "What!!!" Savannah threw her arms around Jake in delight until he yelped in pain. "Sorry," she said sheepishly, but the joy overtook her. "We're going to be in Italy together! I guess I need to ask you an important question."

"Yes, ma'am?"

"Does that mean we get to 'cross the line?'" Savannah was close enough for him to feel her breath.

Jake took her face in his good hand. "Any time you're ready." Their kiss explored all the emotional connection between them that had grown over the last week that felt like a lifetime.

***

Savannah was happier than Duke had seen her since before the accident. Going to Italy and finding a relationship with Jake had opened a future for her. That gave some relief to the ache dwelling in his heart.

Duke had returned to the ranch after the rodeo to find his ransacked room as he'd left it… a reminder of the note Lois had left that sent David and Margaret after her. He had looked some more but eventually gave up any hope of finding it. He had questioned Earl further, but there was no new information about that night at the cabin. When Earl reluctantly handed over full management of Wellington Winery to Jeffrey and Tenuta Piaggi, Duke realized what that night at the cabin had cost him. No one had been left unscathed.

Jake's surgery had gone well. The doctors assured him his shoulder would make a full recovery if he was diligent about the physical therapy.

The grapes had been harvested for the ice wine, and Tiziano was in Asheville before returning to Italy to meet Savannah.

Everything seemed settled. What he couldn't understand was how he could have let Lois suffer alone. He wasn't sure he could ever make peace with himself on that. He walked out to the porch. There was a new dusting of snow collecting on the vines. Knowing Savannah was finishing her packing upstairs and would be leaving gave Duke an overwhelming feeling of loneliness and his own lost opportunities.

He needed to get a grip. Savannah couldn't see him like this. In the distance, Jake's truck appeared, heading up the driveway to pick up Savannah. It was time to drive to Atlanta to catch their flight to Florence.

Savannah stopped at the screen door, watching Duke in this unguarded moment. She hated leaving him alone. She walked out to the porch and went up to her grandfather for a lingering embrace. "I love you so much, Duke. I'll miss you terribly, but I'll be back in time for the late-spring pruning."

Then something occurred to Savannah. "Duke, did you ever look for the note in the library? You know she was always curled up with a book."

Duke saw the effort Savannah was making on his behalf. "Yes, I looked through the desk and around all the chairs. I must accept that it's gone, and I'll never know what it said."

Savannah said quickly as Jake was getting out of the truck, "Well, I know she loved you. I saw the way she looked at you. She loved all of us. I believe that."

Jake picked up Savannah's suitcase and put it in the truck, then came back to shake Duke's hand. "Thank you for everythin', Duke. I'll take good care of her."

"I know you will, son. Safe travels to you both. Let me know when you arrive in Florence." Duke hugged Savannah again. "Now, get goin' before you miss your flight."

Savannah smiled. "We're picking Lizzie up on our way. She won't let us be late."

With a poignant laugh, Jake closed Savannah's door and climbed into the truck and drove off.

Duke went back inside and poured himself a brandy. Taking it into the library, he sat and could almost picture Lois in front of the fire reading. What was the name of that author she loved? She always had that book in her hand. Austen... Jane Austen. That's it.

Something caught his eye on one of the bookshelves, and Duke looked closer. The spine of one of the books was out farther than the others. He didn't remember noticing that before. He stepped over to the shelf and gently pulled it out. *Persuasion* by Jane Austen.

Duke went back to his favorite chair and took a sip of his brandy. He slowly opened the book, noting the dog-eared pages and highlighted quotes. Lois had spent time with this book. Duke moved his fingers across the cover, feeling a closeness with his wife that he hadn't felt in years. When he re-opened the book, it fell naturally to a page with a highlighted quote:

> *"You pierce my soul. I am half agony, half hope."*

Duke's breathing became heavier. He turned to another page.

> *"Tell me not that I am too late, that such precious feelings are gone forever."*

Duke turned to a final page that said it all.

> *"I have loved none but you. Unjust I may have been, weak and resentful I have been, but never inconstant."*

As Duke closed the book, a single tear slid down his face. He sat there, holding the closed book, his brandy untouched beside him. A sound prompted him to look back at the door to the library. Leaning against the doorway, Natalie stood silently, her expression soft as she took in the scene before her. Duke. Lois's favorite book. The full glass of brandy.

There were no immediate words as their eyes searched each other's. Natalie was the first to venture. "May I join you?"

About the Author
Nina Purtee

Nina Purtee is a worldwide traveler, philosopher, and award-winning adventure/romance women's fiction novelist.

Nina draws from her travels to embrace multicultural characters seemingly from different worlds, and allow them to co-exist, embrace each other's traditions, and even find love. Throughout her historical *Annie's Journey Series*, Nina "shares her gift and craft of writing for young women with a strong element of inspiration or timeless message."

"Purtee's sheer brilliance of her pen adroitly explores themes of love, loss, resilience, and courage."

A "natural storyteller, Nina loves to dig into the heart of her stories with touching insights added along the way."

Her love of the sea and sailing brought Nina to the coast of Florida where she calls home when she is not traveling the globe seeking new experiences to write about. A recent two-month author residency in Blue Ridge, Georgia, marked a return to the mountains—and a new creative direction that inspired *Whispers of Blue Ridge*.

Learn more about Nina at **www.ninapurtee.com**